A Thousand Miles
from Nowhere

A Thousand Miles *from* Nowhere

A Novel

John Gregory Brown

A LEE BOUDREAUX BOOK

LITTLE, BROWN AND COMPANY

NEW YORK BOSTON LONDON

Copyright © 2016 by John Gregory Brown

Lee Boudreaux Books/Little, Brown and Company
Hachette Book Group
1290 Avenue of the Americas, New York, NY 10104
leeboudreauxbooks.com

First Edition: June 2016

Gregory Orr, excerpt from "The Ghosts Listen to Orpheus Sing" from *Orpheus & Eurydice: A Lyric Sequence.* Copyright © 2001 by Gregory Orr. Reprinted with the permission of The Permissions Company, Inc., on behalf of Copper Canyon Press, www.coppercanyonpress.org.

Lee Boudreaux Books is an imprint of Little, Brown and Company, a division of Hachette Book Group, Inc. The Lee Boudreaux name and logo are trademarks of Hachette Book Group, Inc.

The publisher is not responsible for websites (or their content) that are not owned by the publisher.

The Hachette Speakers Bureau provides a wide range of authors for speaking events. To find out more, go to hachettespeakersbureau.com or call (866) 376-6591.

Library of Congress Cataloging-in-Publication Data

Brown, John Gregory.
A thousand miles from nowhere : a novel / John Gregory Brown.—First edition.
    pages ; cm
ISBN 978-0-316-30280-7
I. Title.
PS3552.R687T48 2016
813'.54—dc23   2015024561

10 9 8 7 6 5 4 3 2 1

RRD-C

Printed in the United States of America

For Carrie
and for Olivia, Molly, and Walker

Tombstone for my pillow,
Fairground for my bed.

—Robert Pete Williams

I

Let us agree that one of man's most beautiful
postures is that of Saint Sebastian.

—Federico García Lorca

One

In Virginia, three days later, Henry Garrett finally saw it all on TV. He stopped at a motel on Route 29 somewhere north of Lynchburg, the dim outline of the Blue Ridge Mountains rising behind the motel's dusty gray-brick walls, and the short round Indian woman behind the counter, her painted fingernails adorned with glitter, took a look at the address Henry had printed on the registration card, pushed back toward him the three crumpled twenty-dollar bills he'd placed on the counter, and said, "You will stay here with our compliments, Mr. Garrett. You will stay as long as you would like to stay. You have lost everything, yes?"

"Just tonight," Henry said. "Tomorrow—" But the woman reached across the counter and touched his arm. Her fingernails, a pale blue beneath the glitter, gently grazed his skin as she took her hand away.

"With our compliments, Mr. Garrett," she said. "Tonight, tomorrow. As long as you would like to be our guest. We cannot do so much, but this we can do. You have lost everything, yes?"

Everything? Henry thought; he considered the word. Had he lost *everything?*

Again, though, the woman didn't wait for Henry. She swept around the counter, confidently hoisted his canvas bag, and led him out the office door, her red and orange sari glowing like a torch in the dim light of the parking lot. The motel appeared to be empty—*Unoccupied,* Henry thought, as if it were a foreign land—but she led him down the line of rooms to the last one. "Two windows, front and side," she said. "Much nicer for you than the others."

Inside the room, the woman switched on the light, pointed out the coffeepot on the bathroom's vanity, and turned on the television. "Some company," she said, "but it is like the old ones, I do not know why. It requires a few minutes to warm."

She stood there scowling at the television as though it were a disobedient child, so Henry took his bag from her, set it on the bed, and looked around the room. On the wall above the headboard was a painting of what seemed to be a bearded child sailing through the night sky. One of the child's outstretched hands held a feather, apparently plucked from the red swan flying beside him. The other hand clutched a wooden stick, or maybe a flute. Below the painting, on a wicker nightstand, stood a small black lamp with a paper shade depicting a potbellied Ganesh. Henry switched on the lamp, and the figure lit up. He studied the bejeweled crown, the great floppy ears and elephant's trunk. Ganesh was a king of sorts, some kind of Hindu god, Henry knew—but that was all he knew, really. He leaned closer and saw that Ganesh was squatting on a rat, one with an absurdly long tail wrapped twice around Ganesh's corpulent waist. The exact same lamp, Henry now realized, had been on the motel's office counter. Beneath it had been a bowl of green-striped mints and a stack of brochures for someplace named the Lucky Caverns.

Henry stepped back toward the woman, but she hadn't moved. The television still had not come on—the screen was black except

4

for a small circle of gray light at the center—so Henry told her not to worry, that he would be fine without it. "Really," he said, "I'll be fine," which made him want to laugh. He would not be fine.

"Well, I am Latangi," she said, and she began to spell out the name, though she did so in a sort of nonsense singsong verse: "*L* as in *library, a* as in *love, t* as in *telegraph lines flowering above.*"

"I'm sorry?" Henry said. "*A* as in *love*? There's no—"

"Yes, yes." The woman raised her hand, smiling. "Latangi," she said again. "Its meaning is 'slim girl.'" She laughed. "My father was hopeful, yes, but not wise." Her shoulders swung side to side as if she were about to dance.

Henry tried to smile. The woman reached out and handed him the room key, but he suddenly felt a bit dizzy—dehydrated, perhaps—and he dropped the key. When he bent down to retrieve it, he saw that the worn and faded carpet covering the room was printed with an almost invisible purple-and-black-paisley design and that on her feet, beneath her sari, the woman was wearing gold sandals, her toenails painted the same pale glittery blue as her fingernails.

"Thank you so much," Henry said, standing, a bit off balance. The woman reached toward him, gently touched his arm, but then Henry felt her grip tighten. *"Oh,"* the woman gasped. *"Oh, oh."* Henry followed her eyes to the television.

On the screen, a mangy dog stood on a dresser floating in the middle of a flooded street, the houses submerged to the rooflines, the water's surface oily, dappled pink and green. The shot zoomed in so close that Henry could see the dog shaking, struggling to keep its balance on the dresser. Then the images flashed by in a rapid-fire montage of ruin and desperation: a man's body floating facedown in the water, his shirt billowing out around him; two children hoisted in a yellow bucket from a rooftop to a helicopter; a shirtless old man with a scarred chest and long gray beard squatting on the concrete steps of a house that lay in a heap behind him; a man wading through waist-deep water with a bone-thin old woman cradled in his arms, the woman's hands and feet dangling in the water. The volume on the television was turned down, but Henry felt as though he could hear the dramatic music that must be accompanying these images—the martial drumbeats, the groaning strings, the staccato burst of horns. When the red CNN logo swirled onto the screen, Henry turned to look at the woman, and he saw that she was weeping.

"I am terribly, terribly sorry, Mr. Garrett. Your home, yes? You are raised there?" The woman continued crying. "Everything," she said. "Everything."

Henry wanted to tell her that he was fine. He wanted somehow to comfort her.

"Latangi?" he said, trying to pronounce the name just as the woman had pronounced it.

"Latangi, yes," she said.

"Latangi, I—" But he couldn't think of a way to say it, to explain that he had already managed, before the hurricane, to lose every-thing. "Yes, it's my home. I've lived there my whole life. But—"

Now he reached out to touch her arm. As if his hand had some-how set her in motion, though, she began to drift toward the door. Henry thought of the child in the painting with the plucked swan's feather. "You will sleep tonight, yes, Mr. Garrett," Latangi said, her head turned away as if she were afraid that Henry had already begun undressing. "If there is anything at all—" she said, but she gently closed the door before she completed the sentence.

Henry sat down on the bed and stared at the television. He leaned forward and tried to turn up the volume, but there was still no sound. On-screen, a white-haired reporter—Henry knew his name but couldn't remember it right then—stood atop a highway overpass rising out of the water like an amusement-park ride. He pointed behind him and shook his head, flames and black smoke pouring from the roof of a building in the distance, all but its top two floors submerged in water. Henry knew that this was New Orleans, that this was what he had left behind, what had happened these past three days, but he had not imagined, could not have imagined when he left, that it would be so bad. Yes, people had been talking about the hurricane, how it might be more powerful than Betsy or Camille, but he had decided to leave only when he saw, by late afternoon, that Magazine Street was completely empty, as if it were the morning after Mardi Gras and everyone in the city was hung over and sleeping in. Then the police cars had started passing, flashing their blue lights and announcing over a loudspeaker that the city was closed, that everyone had to be gone by dark. *Can you close a city?* Henry had wondered. *How do you close a city?* He'd left without any real sense of panic, feeling a bit like a daydreaming first-grader during a fire drill, dutifully falling into the long line of children shuffling out through the elementary school's heavy double doors.

He'd inched forward for five hours in the traffic until he was finally able to get off the interstate. He found a gas station in Mississippi that was still open, and he waited in line there for another hour to fill up his tank. After that he drove aimlessly along back roads that cut through farmland and pine woods, returning every now and then to the interstate but getting off again when the traffic slowed to a crawl. From time to time he checked the road atlas to make sure he was headed more or less north. He ate fast food, washed his hands and face in the restaurants' grimy bathrooms. He spent the first night at a rest stop because all the motels he'd passed were full, the parking lots jammed with boats and trailers and overstuffed station wagons. All he'd brought was a canvas bag into which he'd thrown some underwear and shirts and a couple pairs of jeans. He no longer owned much else.

Throughout the drive he kept hearing in his head the absurd lyrics of a song some concave-chested, acne-scarred teenager with a tongue stud had played for him a few days ago at the store. *A few days ago—* before everything was like this, before what he was watching on the TV. The song was by a band called the Mountain Goats, though it wasn't really a band, the kid had carefully explained, each flash of metal in his mouth leaving Henry a bit woozy, as if it were his own tongue that had been impaled. The band was really just one guy, the teenager said, a guy who'd been a psychiatric nurse hopped up on amphetamines, though he was now completely clean, a vegan even, maybe a Buddhist or something too, and Henry had listened to the singer's nasally voice and his badly tuned guitar, the song apparently recorded onto a cassette tape in a boom box in this Mountain Goat Man's Portland or Seattle bathroom: *I hope when you think of me years down the line, you can't find one good thing to say, and I'd hope that if I found the strength to walk out, you'd stay the hell out of my way.*

"Ah, a love song," Henry had joked, and the boy had nodded, his head frenetically bobbing up and down.

"You got it," the boy said. "You most definitely have got it."

Henry listened. Everything about the song should have been perfectly awful, but it wasn't—or, rather, it was. It was both perfect *and* awful. It was, indeed, a love song, a swirling mixture of bitterness and bile and desperate longing: *I am drowning,* the singer screamed at the end, which must have been why the song had wound up in Henry's head, that image of water and drowning, the bitterness and desperation, as he drove away from the storm. *I am drowning. There is no sign of land. You are coming down with me, hand in unlovable hand. And I hope you die. I hope we both die.*

Of course. *I hope you die. I hope we both die.* Oh boy.

Henry couldn't explain, even to himself, why he liked such music. He just did. He liked the off-key, the unbalanced, the anguished, the forlorn: the guttural rumblings of Tom Waits, Dylan's scratch and claw, Skip James's cracking falsetto, Lou Reed's drone, Johnny Cash's hoarse whisper, Billie Holiday near the end, when her voice was gone and every word she sang seemed tormented, shot through with pain, doomed. Actually, it wasn't that he *liked* these voices, exactly, or that he thought the lyrics in these songs—in any songs, really—were communicating anything profound. But there was something there, something imperfect, something sharp and bent and rusty, that tore into him somehow, that made him believe the human condition was one great and mournful but still achingly beautiful cry.

Maybe the explanation was as simple as what Amy had said again and again, with ever-diminishing affection: that he was, deep down, still just a dopey adolescent kid, as absurd as that tongue-studded teenager, forever filled with longing, forever admiring all the bruises and black eyes and jagged scars he'd accumulated through the years. But Amy, his wife—*Once his wife? Still his wife? No longer his wife?*—Amy was not a kid. She was anything but a kid. Had that been the problem—that even at forty-one, he was still a child, and she was not?

By Henry's second day of driving, the drowning song had evaporated, drummed out of his head by the sheer monotony of the road, by the trees and utility poles and mile markers and billboards he shot past. He had no idea where he was going. He wound up somewhere in southern Georgia. He bought some fruit at a roadside stand, and as the old man there put the plums and peaches into a plastic bag, he said something about the storm and about rice fields growing best under a foot or more of water, but the old man's speech was so garbled, his accent so thick, that Henry couldn't really understand him.

"Thank you," Henry said, nodding, when the man handed him the plastic bag.

"*Ya bedder schubederee blaterik maneshkin, ike tallin ya,*" the man called out when Henry reached his car.

"Yes, yes, good-bye," Henry said, nodding again and waving as if he understood perfectly what the man had said.

More and more, Henry had realized as he drove away, that was happening to him. People spoke in ways that he didn't understand; their accents, their words, the language that they used—all of it seemed to reach him as if it were being transmitted through tin cans and string.

That night he'd simply turned onto a gravel road and parked next to an overgrown baseball field, the red lights of the scoreboard mysteriously switched on. *Go Spartans!* the scoreboard said, though the home team had been down 3–0 in the sixth.

By the third day—Was it really the third day? Henry wondered— he had no idea where he was. He'd heard a few things on the car radio—reports of a breached levee, of the Superdome crowded with those who'd stayed behind, of Mayor Nagin angrily pleading for help—but he hadn't wanted to hear it, hadn't wanted to know. He no longer wanted information, the endless stream of disjointed facts that his mind took in but somehow couldn't process, as if his brain were a sponge left soaking too long in dirty water. As a kid he'd been proud of his mental acuity, his ability to memorize minute details: baseball players' batting averages and long geometry equations, song titles and the dialogue from TV shows and nearly all the capital cities in the world, from Addis Ababa to Yerevan. He'd come to understand, though, with a kind of sullen relief—no longer would he have to bear the prodigy's awful burden—that he was exactly the opposite of brilliant, the opposite of someone who could, with just a few pertinent facts, solve the most complex of problems. He could memorize an encyclopedia's worth of information and still be able to figure out nothing.

Sometimes, before he'd left his job and everything else behind, when he was teaching his eleventh-grade American lit class—expounding on, say, the narrative tricks and turns that Faulkner is up to in *As I Lay Dying*—he'd step away from the blackboard and realize that he'd scribbled so much there that not one word of it was legible, that he had produced a kind of portrait in black and white of his own addled mind. No wonder his students often seemed shell-shocked, mouths open, pens frozen above their spiral notebooks. How could they possibly figure out what they were supposed to remember?

Instead of listening to the news reports, then, he'd quickly scanned through the radio stations until he wound up tuned to the frenzied sermon of some evangelical preacher. When he moved beyond the reach of that Christian station, he easily found another—and then another after that. He didn't exactly listen to what these preachers were shouting, but he found himself transfixed, just as he had been as a child, by the eerie, discordant music of their voices, by the rising and falling intonation and the congregations' dark murmurings of assent, Hammond B3 organs punctuating the complex rhythms of hand claps and foot stomps and shouts, the rapid-fire ricochet of call-and-response.

Sit at His feet and be blessed! one of these preachers shouted, and a hundred voices, maybe a thousand, answered straightaway: *Amen.*

Keep my mind stayed on Thee! And the voices replied: *Amen.*

Expect to be landed upon the shore! Meet me over in the city that's not made by hand! They tell me that city is made four-square. I want to go there! Gates upon the north and south! Gates upon the east and west! I want to go there! I'm clamoring to go there!

Lord, make a way out of no way!

Amen, Henry had silently chimed in. The cavernous echo of these broadcasts made them sound to him like indecipherable but urgent transmissions from another realm. He thought, of course, about his father, who'd been a professor at Tulane, an anthropologist who'd begun, long before Henry was born, frequenting such churches throughout Louisiana and Mississippi, recording and transcribing the sermons and hymns. Henry's father had written his dissertation on sorrow songs throughout the world, examining the shared thematic strains of Gypsy cantatas, Portuguese fados, black spirituals, and Delta blues. Henry had once heard someone describe his father as a "song catcher," and he remembered as a young child picturing him wearing khaki fatigues and holding a giant net, swinging it in wide circles as if he might somehow sweep these songs from the air the way a scientist would capture butterflies in a field of wildflowers. He remembered his father once telling someone—a colleague? a student? Henry himself or Mary, his sister?—that the only thing he was an absolute expert at was longing and loss.

And now Henry had become an expert on that as well. He had lost everything, yes, just as Latangi had said, but as he'd tried to tell her, it hadn't been the hurricane that had done it. He'd lost everything months ago—nearly a year now, in fact.

Everything, Henry thought, hearing Latangi's lilting voice as he sat on the motel-room bed, still transfixed by the images on the TV.

He had squandered not only his job and his marriage but his entire life, reinventing himself by means of erasure, summoning thin air, as it were, from substance. He'd had everything and then, *poof,* in a magician's cloud of manufactured smoke, he had nothing. He hadn't exactly understood at first that this was what he was up to, couldn't have explained it even to himself. But the hurricane had merely completed the job, had hurled him forward so that finally, lo and behold, he no longer recognized a single thing about his life.

Lone behold, one of his students had once written in a paper, and Henry had loved the mistake. *Lone behold.* He'd added it to the list of delightful errors he kept on an index card in his desk drawer, a list he no longer had because he hadn't bothered to return to pick up anything from school when he quit. *Quit or was fired?* Well, it didn't matter. *Lone behold, hammy-downs, boneified, tale-gating, butt naked, asp burger, peach-tree dish, udder silence.* He remembered all of that, remembered precisely where the index card was in the drawer, re-membered which kid had made which mistake, remembered whether or not he had cringed or winced or laughed or felt a profound com-passion for all that was good and kind and true and dumb in this world.

Udder silence. That's what he needed. For a long time now—he couldn't remember how long—there'd been a strange clatter in his head; he felt as though his brain had been scrambled, pithed, the way he'd been forced to do to the frogs in his high-school biology class when Father Ferguson, skeletal and arthritic, his vestments reeking of formaldehyde and cherry pipe smoke, rattled from table to table to make sure none of the boys were engaged in extracurricular acts of torture. "Your problem, Garrett," Father Ferguson had once scolded him, knocking his pipe against Henry's desk, "is that you can't think straight."

It was true, Henry knew. And it was still true. He could not think straight. He had never been able to. But now it was worse. Now, in addition to his own crooked, winding, aimless thoughts, he heard, not voices exactly, but clatter—he didn't have a better word for it; he'd tried but couldn't come up with anything else that accurately captured the sensation. It wasn't static or interference or noise; it wasn't feedback or reverb or echoing; it was *clatter*. He was besieged by snatches of song lyrics, by lines from poems, by commercial jingles, by actors' stentorian recitations, by bits of conversation from years ago, from childhood, all of it looped and overlapping, endlessly repeated until, for no reason he understood, it suddenly stopped, his brain going quiet.

The clatter, despite the annoyance of it, despite the cacophony, made Henry feel oddly ecstatic, transported, brilliantly alive, as if his brain were finally letting go, bit by bit, of all the useless information he had acquired his whole life. He had never remembered his dreams until the clatter began, but now he woke up with long, intricately convoluted stories spilling through his thoughts, unable to distinguish sometimes what he had simply imagined from what he had actually seen or heard or done. The world—the very fact of his being alive in the world—seemed in these moments incredible to Henry, as if any minute now light would burst forth from his fingertips.

Then the clatter—the ecstasy of the clatter—disappeared, and he was left feeling despondent, shaken, utterly and unalterably alone. His right eye—just the one eye, not the other—began watering for no reason, as if half of his face, half of him, had set about weeping.

Amy, of course, had told him to get help, to talk to someone about what was going on—she'd told him this from the very beginning, in fact, from the first dream he'd had about his father—but Henry hadn't listened. Why *should* he listen? He already knew what was happening. He was merely following in his father's footsteps. He was gradually but inexorably losing his mind.

Going crazy, as Amy knew, as he'd told her a hundred times, was the most distinctive and persistent of the Garrett traits, the deep dark cleft in their familial chin. He'd explained it to her when they first met—not a warning exactly but, well, *information,* he'd said, just something he figured she ought to know. He'd made it sound as though he were joking. He hadn't been, of course. He'd described for her the generations of Garretts who had made the ascent to the rickety, toppling edge of sanity only to peer down into the great abyss below. Most of the stories were mundanely sad ones, stories of quiet disappearances and grim sanatoriums and lonely suicides. Some were so strange, though, that they were almost funny. Before the turn of the century, in the 1880s or 1890s, one of Henry's paternal ancestors had famously leaped from a bank building on Canal Street, his pockets stuffed with cash. Snooks Eaglin, a local musician, a blind man, had written a song about the incident, a song Henry once heard him sing at the Mid-City bowling alley where he performed on Thursday nights, the crowd shouting out requests while dancing on the waxed wooden floor in bowling shoes or sock feet, the thump and rumble of the balls and the crack and echo of the tumbling pins creating the sensation that a mighty thunderstorm was raging outside.

Angel's left his wings behind, Eaglin sang in a comical stage whisper, as if he were imparting a secret he was worried might be overheard. He leaned near the microphone and flashed a smile directly to a young woman in the audience as if he could see her, as if he weren't really blind.

Angel's left his wings behind.
Figures he'll put them to use some other time.
Standing at the edge of that windowsill,
he's betting heaven's got change for them hundred-dollar bills.

Henry had meant to approach Eaglin sometime and ask where he'd heard the story and when exactly he'd written the song, but he never did. He lacked his father's fervor for historical detail. All around, in every way, Henry knew, what he lacked was *fervor.* Instead he possessed *torpor;* he embraced *turbidity;* he welcomed *languor.* He was a *woolgatherer. A coward. A squanderer. A louse.*

Oh, the sweet, sad lamentations of one Henry Archer Garrett, he heard in the radio preacher's singsong voice, *the woeful likes of which this world might be well and goodly blessed to never see hide nor hair of again.*

Amen.

Henry had also told Amy how as a child he'd watched as his great-uncle William Rainey Garrett, his grandfather's only brother, became completely undone.

"Undone?" Amy had said.

"You know what I mean," Henry had answered.

"You mean crazy?" Amy said, and he'd nodded, but what seemed more interesting to Henry was the *manner* in which that craziness expressed itself. His great-uncle had been a municipal court judge who, after his wife died from breast cancer, began handing down increasingly bizarre sentences to defendants. He'd ordered a landlord convicted of beating up tenants late with the rent to leave the state and not return until he'd gotten Willie Mays's signature on a baseball glove, and he'd told a French Quarter stripper convicted on morals charges that she had to adopt three dogs from the SPCA by the end of the week or he'd send her to jail. Finally, his great-uncle ordered a man who'd been convicted of stealing a few hundred dollars and a Doberge cake from Gambino's Bakery to scale the Robert E. Lee monument and scrub the pigeon droppings from the Confederate general's hat; the monument was sixty feet high, and while drunkenly attempting to comply with the order, the man had fallen, breaking his left arm and cracking his hip. He'd made it only about five feet up the column. At that point, Judge Garrett had been quietly removed from the bench.

It had all begun, Henry told Amy, with his great-uncle's wife's death. So maybe it had been sorrow that fueled the madness.

"At least sparked it," Amy said.

"At least sparked it," Henry agreed.

Henry had gone with his father to visit his great-uncle a few months before the old man died. The navy-blue Lincoln Town Car in his garage had four flat tires, and Henry and his father listened as his great-uncle, sitting at the kitchen table, repeated the same story over and over—how he'd once stood with his wife, Maudellena, at the top of Mount McKinley when the wind was so strong it blew pebbles across their feet until they were covered up to their ankles.

"You already told us that one, Uncle Will," Henry's father said each time the story was done, smiling conspiratorially at Henry and patting the old man's arm.

"Did I?" he said, shaking his head, a strange vacant look of horror imprinted on his face, as if each moment contained for the old man some component of recognition of the clarity and reason that had been stolen from him.

Henry's father, before he disappeared, had told Henry, though Henry was too young to understand exactly what his father meant, that this penchant for madness was like a fascinating but exquisitely grotesque family heirloom, one that remained tucked away inside a drawer for years and years until it was finally pulled out for inspection on some appropriately dire occasion.

"No matter how badly you want to see it, don't go looking for it," his father had told him. "Maybe you won't stumble upon it."

Henry had just nodded, thoroughly confused. Who would want

17

to go looking for madness? And what *should* he be doing, what should he be looking for instead?

It was as if his father were talking to himself, though, rather than his son, and yet his father had indeed stumbled upon this grotesque family heirloom. "Carried off by the blues," his mother had once said of his father's disappearance, as if it were something charmingly romantic, deserving of its own musical homage. She had never once acknowledged, despite Henry's and Mary's anguish and confusion, that their father had—*cruelly, unforgivably*—abandoned them, had simply left behind everything, the only apparent clue to his disappearance the words scribbled on a sheet of paper on his office desk at Tulane. They were, Henry eventually learned, the first three lines of a Charley Patton song:

> *I'm goin' away, to a world unknown*
> *I'm goin' away, to a world unknown*
> *I'm worried now, but I won't be worried long…*

His father probably hadn't meant anything by writing out these words and leaving them on his desk. They probably were not a suicide note or a final cryptic fuck-you flourish. His father was always scribbling lyrics in the black notebook he kept in his pocket. When he was little, Henry hadn't understood that his father wasn't making up these words, that he was simply transcribing what he'd heard.

Now Henry had done exactly what his father had done. He had disappeared. He had driven aimlessly until he wound up precisely in the middle of nowhere, in a motel with lampshades printed with the image of Ganesh, the Hindus' crazy deity, a royal elephant astride a rat. Wasn't there anywhere else he could have gone, any friends who would have welcomed him, who would have embraced him and offered a meal and a bed?

Friends. They were already part of the *everything* that he had managed to lose. *Wife, home, job, friends.*

The art of losing. That was part of the first line of a poem he used to teach, a poet losing door keys, handkerchiefs. Even a continent, she said. *A lover? A father? Had she lost a father?* He couldn't remember. *So many things,* the poem had asserted, *seem filled with the intent to be lost.*

He had lost them all, lost everything. He had swallowed ruin and wreckage and despair. He was alone, fully alone, and he could not even bring himself to weep, could not summon that awful cry of loss and longing and regret that would at least announce that he was alive.

Well, he needed to sleep. But he could not stop watching, in silence, the devastation on TV. Even the commercials that interrupted the news—the shiny cars and complicated exercise equipment and scowling attorneys—seemed part of the whole ordeal, a scripted morality play whose message, like that of the hysterical preachers on the radio, was inscrutable to Henry. At first he tried to guess what the reporters must be saying as they stood on wet and dark French Quarter corners—at St. Peter and Royal, at Chartres and St. Louis—or rode through the flooded streets in narrow boats with outboard motors, but as the hours passed he realized that, to counteract the silence, to fend off his exhaustion, he had begun making up their words. They mouthed the lyrics to Bob Dylan's "Don't Fall Apart on Me Tonight," which he'd once proposed to Amy they adopt as their theme song, a suggestion for which she'd only half jokingly slapped him, hard enough to sting. The reporters recited ingredients that Amy used to read aloud to him from the recipes she'd concocted. They counted to one hundred in French and then Spanish—Henry had memorized these words as a kid without bothering to learn the languages—and they sang "The Star-Spangled Banner" in Latangi's lilting Indian accent. He saw the masses huddled outside the Superdome and the convention center, some of them shouting angrily at the cameras, most merely hanging their heads, defeated and grim, and he heard in his head the swelling strings of that endless Gavin Bryars composition, the one that for nearly an hour looped the sad, sweet voice of a bum in a London tube station, the bum singing over and over: *Jesus's blood never failed me yet.*

Udder silence. Lone behold. None of this can be real, Henry told himself, and it was as if he were constructing for his students some complex exercise in grammar and mechanics: none of this *can be, could be, will be, has been, has ever been, will ever be, will ever have been* real.

But it *was* real, Henry knew. He knew that much, at least. He was not that far gone. He kept recognizing the neighborhoods and buildings that popped up on the screen: an antiques store on Royal Street where he once bought Amy a mirror, the plywood covering the store's windows ripped away, the glass shattered; Lawrence's Bakery on the corner of Filmore and Elysian Fields, its metal roof twisted grotesquely, like the recently shed skin of a giant snake; the Robert E. Lee theater, the floodwaters nearly reaching its marquee; the Bucktown shrimp boats pitched up against the side of an elementary-school gym like broken and abandoned toys. In high school Henry had dated a girl from Bucktown, a Mount Carmel Academy girl named Lacey Gaudet whose father had single-handedly built a new house in the backyard of their old one, transferring the bricks one by one from the old house to the new. When he was just about done, Henry had asked him what he planned to do with the foundation of the old house, and Mr. Gaudet said he was going to turn it into a giant indoor swimming pool, each room a different pool but all of them connected by narrow channels of water. "Just like the bayous," he'd told Henry, smiling. "What do you think?"

Henry had believed him, hadn't realized that Mr. Gaudet was pulling his leg. But then he had slapped Henry on the back and said, with a bitterness that caught Henry by surprise, "It's all coming down, son. It's good for nothing."

Henry had liked Mr. Gaudet. He had been a riverboat pilot but retired early when his wife died. Lacey had once proposed setting up her father and Henry's mother. When Henry said he didn't think so, Lacey said, "It might be cool, you know. He's kind of lonely."

"My mother doesn't go out on dates," Henry told her. "You've met her. She doesn't go anywhere."

"Well, maybe she would," Lacey said. "Maybe if he called her and asked her."

"No," Henry said, uncomfortable. How could he explain to Lacey without hurting her feelings that her father and his mother inhabited separate worlds, that they were about as different as two people could possibly be? His mother was—what? An intellectual? An artist? A bohemian? What word would she have used? An eccentric? A recluse? A hermit? A loon?

Henry could still hear his mother's voice, the silly wordplay in which she and Henry's sister had engaged, a kind of game requiring the construction of nonsensical phrases: *Unilateral eclipse. Ecclesiastical ellipsis. Liturgical itinerancy. Truncated vice.* There were rules, but Henry hadn't understood them. He'd sensed that they didn't want him to understand.

When he and Lacey had first started dating, Henry had offered to help her father with the house. "What can you do, Henry?" Mr. Gaudet had asked. "Masonry? Roofing? Tile work?" Henry had been forced to admit that he didn't know how to do anything. Mr. Gaudet had wrapped his arm around Henry's shoulder as if to suggest that he felt bad that Henry didn't have a father to teach him such skills. But Henry's father, of course, hadn't known how to do any of those things either. *He was a professor,* Henry had wanted to say, figuring that would provide sufficient explanation. Even before his father left, nothing in their house—leaking faucets, broken tiles, warped window screens, peeling plaster—had ever gotten fixed.

Breaking things. Breaking down. Those, too, like losing, were the arts that Henry—and so many Garretts before him—had mastered.

Lacey was the one, though, who had broken up with Henry. It was during senior year, after a dance at Mount Carmel, one in which they'd argued the whole time about something—he couldn't remember what—the two of them sitting at the top of the gym's bleachers and shouting at each other over the music.

"This isn't exactly what I'd call fun," Lacey had told him once they'd finally gone outside, and she'd left him there, leaning against his car, an old mud-colored Chevy Impala with torn red vinyl seats, a car that still smelled, a year later, of the skunk he'd run over one night on Pontchartrain Boulevard. After that night Lacey had made a face every single time she got into the car, but Henry had grown to like the smell, the strange acrid sweetness of it.

It had been the very night he'd hit the skunk—in fact, precisely *because* he'd hit the skunk—that Henry and Lacey had first had sex, in a thick grove of magnolia trees in a small park near the lakefront. Earlier, they'd stopped at the 7-Eleven near Lacey's house, and they'd poured a pint of rum into Coca-Cola Icees, their usual concoction. They were driving around listening to the radio and trying to finish their drinks before heading to a party. But when they hit the skunk—they'd thought for a second that it was a squirrel, which was awful enough, but then they were instantly assaulted by the smell, their eyes watering, Lacey suddenly coughing and gagging—Henry pulled over as soon as he could. They scrambled from the car into the magnolia grove only to discover that the smell was still there, that it was on their clothes. So they peeled off their shirts and jeans, but Lacey smelled her hair and then her hands and started gagging again. She started cursing in a way he'd never heard her curse, using the foulest of language, choking it out—*Jesus motherfucking Christ! Goddamned motherfucking sonofamotherfuckingbitch!*—but she was laughing even as she cursed, and Henry was laughing too but also worried someone would hear Lacey, would come running and think he was assaulting her, so he tried to put his hand over her mouth. She snapped at his fingers as if she meant to bite him, but then she licked his palm and said, *Ugh, I can taste it, I can, I swear it's fucking everywhere,* so he started licking her hand and then her arm and then her neck, just to tease her, to make her laugh, and he kept saying *I like it* or *Mmmm* or something stupid like that, and that's how they'd wound up actually doing it, both of them a little drunk, or at least tipsy enough to fend off the shyness and the cringing embarrassment and the ignorance and fear. And it was okay; it was. They both felt fine about it and in the months that followed they got a bit better and managed a kind of patient, fumbling grace, but they never quite overcame the new weight that somehow descended upon their time together, and it was probably that weight, the drag of it, more than any big argument or suspected infidelity, that finally caused Lacey to break up with him.

He wondered now what had happened to Lacey Gaudet. She'd gone off to LSU, he knew, but then he'd never seen her again, never come across her name in the *Times-Picayune,* never heard from someone who knew someone that she'd gotten married or had had a baby or had wound up divorced. How could it happen that people simply disappeared from your life? And her father—was he still alive? Was he still living in that house? Then it occurred to Henry that even if Mr. Gaudet was alive and still living in Bucktown, the house he'd built with his own hands was certainly now gone. Henry closed his eyes and tried to imagine it, tried to envision not just the Gaudet house but every house in the city underwater: his mother's house, Amy's. He imagined water rushing street to street, climbing walls, bursting through windows. Oh God. Was it really possible? Even though he was seeing it on the TV, he couldn't do it, couldn't really create a convincing picture in his head.

Henry stared at the screen until dawn, until he noticed the line of light at the edge of the room's heavy curtains, then he turned off the television and stepped outside, out onto the parking lot, the asphalt glistening, the few cars and pickup trucks there shining with dew. Where was he? How had he wound up here? There was no one, not a single person on this earth, who knew where he was, what had become of him.

No, there was this one person, a complete stranger: Latangi. *L* as in *library*, *a* as in *love*. *A* as in *love*? *T* as in *flowering telegraph lines*?

Nothing made sense anymore.

Henry looked beyond the motel's gray walls and flat roof to the mountains, but the air was misty, and the mountains seemed to have disappeared overnight, seemed as though they had simply been erased.

He stepped back into his room, lay down on the bed in his dirty clothes, closed his eyes, and slept.

Two

As USUAL, his sleep was fitful, littered with the fragments of dreams, each with the same absurd, entirely predictable theme—that he was lost, that the world lay in ruins around him. In each he appeared as a sort of shadowy figure, a phantom or nomad. Or worse: a tourist who had misread his guidebook and had wandered into a neighborhood or across a border where he wasn't supposed to stray.

One moment he shuffled unnoticed through a bustling, dusty market somewhere in Senegal; in the next he bent above a legless Armenian beggar to hear the plaintive strains of a reeded duduk. At a Shinto shrine in Nara, the ancient Japanese capital—a place he'd actually visited with Amy—he knelt on a carpet of cherry blossoms before a mural depicting the sun goddess's brother Susano, the god of storms, brandishing his sword above the roiling waves to slay an eight-headed dragon.

Like a portentous National Geographic Channel special, these fragments of dreams were accompanied by an interminable narration, a relentless litany of woes intoned in a weary, measured cadence. *The world is irreparably in thrall to violence,* the voice declared. *Every-*

where soldiers flash their rifles and spit curses. Men, women, and children cower in the street. Villages burn, cities collapse, cars explode into blossoms of bright shrapnel and black flames. Somalia. Yemen. Sierra Leone. Iraq. All is chaos, misrule. All is fury and vanity and desire.

How is it, the narrator pondered, *that this man who would throw away his life has survived? Why hasn't he been shot or captured and held for ransom or beheaded? This man who no longer believes in luck, in providence, in blessedness or good fortune? This squanderer? This coward? This louse?*

The dreams went on, a turgid and wearying documentary, inexpertly spliced, the narrator's voice a caricature of Henry's own, his baritone deepened to a bottomless bass. Henry watched himself shoving his way through teeming streets, past young girls twirling in the last tatters of taffeta dresses, past boys who bared their scrawny chests and flexed their withered arms as though their bodies were made of steel. Henry saw himself crossing deserts and traversing mountains, braving listing buses and smoke-spewing trains. He had no idea where, in these dreams, he was trying to get to, where it was he thought he was going. He was lost. He was always lost. He didn't need these dreams to tell him that.

And then the girl appeared, as she always did now, and Henry was struck once again by the sheer desolation of his desire. The downy swell of her abdomen, the torturous landscape of still-ripening breasts and thighs. Her delicate hands, the nails jagged, gnawed, unpainted. The melancholy smile, the schoolgirl shrug of her shoulders, the clack of a peppermint, the sweetly indecipherable scent of her skin. The images descended into the obscene, a jumbled litany of erotic enumeration: *lithe folds of labia, dark areolae of breasts, ass and calf and snatch*—all of it tawdry and overwrought, as if the words had been stolen from some slathering poet: *the pouting berry of lips, the jaunty cock of hips, the sinuous stretch and spread and coiling whip of ecstatic release, song of the demonic, protrusion of nipple, juice and sweat, blossom and blossom and ache.*

Oh God. And now, for the first time in all of these dreams, the girl had acquired a name: Clarissa Nash.

Clarissa Nash. Henry had no idea where this name had come from, who the girl might be. She was not one of his former high-school students, thank God, at least not one he could remember. And why— *and how?*—would he remember someone he didn't remember? He tried to persuade himself that she must be simply a character from a book, but he knew that this too could not be true. She was far too real, far too—absurd as it might sound—*detailed.* How old was she? Nineteen or twenty, Henry guessed, maybe a bit older. Not a child. At least not that. Even so, he was forty-one. His desire was unyielding, sublime, pathetic, absurd. Whether or not she actually existed seemed, in a way, the least of his concerns. He just wanted her, wanted these dreams, to leave him alone.

The girl, unnamed then, had begun to appear in his dreams three months ago—in May, when Amy had finally given up on him and left New Orleans. She hadn't cried when she told him she was leaving; she'd been resolute, abrupt, unflinching. He'd asked her to stay, to give him time; he'd explained that he was doing better, that he was figuring things out.

"You're living in a grocery store, Henry," she'd told him. "What is it exactly you think you're figuring out?"

It was true. Nine months earlier he'd moved out. He'd taken everything he owned to the empty grocery store, which he'd bought with his share of the money from his mother's estate. It was a vast, fluorescent-lit aluminum-and-glass building on Magazine Street a few blocks from their house on Prytania—Amy's house, actually, a beautifully renovated shotgun he'd simply moved into when they got married. Everything about the grocery store was tired and sad and downtrodden, the front windows smeared with grease and dotted with the taped corners of old advertisements, the aluminum shelves sagging and bent, the red-tiled floors cracked. Fresh and Friendly had been the grocery's name when it was still operating, though Amy had dubbed it the Stale and Surly. She'd refused to shop there, pointing out that the canned goods were always covered with dust, that the floor was always sticky, that the one shelf reserved for international foods included, as if they were exotic delicacies, anchovies and Vienna sausages. She'd said that Melvin the butcher, in his white shirt and thin black tie and bloody apron, constantly complained about the weather and about foreigners and about children's grimy fingers on the glass of the meat case.

Amy had nearly killed Henry, of course, when he told her he'd used his mother's money, his only inheritance, to buy the building.

She'd shaken her head, disgusted. "You've fucking lost it, Henry," she'd said. "This time you've really fucking lost it."

He'd tried to explain it to her, had begged her to understand. Now, though, to be honest, he couldn't really remember what he'd been thinking or what he'd said to Amy in his defense. He had just felt— he had *known*—that he couldn't keep the money from his mother's estate, that he didn't want it. And when the store had been put up for sale, he'd bought it. It was crazy. He'd known it was crazy. But it had been necessary. That was one of the words he'd used with Amy. *Necessary.*

"Necessary?" Amy had said, incredulous, irate, packing her bags for a trip to Central America, to Guatemala and Honduras and Belize. *Hunting the Palm's Heart: A Hundred Recipes,* her next book was to be called. She'd told him the names of the different trees: the cohune, the waree, the jipijapa, the pokenoboy. She'd told him that each had a different heart. The names had spun in his head; he'd imagined the spiked leaves, the towering trunks. He hadn't been able to respond, to think clearly, to explain what he meant.

"You're going to open a *business,* Henry?" Amy had said, and he'd known from the way she'd said the word *business* precisely what she meant—that he was not equipped to run a business, to run anything: a lawn mower, a vacuum, a blender. He'd tried to think of something he could say that he planned to do with the building—open a bookstore, maybe, or perhaps a concert hall or coffee shop.

"You could have a restaurant there," he'd told her instead. "I bet you could do it."

"If I'd wanted a restaurant, Henry," Amy had responded, "don't you think I'd have mentioned it by now?"

She'd looked at him, fuming, waiting to hear what on fucking God's green earth he might say next. *God's green earth.* That was one of her favorite expressions. He'd said nothing, so Amy had zipped her luggage shut, looked at him again, and sighed. "I don't know what's wrong with you," she'd said, her voice quiet now. "I understand something's wrong, but I can't tell you what it is or how to fix it. I wish I could. Believe me, I wish I could. But you're going to have to do it on your own. You're going to have to find someone, Henry. I've thought about this a lot. Before this. Before now. While I'm gone, you're going to have to find someone. You hear me? You understand what I'm saying?"

"Yes," he'd said, "I understand." And she had just left him there.

No. First she had put her arms around him, told him she loved him, told him that he was the kindest man, the most generous and loving man, she'd ever known. She told him he'd get through this, that she knew he would, but that he needed to figure out how. "You *need* to," she'd said, but he hadn't been sure if that was a plea or a threat. Then she'd left.

He'd stood there in the bedroom, waited, then sat down on the bed. He'd wanted to call out to her, tell her that he had lied, that he did not understand anything, that he was—his mind was—addled. *Disordered.*

Then he'd heard the door close, heard Amy leaving. He understood what he was losing, what he had lost, but he couldn't help himself.

Find someone, she had said. He'd known exactly what she meant: Find a doctor, a therapist, a shrink. Talk to him or her. Take whatever pills were prescribed. Get better. Get himself unaddled, unclattered, de-pithed, unbent.

Instead he had simply moved out of their house and into the store. This, too, he had decided, was necessary, was something he needed to do even though he could hear Amy's voice in his head, even though he knew what she would say, the very words she would use.

Crazy.

Idiot.

Disaster.

Unforgivable.

Too much.

The end.

He'd thought about his father's disappearance—home and then not home, here and then gone. Now and now and now and finally then. These words took on a flavor in his mouth, a certain metallic bitterness. They acquired colors and shades, even shapes. He saw them in the late-afternoon light spilling through the grimy storefront windows and in the dust his feet kicked up off the red-tiled floor.

So unremarkable had been his father's departure that he had no memory of the final words that had passed between them, a final glance or touch. Here. Gone. Now. Then.

With Amy still in Central America, unaware of what he'd done, he'd settled in. He slept on a mattress in the nook of the elevated customer-service counter, all of his possessions—his books and records and CDs and fountain pens and photographs, his clothes and his collection of old inlaid wooden boxes, his father's double bass and beat-up guitars and banjo, a kora from Mali, congas from Cuba, a few of his mother's strange, garish paintings—all of it spread out across the grocery-store shelves as though he meant to sell them. He didn't know why he was there, didn't know what he was doing, what he would tell Amy when she returned. His mind wasn't right—that was about the only thing he knew. He felt sometimes as though his eyes wouldn't quite focus, as if his pupils were dilated and taking in too much light. His thoughts wandered like a dog endlessly tracking a phantom scent, like random musical notes on a staff that, when played, produced something that vaguely resembled a melody but was not, was simply noise. When people started peering through the windows and knocking on the glass doors, asking what he wanted for this or that, he let them in, told them to pay whatever they thought was a fair price. It was usually more than he would have thought to ask for.

He figured that, soon enough, everything would be gone and he would be released from his life, but then at night or early in the morning, people began leaving their own stuff, their own unwanted possessions, outside the door: bags of clothes and toys, toaster ovens and boom boxes and ice skates and prom dresses and bow ties and bicycles and picture books and paperback novels and ceramic vases and dog crates and infant car seats and shoe boxes stuffed with photographs and postcards and letters. Henry hauled everything inside and put it all out on the shelves, and before long there were teenagers with spiked hair and young couples holding hands and old women and antiques dealers spending hours rooting through the junk, homeless men coming inside for the coffee he made in one of the half a dozen drip machines—two Mr. Coffees, two Black and Deckers, a Krups, a Braun—that had been left at the store, men who couldn't manage more than a few words of conversation but liked to pick up his father's banjo or one of the old guitars and pretend they could play, mumbling the lyrics to songs they hadn't heard in years, songs that reminded them, Henry guessed, of women they'd known before their lives had fallen apart.

Just like me, Henry had thought, and a song by Paul Revere and the Raiders leaped inside his head: *It's just like me to say to you, Love me do and I'll be true.*

He recommended books to those who came in looking for something to read, not the books he'd taught his high-school kids over the years—*The Grapes of Wrath* and *Leaves of Grass* and *The Great Gatsby* and *As I Lay Dying*—but old paperbacks with yellowed library cards glued to envelopes on the inside covers, books that he hadn't actually read but that had been left outside, their titles full of a kind of inept promise: *The Estate of the Beckoning Lady, Detour to Oblivion, Wild Angel, Gideon's Mouth, The Bottom of the Garden, Pray for a Brave Heart.*

They might be terrible books, Henry thought, but they would all be good names for bands—Wild Angel, Detour to Oblivion, Gideon's Mouth—and he would use one if only he knew how to play an instrument or sing, if only he weren't completely talentless and also, by the way, *forty-one,* as Amy had reminded him, two decades too old for such nonsense.

He played his records and CDs all day, and soon people began to bring in their own, desperate to share with Henry, as if they were talismanic good-luck charms, their all-time favorite songs: Conway Twitty's "It's Only Make Believe" and King Crimson's "I Talk to the Wind" and Sergio Mendes and Brasil '66's "The Look of Love" and—brought in by one thin, ancient woman, her white hair tied up in a gold scarf, the skin on her arms translucent—Ernestine Anderson singing a Harold Arlen song, "As Long As I Live," the woman twirling down the aisles as the song played, her eyes tightly closed, her arms out as if she were being led by a partner as graceful as Gene Kelly or Fred Astaire. Henry's head was filled not just with these songs and their lyrics but with thousands and thousands more, an endless encyclopedia of rhymes and puns, verses and refrains and choruses and codas.

Of all the regulars who wandered into the store, Henry's favorite was an old man named Tomas Otxoa, a squat, bald man with striking blue eyes and a great hooked nose beneath his broad forehead. He seemed to Henry to have the kind of face you'd see carved in profile on ancient coins, a face that suggested both absolute confidence and implacable serenity, though Tomas was, Henry knew, a profoundly hopeless drunk. He arrived most afternoons with a large plastic tumbler filled with some concoction—Beefeater's and tonic, he told Henry, with a thimble's worth of olive brine—and left an hour or so later, the tumbler empty, one or two of Henry's jazz albums tucked under his arm, albums he would then return the next day, handing them back and nodding in appreciation.

"Very fine, excellent," he said each time in his strange not-quite-Spanish accent, raising the replenished plastic tumbler toward Henry as if to salute his superb taste.

Though the store was usually crowded, Tomas served as Henry's only friend. They would settle into a matching pair of torn corduroy La-Z-Boys at the back of the store, and Tomas would sigh and close his eyes.

Sometimes Tomas asked Henry about his life. Mostly, though, he talked about his own. He had been a businessman, he said, with one home in San Sebastián and another in Caracas. He had finally come to America in search of his brother, Joaquim, who thirty years earlier had escaped from one of the tyrant Franco's prisons by curling himself up inside an acoustical speaker, one that belonged to a group of musicians who had been ordered to play at the prison in honor of the Generalissimo's birthday.

"As you see, I am no one," Tomas said, smiling, opening his eyes and raising his tumbler toward Henry. "I am a tuna fish salesman, an old bachelor. But my brother, you must understand, is Joaquim Xabier Otxoa. Say his name in Euskadi, in the Basque Country, and everyone will know. Recite the words *Ni ez pertson egokia lan hontarako,* and they will tell you that these are the words that begin Joaquim's first and grandest work, *Asmatzailearean Amoranta.* They are to us as resonant, if that is the proper term, as your words of 'Call me Ishmael.' You understand? But there is behind them a sadness as well, for Joaquim was required to compose these words and all the others that were to follow not in his home, not in his own country, but in his secret exile, his hiding place."

Tomas looked up then as if he were confused or as if he only now realized that Henry was there beside him. "How long?" he said. "How long should Joaquim remain hidden?"

"How long?" Henry asked.

"For three decades," Tomas shouted, waving his arms. "For three decades Joaquim is—what? For three decades like a ghost." And he went on with his story, explaining that throughout these thirty years, his brother had dispatched his manuscripts to his publisher's office in the Basque Country's capital of Bilbao not by proper post but by a series of clandestine couriers, many of whom were unaware of the precise nature of their mission. Perhaps they believed they had been entrusted with stolen documents or the blueprints of heavily guarded municipal offices, Tomas said. Perhaps they thought that here were the coded correspondences of the leaders, the so-called terrorists, of ETA, the very plans that would set in motion a spectacular conflagration. Or so his brother might have implied, for who would risk arrest and interrogation, perhaps even torture, in the service of a mere story, an invented tale? "Who would do such as this?" Tomas said, looking at Henry as if he expected an answer, some sort of challenge to the pronouncements he had made.

Henry remained silent.

"They would do so for Joaquim," he said, nodding. "Imagine to be alive at the very time of your greatest artists. Herman Melville. Walt Whitman. Imagine this."

"Would we know, though?" Henry said. "Would we recognize them? Would we know they were among us?"

Tomas nodded. "Perhaps not always," he said. "But *we* know."

And so day after day Henry simply listened as Tomas wound his way through the story of his brother's life, which seemed only coincidently his own as well—how as boys they had stood outside in their father's fields and observed in the night sky the bombs exploding, believing they were merely fireworks announcing the spring festival in Donostia. But their mother had rushed out to call them inside. She was hysterical, weeping, for she had already learned of the previous day's slaughter in Gernika. Then Tomas's father joined the Republicans and six months later met his death in the Battle of Teruel, a futile victory that the Fascists soon reversed. Tomas and Joaquim and their mother attempted to tend to the family vineyard, but the grapes mourned his father's death by turning bitter that first harvest and the next and thus they were forced to leave their village of Getaria so their mother could take a seamstress's job at a factory in Tolosa. "A small, invisible place, this city of Tolosa," Tomas said. He looked at Henry, sipped his drink, and shook his head. "For thirty years I spent every waking hour selling tuna fish to the world. It is true, I suppose, that I was more successful than most men in the earning of money, but now I am merely an old bachelor with arthritic knees and a troublesome prostate and a fondness for American jazz and English gin and the red wines of the Rioja."

Henry had waited patiently for Tomas to work his way through to his story's conclusion—whether or not he had found his brother here in America, whether or not they had been reunited. He assumed, of course, that the ending was a sad one, that the tone of weary resignation with which Tomas spoke implied that his brother had never been found or that Tomas had somehow learned that Joaquim had passed away wherever it was he had been hiding. But Henry never heard the story's end. After about a month of these afternoon visits, Tomas just stopped coming. Henry asked some of the others, those who regularly appeared at the store to sift through the shelves and boxes, if they'd seen Tomas, but they looked back at Henry bewildered, as if they suspected that he had invented this story of the old Basque man with his gin and tonic. For a few weeks, early in the morning and late in the afternoon, Henry would search through the neighborhood for Tomas, walking in circles around Camp and Upperline and Constance and as far south as Tchoupitoulas and then across the train tracks to the loading docks along the river. He suspected, but wasn't sure, that Tomas might have found some other place—a bar or old record shop or coffeehouse—that seemed more hospitable, somewhere he'd have an audience of more than just one person for his stories.

The number of people who occupied the store during the day, though, had continued to grow. A few painters and a potter asked what kind of commission Henry wanted to sell their work, and when he told them he didn't want anything, they came back with the things they'd made and told their friends, who soon showed up with strange watercolor paintings of roadkill and tiny sculptures made from wire coat hangers and Cornell-inspired boxes depicting the Stations of the Cross and a series of hand-printed miniature comic books illustrating the adventures of a pug named Jameson Julius Jehovaseth Jones.

Henry didn't have a license or whatever document you needed to run a store, and there was no sign out front except the old Fresh and Friendly neon, for which Henry eventually found the switch, though only the last bit of the sign lit up, the *endly* part, which seemed exactly right to Henry, and soon he began hearing people calling it Endly's, as if that were not just the store's name but his own: Henry Endly, sole proprietor of Endly's Greatly Used Wares and Whatnots. He figured before long some city official would come by and shut things down, but a few months passed and no one appeared. Henry dragged his mattress to the office in back of the store, and the artists, worried about the safety of their work, set up a schedule for manning the cash register out front, a plastic children's replica that played one of three tunes when the drawer slid open: "Mary Had a Little Lamb" and "Shoo Fly" and one that Henry didn't recognize and that no one else seemed to know either. As the end of summer, when Henry was due to return to Benjamin Franklin High School, approached, Henry called the principal, Paul Kehoe, and told him he wouldn't be back.

"What's going on?" Kehoe asked.

"I've just got my hands full, Paul."

Kehoe didn't even bother to ask what Henry meant. He'd probably heard something from Amy, or maybe he was just happy to no longer have a teacher like Henry to deal with, one who didn't pay a moment's attention to the prescribed curriculum, who simply taught whatever he felt like teaching even though it was supposed to be junior-year American lit and not, as Kehoe liked to say, the world according to Henry Garrett. The students, of course, loved Henry's classes, loved him, mistaking his ineptitude for eccentricity, his disorder for improvisation, his indolence for rebellion. They called him HG instead of Mr. Garrett, and they congregated in the hall outside his office during their free periods so they could listen to the crazy music he always played inside—scratchy LPs of blues or jazz or of the great Amália Rodrigues bemoaning her sad fate or Inés Bacán shrieking through a *siguiriya*—though playing music was, as Kehoe repeatedly informed Henry, both contrary to policy and inconsiderate to others.

In the store, as Henry talked to Kehoe, he had turned up the music, made sure Kehoe could hear it on his end of the line before he hung up the phone. And despite Henry's innate predisposition for ineptitude, rather than floundering, the enterprise that was Endly's somehow managed not merely to make ends meet but to flourish. The old books found faithful readers, the modest dresses acquired admiring ingénues, the more risqué fashions attracted a willing clientele, and the avant-garde artwork brought in adventurous investors, and thus the money—though it was not at all what Henry had intended—began to roll in, spilling out of the plastic cash register and then being stuffed into tins of empty Community Coffee cans that Henry aligned side by side on a back storeroom shelf.

The money disappeared, though, almost as quickly as it appeared, especially during the last few days of the month, when the artists

raided the coffee cans to pay their rent, and the homeless men concocted disjointed tales of wives and children needing medicine or
of on-their-deathbeds mothers in Bogalusa or Grand Coteau whom
they wanted to visit or of Chalmette mobsters threatening to break
their thumbs or slice off their ring fingers if they didn't pay some por-
tion of their gambling debts. Henry gave them all what they asked
for, as much as he had on hand. When Amy returned from Central
America, Henry tried to give her some of the money as well, but she
wouldn't take it, wouldn't even speak to him, really. Once, he spotted
her outside staring in through the windows, her hand shielding her
eyes against the glare. He went out there, tried to talk to her, but she
crossed her arms and said, "You don't have any idea how much you've
hurt me, do you?"

"I do," he said. "I do, Amy. It's just—"

But she turned and walked away, left him there—helpless, perplexed, in agony. How, for the millionth time, had he been unable
to explain what was going on inside his head? He missed her, he did.
And he knew that by leaving her he'd lost more than he could ever
calculate. And yet...and yet...

He didn't know. He couldn't say. The clatter was ruining him,
ruining every thought, slicing every moment into distinct, uncon-
nected fragments.

When someone from the city's commercial registrations office finally did walk through the door—*Jerome T. Burton, CRO Inspector,*
it said on his card—Henry wasn't surprised.

Henry asked if he'd still need a business license if he simply gave
everything away. Mr. Burton made a stern face but allowed that he
didn't really know as he had never been asked such a question; he said
he would get back to Henry promptly. "In a week's time. Five business days," he added decisively, as if the words were a threat.

Henry, though, didn't wait for an answer. He told the artists they could no longer sell their work in the store, and one by one they took away the things they'd made. He put up a sign that told customers they were free to leave with as much as they could carry, and by the end of the week, just about everything was gone. The only item Henry kept, the one thing he'd never agreed to sell, was his father's bass, a great bronze-bodied Kay that for years had stood untouched in a corner of their dining room, the only place in their house where it wasn't in the way. It had always felt to Henry like an uninvited guest who arrived each night at dinnertime but wouldn't sit down and eat. Henry had refused to sell the bass—he'd gotten offers ranging from twenty dollars to two thousand—not so much for sentimental reasons as empirical ones. It was by means of this bass, of his father playing it, that his own undoing had begun, and he thought that maybe one day the instrument might prove necessary—that word again—for him to put himself back together.

This is what had happened: One night in bed, Amy peacefully asleep beside him, Henry had watched as his father—the ghost of his father, of course, because his father was by then undoubtedly dead—stepped into the room, the bass tucked beneath his arm as if it were no larger or heavier than a violin. Henry continued to watch as his father walked forward, stopped at the foot of the bed, set down the instrument, leaned into it, stretched his hands across the strings, and began to play, humming the melody whose rhythm he sustained with his flattened, callused fingers, the bass pressed against his chest.

Henry tried to wake up Amy. He called her name, gently shook her shoulder. She stirred but didn't raise her head. "Listen," Henry said, and he suddenly recognized what his father was playing. It was a Thelonious Monk tune, "Ask Me Now," and though Henry tried again and again to get Amy to wake up, she wouldn't, and when the song was done, his father simply nodded, picked up the bass, and walked out of the bedroom.

In the morning Henry told Amy what had happened, how he'd tried and tried to wake her. They were still in bed, and Amy propped her head up on her arm. "You were dreaming, Henry," she said. "It was just a dream."

"I know, I know," Henry said, but the next night he had the same dream, the same visitation, though this time his father played Monk's "Rhythm-a-Ning," tearing through it at lightning speed, a virtuosic performance of which Henry was sure his father had been incapable when he was alive. He lay in bed and listened, stunned, until his father finished and then, as he had that first time, simply turned and left the room.

The dreams continued night after night, each time exactly the same dream except for the Monk tune his father played; "Think of One" one night and "Hackensack" the next and "Blue Monk" after that and then "Ruby, My Dear" and then "Well, You Needn't." Finally, the night his father played " 'Round Midnight," which was Henry's favorite Monk tune, maybe his favorite song by anyone ever, Henry somehow knew this would be the end. The song had always seemed to him profoundly solemn, unspeakably sad, as if it were not some smoky and romantic ballad but an elegy lamenting a lover's death. As his father played it in the dream, agonizingly slowly, it seemed even sadder, an awful, deathlike dirge, some kind of sigh from the heart's bloody core. And when his father was done, when he picked up the bass and stepped out of the room, Henry understood that this would be the last of these dreams. He wept and wept and woke up still weeping.

"Find someone, Henry," Amy had told him. "Just see someone," she said, pleading, but he couldn't imagine whom he would see, what he could possibly say. What doctor would understand that he wasn't looking to have his mind set right, that he longed not for sanity, not for a clear head, not even for relief. What he wanted was resumption. No matter the suffering, no matter the clatter, he wanted the dreams to come back. What else did he have, after all, by which to remember his father? So he wanted the dreams to continue on and on, his father forever playing the bronze-bodied bass, playing this music that was like nothing else except the sad, slow, and necessary—*necessary,* yes—beating of a heart.

Three

WHEN HENRY woke up, it was almost noon.

So he had slept. That was a good sign. He made coffee now on the
bathroom vanity, standing over the small machine as it sputtered and
spit, then he took the cup outside and went to retrieve the road atlas
from the car. When he'd left New Orleans, he'd sworn he wouldn't
aim for anywhere in particular; he'd be like a wandering troubadour,
content to make the highway his home. In those first hours he'd
thought of the hurricane as a lucky coincidence, the final nudge he'd
needed to truly leave his life behind. Many others on the jammed
highway seemed to think so as well, hoisting bottles and beer cans
through car windows, happy to feel so alive in the face of the storm.
But now, seeing what he'd seen on the TV, Henry understood that
there was no luck, no good fortune, in what had happened. New Orleans was underwater. People were dying. People were already dead.
He couldn't go back even if he wanted to. The grocery store and
everything in it—his father's bass, the few other things still there, the
junk no one wanted to haul away—had surely been obliterated.

He knew, of course, why he'd wound up in Virginia, even if he told himself that it was an accident, that he was just passing through. And he *could* just pass through. He could keep going, head up to Baltimore to see his sister. Mary hadn't spoken to him practically since their mother had died, since Henry had skipped the funeral and left Mary to handle the lawyers and the papers even though he was the one still living in New Orleans, twenty minutes from their mother's house, the house where he and Mary had grown up, where they'd stayed even after their father disappeared. Mary had sent Henry the various documents that required his signature, then she'd sent him the check—more money than he had imagined his mother could possibly have saved—when the estate was settled. It had been signed by a lawyer, but Mary had mailed the check herself. She'd slipped it inside a greeting card with a corny picture of a tropical sunset, but she'd drawn a line through the card's sentimental message, something about beauty and eternal friendship, and written *Fuck you* instead. And beneath that, just for good measure, *Fuck you, Henry.*

Even so, she would take him in, Henry knew. If he called her, she would take him in. She was the assistant curator at a Baltimore museum, but when she was younger she'd wanted to be an opera singer. And Henry knew if he went to Baltimore, she would first force him to endure a performance worthy of the stage: She would weep and put her arms around him, maybe, but soon enough she'd push him away and hammer her fists against his chest. She'd scream that he was an asshole, a bastard, a complete and total shit—then she'd admit to how desperately relieved she was that he was safe. He imagined her slapping him in the face, but even if she did, he knew that he would, in the end, be forgiven. Maybe she'd laugh through her tears and ask about the Broussards—their own private joke, a neighborhood family Mary had invented—and he'd tell her what she wanted to hear: that the Broussards were of course fine, that they had left just in the nick of time, moments before the levee broke and their house was swept away.

All in one piece, he could tell her. *Their house, believe it or not, actually floated.* And he knew he could manage an appropriately detailed description, lace curtains fluttering inside the green-shuttered windows, the house bobbing through the worst of the storm until the wind quieted and then drifting peacefully across the flooded banks of Bayou St. John and out into Lake Pontchartrain, a children's-book miracle, a fairy-tale finale.

And that would do it. Mary would be delighted by Henry's invention—not nearly as imaginative as what Mary used to tell their mother—but of course it would also remind them both that their mother's house, their childhood home, was underwater, had been utterly destroyed. That house could not float; no real house could.

Mary still had friends in New Orleans, he was sure—girls in the neighborhood she'd grown up with, ones who'd married guys who, like Henry, had gone to Jesuit High School and then Tulane and then never left the city, women who couldn't imagine a better place to live. Where were these women and their husbands and their children now? Huddled in hotel lobbies, Henry figured, or sleeping in their relatives' guest rooms or on their friends' basement floors. How many had slept on church pews or park benches or, like Henry that first night, in their cars? How many, Henry wondered, were, like him, unaccounted for, alone?

He needed to see Mary. He needed to get to Baltimore, show up at Mary's door, let her know that he was okay.

Or he could stay here in Virginia. He could stay here and look for Amy. That was his other option. He could find out exactly where she was living, Lexington or Lowesville or Laurel, some place that began with an *L.* She'd told him when she left. She'd given him the address—an old farmhouse or bungalow that belonged to her editor's parents or cousins or someone else who knew someone who knew her editor, he couldn't remember. But she would be staying there, she said, until she finished the Central America book, then she'd decide.

"Decide what?" he'd asked her.

"What to do, Henry," she'd said. "You know. What? Where? Who?"

Who? Oh God.

"You'll come back?" he'd said, meaning to sound hopeful, meaning to let her know that was what he wanted her to do.

"I don't know, Henry," she'd said, her voice flat, uninflected. "I don't know."

One night he'd found the town on an old U.S. road atlas someone had left at the store, a giant book with front and back covers that were somehow cushioned, as if they'd been filled with air. But now he couldn't remember what the town was. Maybe she'd gone to the Lucky Caverns, a candlelit cathedral beneath the mountains, walls of limestone shimmering with specks of mica. He imagined the endless echo of her laughter, her delight at having found such a perfect place to hide from her lunatic, dream-damaged excuse for a husband.

No, that was another of his idiotic delusions. Amy wasn't hiding. She had told him exactly where she was going; it was just that he couldn't remember what she'd said. But he could find out where it was, couldn't he? Or he could somehow make himself remember. And once he did, he knew he could just show up there. Like Mary, Amy must be worried about how he'd fared in the hurricane. No matter what he had done to her, how much he had hurt her, she would want to know that he was okay. She'd want to hear his story, learn what he knew about their friends, about who had decided to leave and who hadn't. He'd have to tell her that he knew nothing, that he had spoken to no one. And then she'd look at him and try to discern how much more unhinged this new circumstance had left him.

Well, I'm not living in a grocery store anymore, he could say, hoping she'd laugh, but the truth, of course, was much worse: he wasn't living anywhere; he had nowhere to go. And she wouldn't laugh, wouldn't find anything he had to say amusing or endearing. He had hurt her—that's what she said, and he had tried to understand what she meant. He *did* understand it. But he couldn't seem to process this understanding, couldn't unscramble it from all the chaos and clatter in his head.

She loved him. She'd said that again and again. She loved his generosity, his gentleness, his hangdog wit. *You've won my heart,* she'd told him, as if he'd accomplished an improbable feat in a rigged carnival game that you were expected to lose.

Hunting the Palm's Heart. That was the name of her next book, but now it felt like some sort of coded message. *Whose* palm? *Whose* heart? *Whose* hunting? The palm, the heart. Love itself. He loved her. He did love her.

He left the road atlas on the bed and took a shower, then he rifled through his bag for a clean shirt, a clean pair of jeans. He needed more clothes. He needed underwear and a razor. He needed to find a phone he could use to call Mary, tell her that he was safe. First, though, he needed to eat something. He grabbed the atlas and stepped outside. Latangi was on her way into one of the other rooms, holding a stack of towels. Henry waved, and she stopped. "Mr. Garrett," she said, smiling. "You slept well?"

"Yes," he said.

"Good," Latangi said. "You will stay again tonight?"

"I'm not sure," he said, shrugging, holding up the road atlas to suggest that he had somewhere to get to.

"I hope you will stay," Latangi said, and she nodded significantly. She didn't believe he had someplace to go, Henry could tell. Maybe she possessed some mystical Eastern clairvoyance, or perhaps she was simply astute enough to know that anyone fleeing New Orleans with somewhere to go wouldn't have wound up, three days later, on this highway, at this dingy motel, five or six states away.

"Is there somewhere to get lunch?" Henry asked.

"You go into town," Latangi said, adjusting the stack of towels. She looked for a moment at Henry. "You turn left on the highway. There is a restaurant. What a Blessing."

She saw that Henry was confused, and she walked toward him. "This is the restaurant's name, Mr. Garrett. What a Blessing." Latangi smiled, then laughed. "They are Christians. Christian Baptists, I believe. Black Americans. You will see. Many *jagannath,* many little statues everywhere, and biblical passages along the wall. *The Lord is my shepherd so I lie down in the green fields.*" She laughed again. "But they are a good and kind family. Very kind."

"The town?" Henry said. "What town is it?"

"Marimore," Latangi said, and she spelled it out for Henry just as she had spelled out her name, her voice like musical notes, like a plucked mbira. "Just a few miles down the road. You will be back, Mr. Garrett."

Henry wasn't sure if this was a question. He thought about what he'd said to Amy: *You'll come back?* A question. He nodded.

"Good, Mr. Garrett," she said. "I would like the opportunity to speak with you later, if I may." She was wearing a different sari today, Henry noticed, this one a pale blue, the same color as her nails, and Henry wondered how she had come to be living so far from her own home, what sort of misfortune had propelled her here. Perhaps that was why she wanted to speak to him—to recount, like Tomas Otxoa at Endly's, her own sad tale of desperation and loss. People always wanted to tell him such stories, to unburden themselves. Why they would do so to such a man as him, Henry did not understand. Did they sense that they were in the presence of a kind of human sponge?

"Thank you," Henry said. "I don't know—"

But Latangi smiled, walked away, and disappeared into the room. As Henry headed across the parking lot, he could hear her singing inside, her voice faint but sharp, almost metallic. The mist had evaporated and the mountains had appeared again over the motel, a gray-blue silhouette against the sky. It was hot outside, and even hotter in the car. Henry put the windows down, then he pulled out onto Route 29 and headed north. Lining the highway were the same kinds of ramshackle buildings he had seen throughout his drive— used-car dealerships and body shops and beauty salons alongside tiny brick churches and clapboard houses and narrow trailers ringed by overturned plastic furniture and children's toys. Everywhere there were portable signs facing the road, black plastic letters arranged in rows announcing sales and specials, births and deaths, ice cream flavors and fire-station pancake breakfasts. Even the churches had these signs, offering witty teasers for Sunday sermons or snippets of scripture. *Except the Lord build the house...* one of these signs declared, and Henry wondered, as clearly one was intended to, what the rest of the verse might be. And another church sign left him puzzled. *Eternity,* it read, *is to long to wait for redemption.* How exactly, he wondered, did one "long to wait for redemption"? Then he realized that the sign was, of course, supposed to say *too long,* that eternity is *too* long to wait for redemption. It was the sort of spelling error that, a year ago, he would have told his students about, one that would have made them laugh.

He drove now past a John Deere dealership with spectacular green-and-yellow farm equipment lined up in a row like gigantic children's toys. Just beyond the dealership, parked on the highway's shoulder, was a light blue bus, and beyond that stood a ragged line of men in orange reflector vests carrying garbage bags. These were prisoners, Henry quickly realized, because farther ahead, walking backward and smoking a cigarette, was a guard with a rifle resting on his shoulder. The guard nodded sternly as Henry drove past as if to point out that he hadn't missed a thing, that he had taken note of the Louisiana license plates on Henry's car and all the mud and dust the car had gathered from the back roads in Georgia and South Carolina. Henry thought again about Lacey Gaudet, about the skunk and his old car, about peeling her underwear down across her hips, the frightening thrill of it, and the fallen magnolia blossom she reached for and brought to her nose to fight the stench of skunk or maybe, he realized later, to hide the fact that she was crying. It was her first time, and it must have hurt. He heard Amy's voice: *You hurt me, Henry.*

He had not ever wanted to be cruel, to hurt. Was that not enough?

He turned on the car radio, still tuned to a religious station, a man with a thick Appalachian twang asking listeners to pray for Mrs. Audrey Henderson, a shut-in living over in Monroe. Music started, a bluegrass song about a great mansion in the sky, and Henry followed the sign for Marimore.

The restaurant was in a small aluminum-and-glass strip shopping center with a fitness and tanning salon, a florist, a state-run liquor store, and a doctor's office. The restaurant's sign was a wooden block, cut and painted in the shape of a red-tasseled Bible, the words *What a Blessing* scrolling across it in gold letters.

Inside, the restaurant was decorated precisely as Latangi had de-scribed, with embroidered Bible verses framed on the wall, display shelves of ceramic statues of praying hands and twig-bearing doves and Baby Jesuses lying in miniature mangers and Ten Command-ments tablets shaped like matching tombstones. But the music—coming from a boom box positioned behind the register—was not at all what Henry would have expected. Instead of gospel—or even pop or R&B—the music playing was Miles Davis, a live version of "If I Were a Bell," Davis's fluttering trumpet speeding through the melody, somehow managing to suggest both uncertainty and resolve. A young girl, a teenager, her hair pulled tight behind her head, smiled at Henry, picked up a laminated menu, and led him to an open table.

"The music?" Henry said as he sat down.

"Not me." The girl laughed, shaking her head. "That's my grand-father. He's crazy for this stuff."

"You don't like it?" Henry said.

The girl glanced behind her and shook her head again. "No words to it."

"It's Miles Davis," Henry said, and the girl looked at him as though trying to figure out something, whether he was dangerous, maybe, or what kind of accent he had. "I like it," Henry said.

"Most people don't. They just want it turned down," the girl said. "Papa can't hear so well, so all day he turns it up bit by bit until it's blaring."

"It's meant to be loud," Henry said.

"Well, I'll tell Papa someone finally likes it."

"Wait," Henry said as the girl started to go. "Listen," he said, and he was surprised by the pleading tone in his voice. The girl stopped and turned her head to the side as though she was indeed listen-ing. She had a small scar on the bottom of her chin, a thin pale line against the brown skin, and she raised a hand to cover it. Maybe she had noticed Henry looking. And that moment, as if Henry had orchestrated it, the trumpet fell away just as the tenor sax took over, a spiraling line of exquisite power and grace. "That's Wayne Shorter," Henry said, surprised that he knew this. "In 1965," he said. "Live at the Plugged Nickel." He shook his head. "It's a crazy thing to know," he said. "It's just—"

The girl looked at him, her hand still at her chin.

What was he trying to say? He couldn't explain that it was this kind of thing—insignificant, useless—that always popped into his head.

"Well, you sound just like Papa," the girl said, stepping away now, hurrying toward a table where a man was holding his check in the air.

What he truly sounded like, Henry knew, was his own father, leaning near their old Philips stereo, the receiver's tubes casting a faint green light onto the wall behind the stereo's wooden cabinet. Henry sat and listened now, in this crowded restaurant, as he had sat next to his father, both of them absolutely still, Henry standing up only when one record ended and the next one dropped into place. He'd liked to watch the records spinning around, liked to try to decipher the label as the disk spun and spun. "Listen," his father would tell him, a hand on Henry's shoulder. "Listen to this." And now, though for the life of him he couldn't say why, Henry felt as though he were hearing this music, truly hearing it, for the very first time, as though he could finally detect what he had never been able to before—the distinct pattern that all the instruments, weaving this way and that, had stitched together.

Though Henry had listened, through the years, to nearly all of the music his father had left behind, he'd never understood it the way his father had. Henry had made his way through his father's reel-to-reel and cassette tapes and dusty 78s, through the recordings of Algerian rai and Ethiopian jazz, Cuban *son* and Congolese rumba and Andalusian flamenco, Caribbean gospel and Texas and Delta and Memphis blues. He tried to listen to the scratchy Folkways' recordings of slaves' sorrow songs and Baptist hymns and prison chants and sea chanteys and Appalachian ballads. Henry could usually distinguish one style from another, could sometimes name the particular artist who was playing, but he lacked whatever talent his father possessed that allowed him to perceive the way all of the world's music was, as his father had explained it, a single song.

Henry could even remember how once, on a world map laid out across the kitchen table, his father had shown him the routes that music took as it spread through the centuries from one continent to another, from one region to the next, from city to city and town to town, transforming each time into something new that nevertheless contained vestiges of what it had once been. Henry had been too young—he had always been too young—to really follow what he was saying, to even care enough to try to understand. But he did understand, when his father spoke, that this subject mattered to him more than anything else in the world. It mattered in a way that was unsettling, even frightening, to Henry, as if his father were a swimmer kept afloat in the ocean not by his body's natural buoyancy or by the careful movement of his arms and legs but by something much more mysterious and terrifying—something just like the painting he'd once seen that depicted beautiful Sirens perched on jagged rocks, sharks and stingrays and other deadly fish swirling around them, the Sirens calling out in strange, piercing cries that Henry imagined he could hear just from the way the Sirens were drawn, their heads thrown back, their mouths wide open.

"Music speaks what otherwise cannot be spoken," his father liked to declare when someone asked him why he studied what he did. "Each melody, each song, is like a dream," he'd say, and though Henry knew his father was just speaking the way professors spoke, he somehow also sensed that there was desperation as well as comfort in this pronouncement.

Yes, Henry understood that songs were like dreams—even though throughout his childhood, throughout his whole life, in fact, up until his father's ghost appeared at the foot of his bed, Henry didn't dream.

Everyone, of course, insisted that Henry *did* dream, that he simply didn't remember these dreams. Amy had told him that he was lucky. She'd often felt besieged by her dreams, which were so astonishingly vivid, so rich with detail, that Henry once joked that she spent more time recounting them than she'd spent sleeping.

What Amy could not do, though—and what Henry, oddly enough, did quite well—was interpret these dreams. Henry seemed to unravel their mysteries with such effortless confidence that Amy would not, even when Henry begged her to, stop telling him every detail. She did not understand that his skill was simply the result of his having loved her, of having watched her so closely for so many years, of sensing that her life was somehow decidedly more real than his own, as if her every footstep left a permanent mark while his were far too ephemeral to leave even the slightest trace. He remembered everything Amy had ever told him about her life—the boys and books and college classes and pets she had adored, the places she and her brother had visited with their globe-trotting parents, all of them floating down the Nile on a wooden raft, riding leathery, mud-caked elephants in India, climbing the trash-strewn path to Machu Picchu, sailing to England on the *QE2*, kneeling in a bamboo cage above the scorpion-infested floor of a Buddhist temple on an island in the East China Sea. He remembered every meal she had cooked, every outfit she had worn, every present she had given him. He was certain he could remember, if he tried, every time they'd had sex— or not remember, exactly, because he did not need to remember, his body imprinted with her touch. Amy was so calm and rational in her commerce with the world that he had been shocked and embarrassed by how imaginative and daring and vocal she became in bed, her hair unleashed from the complicated knot into which she wound it each morning, like the demure librarian who, in the final pages of a romance novel, abandons her painfully prim demeanor and whispers *Take me now* into her hero's ear. Henry, though, was the one who always felt *taken*.

He hated his silence, his inability to announce his own desire, to tell her what he wanted to do to her, what he wanted done. With his high-school students, in conversations about the stories and poems and plays they read, he was forthright, casually explicit, when discussing sex. Paul Kehoe had warned him, of course, that he had to watch what he said, that there were parents who didn't approve, who perceived his candor as a dangerous enticement.

All art, Henry had wanted to tell Kehoe, *is a dangerous enticement,* thinking of his father's passion for music, his mother's paintings, but he'd said it to Amy instead.

"And food," Amy had answered. "Food is the first enticement." It was food, Amy claimed, that had lured the fish from the sea, that had drawn man from his cave, that had led him to spark fire from the dull inertia of tree and stone.

It was indeed food that had enticed Henry to ask Amy out on a date. He'd approached her at a local bookstore where she had set up a table of dishes she had prepared, the scent of each dish so wonderful that at first Henry didn't notice how beautiful Amy was—or how ridiculous she looked in the tall white chef's toque and matching white canvas apron she was wearing, a silk-screened portrait with her signature beneath it on both, something her publisher had insisted she wear. She was the author of a series of witty cookbooks that led the reader on fanciful, intrepid excursions across various continents in search of exotic meals; she was at the bookstore to sign copies of the latest installment.

A Pilgrim's Provisions, the series was officially titled, though Amy told Henry over drinks that night that she preferred her original alliterative proposal, A Forager's Feasts, which seemed more in keeping, she said, with her modest, decidedly secular aims—and the books' equally modest sales, she added, which were just enough to send her to her next volume's exotic destination.

"Which is where?" Henry had asked her.

"Japan," she said. "In two months."

And Henry had ended up going with her, even though he hated traveling, hated the dislocation of it, the sense that he had been set adrift. Right after they returned, he suggested they get married. "That way," he said, as if the issue were one of logic and convenience, "you could, for instance, get a dog and not have to worry about how long you were gone. You'd have someone to watch him for free."

"What if I don't want a dog?" Amy had answered, laughing.

"Even better," he'd said. "The truth is I'm not very good with dogs."

"So what are you good at?" she'd asked him, and he'd just looked at her, then he'd lowered his head as if he were thinking, and he'd waited until his silence had become comic, had set Amy to laughing again.

"Nothing," he said finally. "I'm good at nothing."

He understood, of course, the charm of such apparent modesty.

But in this case, what he'd said was actually true. He didn't have a clue, really, about history or philosophy or biology or chemistry or economics. He was at a loss on the subjects of medicine and law and meteorology and comparative religion. He could not play chess or garden or sew and did not understand the stock market or car engines or actuarial tables. He could not locate or name any constellations; he could not tell a finch from a nuthatch, a birch from a cypress. He had never held a gun or a blowtorch or a power saw; he'd never been a bartender, a roofer, a ranch hand, a roughneck, or a smoke jumper.

"Sex," she'd said. "You're good at sex."

"No," Henry said, more seriously, more honestly, than he had intended. "*You're* good at sex. I'm just the student. An *eager* student, mind you—"

"Books," Amy said, triumphant. "You know books. That trumps them all."

No, he'd said. There too he didn't know most of what he was supposed to know. He hadn't read *The Iliad* or *The Odyssey* and certainly nothing obscure like *The Tale of Genji* or *Tristram Shandy* or *The Faerie Queene* or *The Decameron*.

"Yeah, well, who has?" Amy had said, but he held up his hand.

"Listen," he said—like his father, or like some reverse image of his father, who had of course known everything he was supposed to know and a million other things as well: how to open a wine bottle without a corkscrew, how to count cards in blackjack, how to make a Sazerac and an Old Fashioned.

He hadn't read Henry Miller, he told Amy, much less Henry Fielding or Henry James. "You'd think, you know, given my name, that I'd have read at least some Henrys."

"O. Henry?" Amy asked.

Henry shook his head. And he hadn't, he said, read Jane Austen or

Tolstoy or much of Hemingway besides *The Old Man and the Sea.* In a seminar in college he'd been forced to make his way through Malcolm Lowry's *Under the Volcano,* about which he now remembered exactly nothing, and *Moby-Dick,* much of which he couldn't remember even as he'd read it. Mainly, he told Amy, he had tried to figure out which of the two books was a more useful prop to spark conversation with the beautiful, sullen young graduate students who, with their spiked bangs skimming their lashes, studied at the café tables in the student union.

"Which one *was* better?" Amy had asked.

"Neither one. Nothing," Henry had said. "I tried everything. Kerouac and Ginsberg and Bukowski and Borges. I even sank as low as Kahlil Gibran. Nothing worked."

"Well, now it has," Amy had said, taking his hand.

"You're a sucker for Kahlil Gibran?" Henry had said. "Do you know how pathetic that is?"

"Not Kahlil Gibran," Amy had said, smiling, crying now. "You. I'm a sucker for you."

"Worse," Henry had said. "Much, much, much worse."

He hadn't meant it, of course. He had believed that he could make her happy, that he could offer her his devotion, his attention, his admiration. And he had believed that she would erase—that she had already erased—his peculiar proclivity for melancholy, his abysmally romantic attachment to sorrow. He was, had always been, his father's child, not in intellect but by temperament—and yet for five years with Amy, he had mostly managed to swear off the pallid and grim, the mournful and forlorn. Amy had cooked for him, and just this was enough to summon in him a dazzling joy—the real thing, complete and total. He felt the same mixture of delirious gratitude and dizzying overindulgence after Amy's meals that he felt after sex. Amy, notebook in hand, planning her next book, bombarded him with questions, the very questions he might have asked her when he lay exhausted in bed: *How good was it? What in particular did you like? How soon would you want it again?*

What man would walk away from such a woman, would hurt her the way he had hurt her?

Yet he *had* walked away. He *had* hurt her. And now—now he had lost everything. He had executed with unlikely depth and precision his grand and transcendent plan for ruin. Sitting at his table at What a Blessing, listening as Miles Davis gave way to Oscar Peterson and then to some tenor player he didn't recognize, he tried to picture the past year or so of his life as a line drawn on a page. It looked like a child's scribbles, like a madman's preposterous treasure map. He finished his lunch, paid the check, and went back to his car. He took out the road atlas, pulled out a pen from the windshield visor, and put an *X* over the spot where Marimore stood.

Here, he said to himself. *Here.* He carved the *X* into the page as if that would make everything more concrete, more real. *Here is where I am.*

And where would he go? How far might he get? He considered the fact that Amy, somewhere near, would be only an inch or two away on the map. An inch or two. Maybe he would find her if he just drove and drove, winding his way from one town to the next, looking for the sort of farmhouse where Amy would be living, some beautifully weathered clapboard and tin-roofed cottage tucked beneath great towering trees, surrounded by a garden of hostas and peonies and phlox and a dozen other flowers and plants whose names he knew from Amy but couldn't identify, not even if a gun were put to his head. Maybe he could roll the car windows down and drive until he detected the scent of her cooking, of whatever recipe she was trying out.

Was it possible that Amy already knew he was here, had felt some change in the atmospheric pressure, some subtle signal in her dreams that announced his arrival, the same way she'd known, three years ago, that she was pregnant but that something was somehow wrong, that her body and the baby weren't right?

She'd had a dream, she told Henry, that she was growing taller, a little more every day until she no longer fit into her clothes, her sleeves inching their way up her arms, her toes punching through her shoes. She had to bend down to step through doorways, had to sleep curled up on the bed. This time she hadn't asked Henry what the dream meant, hadn't wanted him to explain. Six weeks later she'd had a miscarriage, and for the next few months she'd cried every night when she got into bed, curled on her side exactly the way she had imagined herself curled up in her dream, her hands tucked between her knees. Henry, who had been both terrified and thrilled at the prospect of being a father, had not known how to comfort her except to say that they could try again, that he was sure the next time everything would be fine.

But there had not been a next time, and Amy had gradually set aside her sadness in the manner she always did, with a kind of ferocious energy that Henry admired but could never muster for himself. He was always amazed by Amy's capacity for joy. She'd had plenty of tragedy in her life—her parents had died a few years before she and Henry met, in a plane crash on their way to visit her brother in Sierra Leone, where he worked for a relief agency. But sadness never managed to take hold of her the way it did Henry; she seemed to emerge from it with a kind of burnished regard for all that was remarkable and fortunate in her life.

"It's all a wonder," she'd said one Saturday morning to Henry as he lay next to her in bed. His eyes were still closed; he hadn't moved but she knew he was awake. It was spring, and when he opened his eyes he saw that she was sitting up and looking out the window, running her hands through the tangle of her hair. He told her he'd misunderstood her for a moment, thought she'd said *wander.*

"That too," she said. "It *is* all a wander." And she lay back down and started in on one of her favorite games, reciting whichever list she'd been forming in her head: ideas for future volumes of A Pilgrim's Provisions, or the places in the world she'd like to go that she had not yet been, or the foods she most longed to eat again—tropical Filipino fruit salad and Indonesian fish eggs and Australian wild boar and roasted Basque peppers with cider.

"I don't want to go *anywhere,*" he'd once said to her as she spoke, her eyes closed as she imagined a trip down the Amazon, stopping at each village along the way to find out which foods they considered their greatest delicacy. Everywhere in the world, she'd once told Henry, it was the foods that were considered aphrodisiacs that were deemed to be the most delicious, no matter how disgusting they actually tasted.

"Except here," Henry had added, sneaking his hand beneath the sheet, beneath her nightgown. "I don't want to go anywhere except here."

"You're an idiot," she'd said, but she kept her eyes closed, let his hand work its way up her leg.

"Yes, but I'm *your* idiot," Henry had said.

"My idiot, yes," she'd said. "All mine."

He returned to Route 29 and headed back to the motel. He figured he would get his bag and say good-bye to Latangi. He would thank her for her kindness, ask what it was she wanted to speak with him about, and then be on his way. Only then would he decide where it was he was going next. To stay with his sister. To find Amy. To continue wandering. To decide to decide what he needed to decide.

Up ahead, Henry could see, the pale blue prison bus was still parked on the highway's shoulder, exactly where it had been before. The prisoners, though, had switched sides, as had the rifle-toting guard. Most of them were scattered across the sloping berm at the highway's edge, slowly moving forward in unison, but three of the prisoners stood just beyond the yellow stripe on the shoulder.

The men appeared to be staring at something on the ground or perhaps shielding their eyes from the sun as they talked. Just as Henry approached, he saw one of the men, an old black man with gray hair, step across the yellow stripe. Henry wasn't sure what was going on. Then the old man took another step and then another and then, now, he was directly in front of Henry's car.

Henry did not have time to swerve or even slam his foot on the brake before the awful collision.

Later, when it was done, he would wonder if he really had seen what he thought he remembered seeing: the old man, as soon as he was out in the road, raising his arms at his sides, raising them as if what he meant to do, in the moment before Henry's car struck him, was fly.

Four

It MADE no sense to him. A man was dead, not by his hand but by his car. Not by his choice but by the man's own choice. Even so, a man was dead, and Henry had killed him, had spilled the man's red blood all over the black stink of the highway and across his car's bumper and hood and windshield, the bumper and hood now smashed as if he had struck not a man's body but a tree, the windshield cracked into a jagged puzzle. Henry lived nowhere, had nowhere to go—yet he'd been told that although it was clear he wasn't to blame, that he bore no responsibility for what had happened, he ought to stay put awhile.

Those were the precise words the Marimore County sheriff had used, and though he had posed it as a question, Henry had understood it was not a question. "You'll stay put awhile, Mr. Garrett?" the sheriff had said, peering up from the papers on his cluttered desk, the late-afternoon light angling through the windows, illuminating the dust, and Henry had nodded, his hands still shaking, knuckles white as though he still gripped the steering wheel. He had never been in a sheriff's office, had seen them only on TV and in the movies, but this one looked exactly like those, like a stage set from *The Andy Griffith Show* or some John Wayne Western. The wooden furniture was chipped and faded and worn. Giant hoops with large keys hung on the wall near two cells with sliding metal-bar doors. A bulletin board displayed faded posters of wanted men, their faces unshaven and their eyes glazed, and of missing children, and on a bookcase beneath a dirty window, dishes and wooden plaques were stacked haphazardly on the top two shelves while old magazines and plastic three-ring binders spilled out of the shelf below.

When Henry looked out the dirty window, he saw a young woman and a little boy stepping out of the hardware store across the street. The young woman was carrying the boy's stuffed animal—it looked to Henry like an elephant, like Ganesh on the lampshade at the motel, but he figured that he must be wrong, that it must be something else, a bear or dinosaur or pig or some fanciful imaginary creature. The woman was also holding a brown paper grocery bag, her purse slung over her shoulder. Henry watched as the woman awkwardly tried to shift everything to one arm so she could take hold of the boy's hand, but the boy ran down the block ahead of her. Henry could see that the woman was shouting for the boy to wait but couldn't hear her. He felt panicked, as though the child were in terrible danger of darting out into the street, of getting hit by a car—or maybe just of winding up lost for a few awful, frightening moments. He turned away and looked back to the sheriff, who was saying something that Henry had missed.

"Excuse me?" Henry said, and the sheriff explained that he'd provide Henry with a copy of the report once it had been processed.

Earlier, right after the accident, a deputy had arrived at the scene, asked Henry a few questions, and then driven him into town to the sheriff's office and brusquely handed him over to the sheriff as though

Henry were being taken into custody. Henry figured he must be in shock. He had considered giving the sheriff a false name when he began to fill out the report. The idea had come to him almost immediately when he stumbled from his car. He'd blindly hit the brakes after he struck the old man, desperately trying to see through the broken windshield as the car skidded off the road and slammed into something. He had pushed open the car door, heard pieces of the windshield crack and fall, felt his legs give way as he tried to stand. A small V-shaped cut on his forearm bubbled to his pulse; he put his hand over the cut and slumped down to the ground. He heard shouting and saw the guard herding the prisoners across the highway and back onto the blue bus; he heard the prisoners yelling, cursing, saw them waving their arms in protest. Only then did he see the man's body, all the blood. He retched and looked away.

Who are you? Henry had heard in his head, the question somehow a threat, and he had begun to scroll through a list of names as though he were randomly calling the roll on the first day of classes at Ben Franklin: Louis Stieb, Arthur Ganucheau, Harry Tomeny, David Delery, Jerry Giorlando, Emile Broussard.

Emile Broussard. No, that wasn't a real name. That was the father in the family that Henry and Mary had invented—that Mary had invented, actually. It was Mary who'd come up with it all on her own. Henry had simply agreed to play along.

He'd sat on the ground, felt the heat against his thighs and hands, the small trickle of blood beneath his fingers. He looked again at the man lying there, his body circled by the dark stain of his blood. A few cars had stopped; people rolled down their windows, stared. No one spoke to him, though. A crowd gathered on the side of the highway—men with sunburned faces and arms, a woman wearing a green scarf and sunglasses, her hands covering her mouth—but no one approached him. No one approached the dead man facedown on the road either. Maybe they thought Henry was dangerous; maybe they thought he had killed this man on purpose. But why didn't someone rush over to the dead man, kneel beside him, turn him over? Henry waited, trying to calm the shaking in his arms and legs. He took his hand away from the cut. It had already stopped bleeding.

Emile Broussard. Emile Broussard. It was two years or so after their father had left them. Henry was seventeen, so Mary would have been fourteen, and their mother had begun spending all day every day in her bedroom, which soon became crowded with books and newspapers and magazines and paint-smeared cloths and an ashtray for her thin cigars, whichever canvas she was working on perched on a low easel by the bed—landscapes with fiery-red hills and trees bruised with purple-tinged leaves and clouds as dense and dark as smoke. A small gallery uptown sold his mother's paintings, most of which Henry found frightening, nightmares of color with titles that bore no apparent relation to what was depicted in the paintings—*Erica Controls the Weather, Waving at Trains, The Gatekeeper's Forgotten Garden, The Florentine's Leaves*—which somehow made them even more disconcerting.

The gallery owner, an Italian woman named Marianna Greco, would stop by the house sometimes when his mother finished a canvas or needed more supplies. Marianna usually arrived with a bottle of wine or champagne, and she and his mother talked for hours, Marianna laughing and cursing and recounting long stories that Henry could never follow. He had no idea who bought his mother's work or what they paid for it, though once, when Henry was still in high school, a man in a gray flannel suit had knocked on their door at home and asked to speak with the artist Jocelyn Garrett.

Henry had hesitated, surprised that anyone other than Marianna knew who his mother was. The man then held out a card with the name and address of some gallery in New York: *Maldich and Lietche,* it said in gold-embossed letters, *46 East Seventieth Street.* Henry left the man in the front hall and took the card to his mother's bedroom. She looked at the card, frowned, and handed it back. "Tell him he needs to speak with Marianna, Henry," she said. "Tell him I'm not here."

"But you *are* here," Henry said.

"Then tell him I'm not available," she said.

"But he might be important," Henry said. "He might be somebody it would be good for you to know."

His mother put her hands on his shoulders. "I don't want to speak to him, honey," she said as though she were merely trying to comfort Henry. "I just want to be left alone to paint."

And Henry had looked at her for a few seconds and then said okay. He nodded and said that he understood. Then he walked back to the front of the house and told the man that his mother wasn't available just this moment, that he should please talk to Marianna Greco at her gallery. Henry shook the man's hand. He had tried to make his voice sound both professional and casual; he hoped that he'd conveyed that, although his mother was a bit shy and strange, there was nothing truly disturbing about her.

When the man left and Henry closed the door, he wondered again, as he'd wondered before, if it was somehow because of his mother, because of something she had said or done or simply because of who she was, that his father had decided to leave them. Who had been the crazy one? Maybe she'd told him to leave, told him she just wanted to be left alone, told him she was done with their marriage and from that moment forward just wanted to paint. Maybe she had somehow convinced him that it would be best for Mary and Henry not to know where he was going, or even why he had to go.

"You understand the problem?" he'd asked Amy after recounting what had happened. "I could never figure out which part of my life was the *most* fucked up. All of it was fucked up, I knew that. But it seemed important to clarify what the *worst* part was."

A few months after his father left, shortly before his fifteenth birthday, Henry had come across an old photo album tucked beneath some books on a shelf in the living room. Paging through the album, he'd stared at each picture as if it might contain some kind of clue. There were black-and-white photos from his parents' honeymoon in Jackson, the two of them sitting side by side on a porch swing, looking like teenagers out on a date, their hands clasped together, fingers entwined. There were photos from his father's research trips, his father dressed in a seersucker suit and standing in front of old white clapboard churches next to ministers in red robes, Bibles clutched to their chests, and women in elaborate hats and matching dresses who smiled but also seemed to regard the camera with suspicion. He had no idea who took these pictures—his mother, maybe, if she'd been with him. One of the photos from a trip his parents had taken to New York showed them both at some crowded, smoky jazz club sitting with their arms around each other at a small table with people Henry had never met, all of them laughing and raising their glasses for the camera. These photographs seemed to depict the life of two strangers, of some couple Henry only vaguely recognized.

But his parents had always been, if not exactly affectionate with each other, then at least gentle and soft-spoken and kind; he didn't remember ever hearing them argue, didn't remember them talking about anything except art and literature and music, as if the real world didn't exist. Surely there had been other things that required their attention—bills and pediatrician appointments and parent-teacher conferences and their children squabbling or outgrowing their clothes—but Henry couldn't remember any of this. It was as if he and Mary had been merely angelic, mildly entertaining sprites who floated—vaguely, indecipherably—in their parents' midst. Why, then, hadn't his mother been enraged or despondent or even discernibly surprised when her husband, their father, had left? Why hadn't she been, like Henry and Mary, stricken with grief, reduced to a numb, staggering silence, as though their house had become shrouded in an impenetrable fog that they would be forced to wander through for the rest of their lives? Wouldn't she, if they had loved each other, if they had been happy, have done anything to find her husband? Wouldn't she—wouldn't anybody—have told them what had happened, how they were supposed to carry on with their lives? Wasn't what his mother had done as inexplicable, as unforgivable, as his father's leaving, even if he had betrayed her in some shameful, unspeakable, detestable manner?

How hard was it to list the possibilities? A murderer, bigamist, homosexual, drug addict, epileptic, amnesiac, con man, philanderer, incorrigible cad, compulsive gambler, Mob boss, hit man, foreign agent, a black man passing as white. And which of these would have been, in his mother's eyes, sufficiently worthy of shame? Which would have convinced her to declare, again and again, that he'd simply been some kind of helpless dreamer, a man carried off by the blues?

Henry knew, of course, that other people didn't live like this. He didn't know anyone whose father had simply disappeared; he didn't know anyone whose mother was an artist who shut herself off from the world, who spent days and days without getting dressed, who was content to eat bread and fruit and cheese and canned soup for dinner, who didn't watch television, didn't call on friends or seek any commerce with the world. Everything in his mother's bedroom had wound up covered with paint: her pillows and blankets and sheets, her nightstand and alarm clock and slippers, the carpet and closet doorknobs and drapes, the window sashes and windowpanes. When Henry complained about the mess, when he told her she needed to get out of the house and they really ought to clean her room, she had simply laughed; she said she liked being at home, liked working in the bedroom, liked that it had become her studio. "It's not dirty, honey," she told him. "It's paint. It's pigment. It's all just light." Having everything around her, living with her work, made her feel comfortable, she told him. It made her feel free. She was more than okay, she said. She was content.

And she *was* content, it seemed to Henry, more content than she'd been before his father left, when she had spent her days attending to his father's academic career, organizing his field notes, typing transcripts of his interviews, cataloging the recordings he made, proofreading drafts of the articles he wrote. She had lunch with his colleagues' wives, prepared dinners for his graduate students, accompanied him to lectures and concerts. In the midst of all this activity, she had seemed almost normal, though Henry had also sensed, as though it were a menacing villain standing just beyond the stage lights, poised to make an entrance, the presence of despair.

At night, his mother painted. She shut herself off in the spare room she had used as her studio, a room across the hall from where Henry slept. He would wake up sometimes before dawn and know that she was still working. He'd hear a brush clattering in a can of turpentine, the palette knife scraping again and again against the canvas as though she were erasing everything she'd just done. He'd hear her pacing back and forth, talking to herself; even under the covers, he could smell the oil paint and the turpentine and the smoke from her cigars. By the time morning arrived and he had to get up for school, she would be in bed, asleep next to his father, as though Henry had merely imagined her working through the night. He had wondered why his mother's painting seemed somehow furtive, a secret she did not want to share.

Though she appeared to be happy as a recluse, though she let Henry be, rarely asking where he was going or how he spent his free time, she never wanted Mary to leave the house except to go to school. It seemed strange to Henry that this was the one thing she took the trouble to care about, as if all the usual parental concerns had been boiled down or stripped away to this single preoccupation. Henry wondered if she was somehow worried about boys, worried about what kind of trouble Mary might get herself into. She liked to say that Mary was *saucy*, and though Henry wasn't sure exactly what she meant, he understood that there was both pride and disparagement in this description. She would keep Mary busy, asking her to read out loud—they both liked Shakespeare's plays and Victorian novels—or hunt for particular paintings in the art books stacked on the floor in her room. She taught Mary to stretch and prepare canvases, to name the constellations and types of cloud formations. They designed their own tarot decks with a ludicrous cast of characters, ones they'd made up together: the Pigeon-Toed Gardener, the Belated Henchman, the Flummoxed Maiden, the Angel of Debt, the Alabaster Raven, the Coruscating Fool. And his mother talked with Mary in a way she did not with Henry, the two of them curled up on the bed together, whispering and laughing. Once Henry had asked Mary what they talked about, and she'd shrugged and said, "I don't know. Nothing, really. I think she just likes to hear my voice."

"All the junk in her room, the mess—doesn't it bother you?" he'd asked her.

Again Mary had merely shrugged. "She's not exactly the most normal person in the world, if that's what you mean."

He wasn't sure exactly what he'd meant. He wanted to ask Mary what she thought was wrong with their mother, why she lived the way she did, but the question seemed too important to speak out loud. And besides, Mary was nearly three years younger than he was—what would she know, what would she understand, that he didn't?

The one thing their mother didn't seem to mind Mary doing was babysitting for neighborhood families on Friday and Saturday nights. If Henry was around, if he didn't have plans with his friends, he'd sometimes go with her. They'd watch television together once the kids had been put to bed. Mary was good with the children she watched—she'd get down on the floor and pretend she was a pony or a dog; she'd hold them when they cried; she'd patiently read them the same book over and over. Her greatest gift, though, was her voice. She could quiet even the most distraught child by simply singing. She sang lullabies and nursery rhymes, but she also sang some of the blues songs they'd heard their father play on his stereo, songs whose lyrics made the little children laugh: *Let me be your wiggler until your wobbler come,* she'd sing, dancing, flailing her arms. *If she beats me wigglin' she got to wobble some.*

Or she'd sing, *I've got a merry-go-round, little girl, don't you want to ride?* And she'd grab the children's hands and swing them around and around.

All you ladies gather 'round, she'd sing, glancing at Henry, raising her eyebrows and smiling. *That good sweet candy man's in town.*

Henry would look away, embarrassed that his younger sister understood what these songs were really about, that in one way or another, they all had to do with sex.

72

His stick candy don't melt away, Mary would sing, clearly enjoying Henry's discomfort. *It just gets better, so the ladies say.* And Mary would strut back and forth, stick out her bottom and shake her hips. *Saucy,* Henry decided, was exactly the right word for what Mary was.

Eventually, Mary began babysitting on Saturday nights for the Broussards, a new family, she said, that had just moved into the neighborhood. They had twin blue-eyed boys who were two years old. She told her mother that the Broussards lived over on Chamberlain, that Mrs. Broussard was young and blond and beautiful, that Mr. Broussard looked like a movie star, handsome and broad-shouldered and very, very tall, with a cleft in his chin like Kirk Douglas's, a voice as deep as Gregory Peck's. He'd told Mary he worked for the government but also suggested with a shrug of his broad shoulders that he couldn't talk about it, couldn't tell her much more than that. He'd wanted to know if she could be discreet, and she'd told him that she could, that she wouldn't give out their address or phone number, that she wouldn't let anyone know where they'd gone to dinner, when they'd left or when they'd be back. He didn't say so, Mary said, but she figured he must be some kind of special agent or spy.

"Maybe he's in the Mafia," Henry had said, thinking about an elementary-school classmate named Sandra Corso. When she and Henry were in fourth grade, her father had been shot dead in his bed by a man who had broken into their house. Word spread around school that her father had been part of the Carlos Marcello crime family, that he'd been a hit man himself, dumping bodies in the swamps out in St. Bernard Parish, leaving them as delectable dinners for the alligators there.

"He's not in the Mafia," Mary said, looking from Henry to their mother. "I know he's not."

"Of course not," their mother said. "Not with a name like Broussard."

"Maybe he changed his name," Henry said, but then he saw that Mary was on the verge of tears.

"That's enough, Henry," his mother said. "You're frightening her."

Mary came back home with stories about the cute things the Broussard twins had said or done, about the beautiful dresses Mrs. Broussard wore, about what she'd learned of their life—how they'd lived in New York for a while and then in San Francisco, how they'd spent two years in London and one in Paris. "They both speak French," she told her mother. "It's so beautiful. You should hear them."

It was a while before Henry discovered that the Broussards didn't actually exist, that Mary had invented them as a way to go out with her friends. He'd offered to keep her company one Saturday night when he had nothing else to do, and Mary had told him that he didn't need to, that the twins kept her busy. "Well, I want to meet this guy," he told her. "I've never met a spy."

Mary said she didn't know if that was a good idea, but their mother said she was sure the Broussards wouldn't mind if she brought her brother along. Mary turned to Henry; he could see the pleading look in her eyes but didn't understand it. "It'll be fine," he said. "I've got nothing else going on."

When they left home, Mary walked down to the end of the block and then headed in the wrong direction, away from Chamberlain, the street where she'd said the Broussards lived.

Henry stopped and Mary turned to look at him. Just from her posture, from the way she stretched out her arms, the palms of her hands turned toward him, her shoulders slumped, he realized what was going on.

"Oh my God, Mary," he said.

"Please," she said, desperate. "Please don't tell her, Henry."

He shook his head and laughed. "They don't exist?" he said. "You just made them up?"

"Please," she said. "Please."

And he'd laughed and laughed, amazed—and a little frightened—by Mary's imagination, by the fact that she had conjured this family from thin air, that she'd had the nerve not just to create such a lie but to embellish it from one week to the next. What else had she said she'd done that hadn't been true? "What do you do?" he asked her. "Where do you go?"

"We just hang out," Mary said. "Just Julia and Eleanor and me."

"But where?" Henry asked.

"Just around. Julia's got keys to her father's office."

"His office?" Henry said. "What does he do?"

"He's an optometrist," Mary said. "He doesn't care what we do as long as we stay out of the examination rooms and don't mess with the machines."

"What do you do, then?" he said.

"I don't know. He's got a radio there. We listen to music. We talk."

"And boys?" Henry said.

"Jesus, Henry," Mary said. "It's nothing. We just all hang out. It's just I know Mama wouldn't understand. She wouldn't let me."

"What happens when she finds out?" he asked.

"She won't," Mary said, and she gave Henry the same pleading look she'd given him earlier. "She won't find out," she said.

"Okay, okay," he said. "It's not like I'm going to say anything."

"Yeah, but now she thinks you've met them." He watched Mary stop and reach into the pocket of her jeans. She pulled out a crumpled pack of Camels and some matches.

"Jesus, Mary," he said, pointing to the cigarettes.

"And Joseph," she said. "Get it? Jesus, Mary, and Joseph." She lit a cigarette and expertly flicked the match away. "So now you've got to help," she said, exhaling the smoke. "You've got to make her keep believing it."

Why? Henry almost said but didn't. He already knew why. Without this family, without somewhere she could go, his sister would be trapped at home with their mother, and the idea of that was too awful for Mary, too awful for both of them.

So Henry did what she asked him to do. When he got home that night—he'd met up with Mary at midnight in front of their house—he'd told his mother all about the Broussards, about the twins crawling over him, wrestling him to the ground.

"Is she as beautiful as Mary says?" his mother asked, patting the bed for Henry to sit down next to her.

"I guess so," Henry said, embarrassed. "She's pretty."

"But is she beautiful?" his mother said, and though Henry didn't know why Mrs. Broussard's appearance would matter to his mother, he understood that it did.

"She's very beautiful," he said. "She was wearing a long black dress and she had her hair up, with a pearl necklace, like she was a princess or something." In his head he pictured an actress he'd seen in a magazine. It had been an old picture, black-and-white—of Audrey Hepburn, he thought.

"Hmm," his mother said, kissing Henry good night. "A princess."

And Henry felt as though he'd found himself in some strange new place. The house, his mother, Mary, the sound of his own voice—everything seemed somehow different, unfamiliar. It even felt strange to him when he lay down in his bed and pulled the covers up, as if he weren't sure exactly where he'd wake up in the morning.

He couldn't fall asleep and so instead had tried to picture Mrs. Broussard as he'd described her for his mother—in the long black dress, the shiny fabric tight against her breasts and hips. He imagined her removing the strand of pearls, loosening her hair, twisting and reaching behind herself to slowly unzip the black dress, and stepping out of it, her feet delicate and tiny. And what would happen then? He couldn't really imagine it, couldn't conjure up the story, couldn't complete the picture. All he could do was feel the rush of desire, the swell and ache in his groin. All he could do was provoke, with his hands, some rough approximation of relief until, exhausted and ashamed, he fell asleep.

Five

HENRY HAD wanted to run. He had considered standing up and walking out the door and seeing just how far he might get, seeing whether or not they'd grab him, throw him to the ground, and toss him into one of the two empty cells.

But he hadn't, of course. The sheriff had finished his report and then driven Henry back to the motel. They drove straight past the spot where the accident had happened—it had not been an *accident,* of course, but what had it been? What were the words he was supposed to use? The sheriff simply glanced over at Henry as they drove past and let out a long breath. "Awful business," he said, and Henry turned and looked out the window. His car was gone, towed away, but the highway was still stained, a darker black against the black, bits of glass shining in what was left of the daylight. *Awful business.* Was that how Henry was supposed to think of this?

The sheriff pulled into the motel parking lot, stopped in front of the office, and kept the patrol car idling while Henry got out, fished the room key from his pocket, walked down to his room, and opened the door. His hands were still shaking. Henry looked back and waved, and only then did the sheriff nod and drive off.

It just made no sense, Henry thought as he lay on the motel bed and stared at the ceiling. It made no sense that a man was dead and that his city was in ruins and he had no wife or friends or family to whom he was able or willing to turn and that what he felt was not anger or grief or loneliness or guilt.

He felt nothing.

No, to feel *nothing* would be a relief.

He had wanted that child. Why had he not managed to tell Amy how devastated he'd been? What had prevented him from speaking?

Why had he walked away from what he wanted, the only thing he wanted—but there had been all that blood on the highway, and the single V-shaped scratch on his arm, and the thousands and thousands gone in New Orleans, and Amy, and the girl, *this* girl. For the first time he did not require sleep, did not need the absurd machinations of his dreams, to summon her. Oh, he did not feel *nothing*. What he felt—what he had become—was desire.

He did not understand his own thoughts, his own mind. How, in the midst of such ruin and horror, was there this: He watched, his eyes closed, as the girl stepped to the foot of the bed, stood there exactly as his father had stood there holding the bass, though that was in a house that was now gone, a house that was underwater or had been washed away, a life that he had given up, that he had forsaken. The girl wore faded jeans and a red T-shirt, low-rise jeans that rested below the bones of her hips, a torment of bare skin between jeans and shirt. She smiled at him, coyly slipped her hands into the pockets of her jeans, and said, *Oh, you know who I am, you just won't remember.*

"I don't remember," he said. "Tell me."

Henry, she said, and he felt a sharp stab in his back, a pain that arced up through his ribs and then down along his left leg. The girl knelt on the bed, leaned forward, and cradled his feet in her tiny hands. He closed his eyes, felt her press her breasts against his thighs, felt her hands reach beneath his back, her fingers tapping along his spine as if she were searching for the precise place where the pain had begun. *You don't have to remember,* she said, whispering now, playful. *You don't have to think at all.*

"Please just tell me," he said, or tried to say, and he felt the girl stretch over him, felt her tiny hands, her fingers, brush against his lips, felt her hair spill across his chest.

"I killed a man," he said. "A man is dead," he tried to say, but he knew that the girl couldn't hear him, wasn't listening, and he lay there with his eyes closed and heard the slow thrum and groan of his father's bass and he tried to speak, tried to say the girl's name, *Clarissa Nash,* but he knew now that he was asleep and so did not have to open his eyes to see that the girl was undressed, that she understood the delicious agony of her breasts and thighs, her scent and skin, that he could do anything to her, that he could do nothing, that he *was* nothing but his own desperate longing.

He was asleep, of course. He had been asleep all along.

How long? When the man stood in the road and raised his hands and the car struck him and there was terror and blood and the skunk smell of death?

Had he been asleep then? Had that, too, please God, been a dream?

He woke up to a knock at the door, a pause, another knock. Before he could move, he heard the jangling of keys, and he opened his eyes to see the door swing open and Latangi step inside.

"So sorry, Mr. Garrett," she said, and she stepped back out of the doorway, surprised. "The light was off and I knocked. I thought perhaps you were out."

"No, no," he said, sitting up, his back sore. "I'm here." He reached over and turned on the lamp by the bed, the shade swinging side to side, Ganesh swaying as if the earth beneath him were quaking.

Latangi remained outside a moment and then walked into the room. "Again I am so sorry," she said. "There was a telephone call. They asked if you would appear at the courthouse at nine o'clock." Henry turned to sit on the side of the bed, put his feet on the floor. He ran a hand through his hair, then looked at the clock. It was a few minutes past eleven. At night? In the morning?

"There was an accident," he said.

"Yes, yes," Latangi said. "I have learned. Sheriff Roland telephoned. He explained. I am so sorry. How terrible. These men on the side of the highway road, I have seen them. Such a terrible fate. And this man—" She threw her hands up, just as if she had watched it happen.

"I am so sorry for him and for you and—well, it is terrible, all this." She walked over to him now, her hand outstretched. "Sheriff Roland will send a car for you, he says. Eight-thirty pickup. I was bringing you this note."

"Yes, okay," Henry said, accepting the paper from her. He saw Latangi take a quick look around the room.

"You have not had your dinner," she said.

"No," he said. "I fell asleep. I—"

"I have made a dinner. Would you please join me?"

"It's very late," he said. He could not get himself properly awake. His father. Amy. The girl. The old man stepping out onto the highway in front of his car, directly in front of him—he had been real— the man who had raised his arms as if, absurdly, to fly. Or had he been trying to suggest that he was a target, that he meant for Henry's car to strike him?

"It's very late," Henry said again, closing his eyes, opening them.

"I am accustomed to eating late, Mr. Garrett. Plenty of work to do and little time for food. That is how I keep this figure." She smiled and stepped awkwardly to the side, shifting her weight as if she might spin around in her sari, the red and orange one she had been wearing when he arrived yesterday. He thought about Mary dancing while she sang for the children she watched. He needed to call Mary. Why hadn't he called her?

"Even so, we must eat, yes?" Latangi said. "You must eat."

Henry nodded. Yes, he needed to eat.

"Ten minutes, then?" she said. "Will that be enough?"

Again Henry nodded.

Latangi brought her hands together as though she were going to begin clapping. "Through the office," she said. "It is modest but clean. And I am an excellent cook, you will see."

Latangi was waiting in the office when Henry arrived. She led him through a door behind the counter to her apartment, the living room larger than he would have predicted for so modest a motel but crowded with so much furniture—sofas and slipper chairs and ottomans and end tables and lamps—that it reminded Henry of Endly's. In one corner of the room was a tower of woven rugs, in another a stack of wicker baskets. Latangi noticed Henry looking around and said, "Yes, it is a mess, I know, Mr. Garrett. My husband, he passed away five months ago. He operated a business. Imports from India. This is how we lived, I am afraid, like bulls in a china shop, as they say. I am forever knocking into this and into that, and he says, 'Latangi, you are as graceful as a butterfly. You go here, there, here. You must be graceful as a snake instead, moving carefully, twisting and turning.'" She smiled and then sighed.

"I'm sorry," Henry said.

"He was a clever man," she said. "A good man. When he was ill, he told me that he had been wrong. 'All that flittering and fluttering,' he said. 'It is indeed better to have a butterfly than a snake for one's wife.'" She looked around as if she might begin trying to straighten up the apartment, but instead she threw up her arms and turned back to Henry, tears in her eyes. "Yes, he was a good man."

Henry did not know what to say, but Latangi stepped toward him. "Also this, Mr. Garrett. Mohit was a poet as well. More of a poet than a businessman, you see."

Latangi looked closely at Henry as if she were studying him, attempting to discern some hidden quality or avocation of his own, then she went to the table and reached for a bright blue teapot. "He composed long works of poetry, so very many pages," she said. She made the *rat-tat-tat* noise of a typewriter. "Page upon page. Poetry of a spiritual nature but also poetry of love, if you understand."

Henry nodded, and Latangi poured the tea from the bright blue pot into two small cups.

"I am afraid I am not much for poetry, Mr. Garrett. I am not equal to it, I would say. Mohit, he loved these words more than food. Once, he said to me, 'I have married you, Latangi, for your words the way other men marry for wealth.'" She laughed and sipped her tea. "Yes, you should hear him. 'You are a bottomless well of words, Latangi, and so you are a treasure to me,' he would say. Even upon our marriage he declared that my only task was to fill his life with words."

"Did you?" Henry asked, accepting the cup of tea that Latangi offered him.

"Yes, yes," Latangi said, laughing, leading Henry through the living room into a small kitchen with a Formica table spread with ceramic pots, a vase of dried flowers at the center. "I am so full of words, I am afraid, Mr. Garrett, I have allowed you too few."

"That's fine," Henry said, sitting down. "I don't have so many. They stay here," he said, pointing to his head.

"Yes, yes," Latangi said. "When Mohit passed away, I no longer wanted to speak. My whole life I had done nothing but speak. Suddenly the words were gone. Without Mohit's ears to listen, I felt as though I had no mouth."

"Yes," Henry said. "I understand."

"This hurricane," Latangi said. "So terrible. It is all beyond words."

"Yes," Henry said, and he realized that he had not turned on the television again, that he had no idea what was happening in New Orleans. He wondered if the water had receded but then realized that it could not have. Where would it go? As a child, he had marveled every time he and his father drove past the Orleans Canal pumping station, its smoky red-brick walls pierced by the giant green metal pipes that emerged from the ground like secret passageways to the underworld. Would the city simply rot away beneath the water? Who was left there now? Who had failed to obey the order to leave? How many had not been able to get up from their beds and so were now dead? How many had climbed stairs as the water rose and then could climb no higher?

Henry looked down at the plate Latangi had placed before him. He wondered if anyone he knew had stayed there, had died in the storm. He tried to think of who might have been foolish enough to remain in the city, who might not have had the means to get out. There had been so many people coming in and out of Endly's— homeless men, their heads filled with voices, too angry or disturbed to distinguish the real threat of a hurricane from the threats they lived with every day, the snakes that leaped from the mouth of anyone without a beard, as one man had told him, or the deadly poison that women could inject through your ears simply by speaking at a certain pitch. Henry thought about Tomas Otxoa, whom he hadn't seen in weeks. Maybe he had already left New Orleans, had gone back to San Sebastián or Caracas. Or maybe he had taken his own life, drunk and consumed by despair, certain he'd never find his brother. Henry tried to listen to Latangi, tried to quiet the clatter in his head, but he could not stop himself from hearing Tomas's voice—the way he cleared his throat and closed his eyes before speaking, as if he were trying to summon the smallest details from his memory.

"There was, in the city of Tolosa," he'd begun one afternoon, "as there is, I suppose, in every small town, a person who in English is called, I believe, a village idiot. Village idiot, yes?" he'd said, and Henry had nodded even though Tomas didn't open his eyes.

Latangi was saying something about one of the dishes she'd made, but Henry felt his temples throb, felt shooting pains behind his eyes, and he couldn't get Tomas Otxoa's voice out of his head.

"A village idiot, then, though Bernardo Belaga was not so much an idiot as a drunkard," Tomas had told him, sipping his gin, and Henry had known what would come next, Tomas's meandering description of this man Bernardo Belaga—how he'd worn a dusty navy beret to hide the few strands of straw-colored hair remaining on his head, how his tattered clothes were forever stained with the cheap wine from the Navarre by which he achieved and perpetuated his intoxication, how he had worked for his father, a butcher, but after slicing off, on three separate occasions, two of the fingers and half of the thumb on his left hand—in the final incident, the digit in question had been wrapped in paper and taken off by a customer before the drunk Bernardo recognized the extent of his injury—he had become instead a crossing guard for Tolosa's primary school, though his habit of studying too closely the legs and hindquarters of the children's young mothers as they paraded before him, as though he were peering at deliveries destined for his father's shop, ensured that Bernardo was quickly deemed unqualified for this position as well, and how, after that, Bernardo no longer pursued employment of any kind, content to spend his days happily wandering Tolosa's streets, sleeping on hot afternoons in the city square beneath the shadow cast by the Convento de San Francisco, though, by some miracle, even three hours' sleep did nothing to diminish his intoxication, nor did the news one day that his father had died of a heart attack after hoisting a particularly large lamb's leg upon the scales for sale to Mr. and Mrs. José Domingo Azurza, whose youngest daughter was to be married that Sunday morning.

"You are not hungry, Mr. Garrett?" he heard Latangi say. He tried to remember the last time he'd seen Tomas, what Tomas had said as he left the store, if he had said anything at all to suggest that he wouldn't be back.

"Are you feeling unwell?" Latangi said, reaching across the table to touch his arm.

Henry saw again the man on the highway, his twisted form, all the blood. He did not feel well.

But he needed to eat. "No. I'm fine, thank you," he said to Latangi, picking up his fork. "I'm sorry."

The food was good, the same kinds of dishes, with the same scents and spices, that Amy had made for him—when? A few years ago, when she was working on one of her books. Henry didn't know what he was eating, but he remembered Amy reciting the names of different dishes: *dal bukhara, chickpea and tomato rajma, pulao, murgh musallam, lucknowi biryani.* He remembered Amy explaining, as if he were an idiot, as if he indeed knew nothing at all, that, just like in the United States, the different regions of India all had distinct cuisines.

"Thank you," Henry said again when he was done.

Latangi stood and took his plate. "It is not so easy here in Virginia," she said, "to acquire the ingredients, the spices, for Bengali dishes."

"It was all delicious," Henry said. "Everything."

"Thank you, Mr. Garrett," she said.

"Henry, please," he said.

"Mr. Henry," she said hesitantly, "I do not cook so often anymore." She placed his plate in the sink, wiped her hands on a towel, and turned to him. "I wished to speak with you, Mr. Henry, before today's accident. I do not know if you have family, if you have lost your loved ones in this storm."

"No," Henry said. "There's no one—" He tried again to think of a way to explain his circumstances. Once again he pictured Amy living in the Lucky Caverns, the limestone floor covered with ornate Persian rugs, a long table spread with a starched white tablecloth, with steaming dishes and wine bottles and candles, Amy's hair unwound from its knot, long curls resting against her bare shoulders. He imagined her wearing an elegant black dress, the one he had told his mother Mrs. Broussard was wearing. "My wife," he said, resting his hands on the table. "We're separated. She's here." Latangi looked at him, seemed to be studying his expression. She waited, but he could not explain. "In Virginia," he said.

"And you will see her?"

"I don't know," he said. "I—"

"I am sorry, Mr. Henry." Latangi stepped toward him as though she meant to embrace him. "I do not mean to be too inquisitive." She stopped, then she began to clear away the remaining dishes from the table. When Henry attempted to help her, she placed a hand on his shoulder. "Sit, Mr. Henry," she said. "I did not envision, of course, an occurrence such as today's when I suggested I wished to speak with you, to request your help. We can speak about this tomorrow if you like. There is no hurry."

"No," Henry said. "You've been very kind. Is there something I can do?"

Latangi put the last of the dishes on the counter and sat down at the table. "Perhaps you would like more tea?"

"No," Henry said. "I'm fine."

"Then I will ask your help," Latangi said. "It is an unusual request, I know. Perhaps it is nothing, a woman's sentiments, that is all." She looked down at her hands, and Henry thought he could see the traces of designs there, as though her hands had not long ago been painted with henna—for her husband's funeral, he imagined. But Henry knew from Amy—everything he knew seemed to have come from Amy—that henna was used not for funerals but for weddings, for the bride and her family. Amy's book of Indian recipes had included a photograph of a bride's elaborately hennaed hands next to a recipe for making an aromatic henna paste with lemon juice and cloves. He wondered if perhaps Latangi had a daughter who had recently gotten married.

Henry waited for Latangi to speak. He figured that she would ask him to help with some manual labor that she couldn't manage, hauling away musty old mattresses or pulling up a particularly worn carpet in one of the rooms. But what did that have to do with sentiment? *A woman's sentiments,* she had said.

"You are a teacher of English, yes, Mr. Henry?" Latangi said hesitantly, and Henry looked at her. "At Benjamin Franklin High School?" she said. "This is you?"

He did not understand how she could know this about him. He had not told her. "I'm sorry," he said, "but how did you—"

"Aha!" Latangi said, smiling, clapping her hands. "Am I not clever?"

Henry still did not understand. Perhaps he had been right and Latangi did indeed possess some kind of clairvoyance—though it was an imperfect clairvoyance, since she did not seem to know that he was no longer a teacher, that he had quit his job more than a year ago. Then it occurred to him that maybe somehow, by sheer coincidence, she happened to know Amy, that they had met and talked about him, that she might have called Amy and warned her that he was here, that he might be looking for her.

Latangi seemed to be enjoying Henry's bewilderment. Then she clapped her hands again and said, "The Internet, Mr. Henry. Yahoo. I searched your name. *Henry Garrett. New Orleans.*" She wiggled her fingers as though she were typing. "So large a city and thus there are many Henry Garretts. But I knew this one, teacher of English at Benjamin Franklin High School, was you. Yes?"

"Yes," Henry said, "that's me," and Latangi's delight with her discovery was so clear that Henry couldn't help but smile. "You are indeed clever, Latangi," he said, and she laughed. "But I don't teach there anymore."

"No," she said, shaking her head. "This hurricane of Katrina—"

"Not the hurricane," he said. "I quit long before the hurricane."

"Why did you quit your teaching, Mr. Henry?" she said.

Why had he quit? What could he possibly say to this woman without sounding like an idiot, a complete and utter fool? He thought of how Tomas's story of Bernardo's life had ended—with Bernardo falling to his death in a silo of shimmering grain, Tomas claiming that Bernardo had been captivated by its beauty. Could he say to Latangi, *I was searching for beauty; that is why I quit my job?* Was there any truth at all in such a claim? No, there was no truth. There was a difference between searching for something and being lost. They were not the same. He had not been searching for beauty; he had attempted to escape it, the sorrows of childhood, of losing so much: a father, a baby, his own fragile mind. And he had not quit merely his job; he had quit his life—or he had tried to quit it and had failed. He had failed because he could not clear his head, could not remove all the detritus there, the clatter—the memories and voices and desire, Amy and her cooking and their sex and the baby they lost and this girl Clarissa Nash whom he couldn't even properly remember. Where had she come from? He didn't know what would be worse, if he had made her up or if she was real.

"I just quit," he said, looking at Latangi, at the expectation in her eyes.

"Why, Mr. Henry?" she said.

"Well, that's one of those things I don't have words for."

She continued to look at Henry as if certain he would resume, offer some explanation, but then she bowed her head. "Yes, I understand," she said. "I will not inquire." She pursed her lips and raised a finger to them. Was this a universal gesture for silence, for acknowledging secrets that must not be spoken aloud?

"But you did want to ask me something?" Henry said.

"Yes," Latangi said, looking up again. "It is an unusual request, but it is a task for which I am not equipped. You are an English teacher, Mr. Henry. You could perhaps do what I cannot." She leaned forward now, her elbows on the table. "It is late, I know, but I must tell you a brief story. When Mohit and I were married, I was very young—sixteen years old. Mohit was five years older. Twenty-one. Our marriage was arranged by our families, but no matter. We were already in love. I could show you a picture of Mohit in his sherwani. So handsome. I was a good student, a smart girl, but this was to be the end of my education. We were to leave our home, our families, for Calcutta, where Mohit was to continue his education to become a doctor. I was, of course, to be a wife and mother. All this was determined, you understand."

Latangi paused and looked down at her hands, and Henry guessed what would come next—that their lives had not gone as planned, that Mohit had failed in his studies, that there had been no children or there had been a child but the child had become sick and had died. Every story, in the end, was a sad one.

He heard the office door open, the bells above the door chiming, and Latangi stood up. "Just a moment, Mr. Henry," she said.

When she stepped into the office, Henry got up and walked around the apartment. On the living-room walls were framed pictures of the sort he'd seen before at Indian restaurants, cartoonishly colorful depictions of what he assumed were Hindu deities: a man or woman—he couldn't tell which—in a skull-covered cape and riding a bull; a four-headed, four-armed bearded man standing on a lotus flower; the elephant-headed Ganesh wearing a crown and perched on a throne, two young women at his side; a figure with three eyes soaring through the sky, a woman's body draped over his shoulder. The pictures were webbed with cracks, as though they had been painted on cheap wood or cardboard. Each had a price tag affixed to its frame.

Henry heard the front door open again, and a few moments later Latangi stepped back into the apartment. "So sorry, Mr. Henry," she said. "A guest was in search of a man he has met too many times." She pretended to raise a drink to her mouth. "Mr. Jack Daniel's."

Henry laughed. "Yes," he said.

"Though some prefer the Wild Duck," she said.

"You mean Wild Turkey," Henry said.

"Yes, the Wild Turkey," Latangi said, and she sat down in a wicker chair and motioned for Henry to sit down as well. "I must let you sleep," she said, "so I will finish my story. We went as planned to Calcutta, but Mohit did not begin his medical studies. He had never had any intention of becoming a doctor, but he had been too afraid to tell his parents. He was, as I said previously, a poet. That was his only interest. He worshipped Rabindranath. You know of Rabindranath Tagore, Mr. Henry?"

"I've heard of him, I think," Henry said. "I'm afraid I haven't read any of his poems."

Latangi leaned forward and whispered, "Nor had I, Mr. Henry." She laughed. "Ah, but Mohit demanded I read the great Rabindranath. He was a forward-thinker, Mohit, and believed I must continue to learn even without a university education. How else was I to fill his life with words? he asked. He had written his poetry in Bengali, but already he was writing over again in English, as Rabindranath had done. Now, Mohit insisted that my English was far better than his own, but this was not true, Mr. Henry. This was Mohit's kindness speaking. He said I would assist him in the translation of this poetry, and the world would one day recognize the two of us together. 'You have the gift of words, Latangi,' he declared. But I had no such gift, Mr. Henry."

She adjusted her sari and then leaned back and folded her hands in her lap. "I did try, however. Every verse of his poetry that he wrote in Bengali, I wrote again in English. I wrote every line again and then again until Mohit agreed I had revealed the meaning of his words. Forty-five years of this writing, Mr. Henry. Forty-five years in Calcutta and Allahabad and then London and then here, for the end, in Virginia. He worked very hard, Mohit, to succeed, but he had no more luck with this poetry than he did with *this*"—and she raised her hand to indicate the crowded room.

"I'm sorry," Henry said. "It must have been difficult."

"Difficult? No, no," Latangi said. "I have not been clear, I'm afraid. There is no regret. Mohit was a great man. By what other means than love is greatness determined? Those are Rabindranath's words, Mr. Henry. Or perhaps they are Mohit's. I cannot remember." She smiled. "You see, I was not so fine a student as Mohit believed. Now, though, I would like to see if perhaps I might return his love more perfectly. I do not care if the world sees this poetry, Mr. Henry. I am old enough myself not to care for such things. All the joy for me was remaining at Mohit's side, sharing in his endeavor."

She leaned forward in the chair, and Henry saw the expectation in her eyes.

"I'm not sure I understand," Henry said.

"I would like these verses to be read," Latangi said. "Not by the world. By one reader."

Henry looked at Latangi. Her face was flushed, as though she were holding her breath. "By one who can truly hear the words, Mr. Henry," she said. "That is my request. I would like you to read Mohit's words."

Henry began to answer, but Latangi raised her hands to him. "I will prepare your meals, Mr. Henry. I will keep your room in order. You will stay as long as you would like to stay. There is nothing else of this to discuss."

"Then, yes," Henry said. "Of course. Of course I will read Mohit's poems."

Latangi leaped from her seat and embraced him.

"I knew," she said, crying now. "I do not know how I knew but I did. You may not believe in such notions, Mr. Henry, but I am certain."

"What?" Henry said. "What are you certain about?"

She walked over to a small glass-topped table, opened a wooden box, and removed a key from it. She placed the key in Henry's hand. "This is the first room, room one, all the way at the other end from your room. It is the room Mohit used as his study. All his poetry is there. Now, though, you must sleep. Tomorrow, when you return from the courthouse, I will show you, or you can go in on your own. Mohit was very organized, you will see. With everything else, it was all mumble-jumble, Mr. Henry, but not with his poetry."

She led Henry out to the office and through the front door. The bells on the door chimed, but otherwise everything was silent. No cars passed on the highway, and even the fluorescent lights in the parking lot seemed to have dimmed, casting only a faint pink light onto the motel's gray-brick walls. "I will sleep very well tonight, Mr. Henry. Thank you for your kindness. You will sleep well too. I know this." She raised one hand, as if she were offering him, in the quiet of night, a final blessing, and Henry thought of Tomas Otxoa's description of the idiot Bernardo raising his hand like a priest making the sign of the cross before falling into the silo. *How would Tomas have known such a thing?*

Henry looked down the row of rooms to the one that Latangi's husband had used as his study. He had no idea what he might do for Latangi, why his reading her husband's poems seemed to mean so much to her. He thought about his mother and Mrs. Broussard, about how his mother had wanted Mrs. Broussard to be beautiful, as beautiful as a princess. "What were you certain about, Latangi?" he asked again, slipping the key to Mohit's study into his pocket and removing his own key.

He waited as Latangi once again adjusted her sari. "I am certain, Mr. Henry, that they were waiting for you," she said. "Perhaps you do not believe in such things, but there it is. I am certain that Mohit's words have been waiting for you."

94

Six

HE DID not sleep well, despite Latangi's assurances, her benediction. He woke up again and again covered in sweat. The room's air conditioner seemed to have quit working, so he kicked away the covers and peeled off his soaked T-shirt. He lay there on his back, awake, restless, sore, his legs twitching. Even in the dark he could see the pattern of thick swirls on the ceiling, the same design as the one inside the old theater on Prytania Street where he and Amy had sometimes gone on Monday nights to watch double features of French melodramas or Scandinavian epics or corny Gene Kelly musicals.

Amy loved movies, though she'd told Henry when they'd first met that she didn't like severed limbs or bloody axes or skeletons, and she didn't like guns or car chases or abducted children or stories about sports, except the ones, she'd explained, where some athlete or team overcomes incredible odds. Documentaries were fine as long as they weren't about serial killers or sex-change operations or political assassinations or animal cruelty.

"I like wholesome movies, I guess," she'd said, and Henry couldn't help but think about the sex they'd been having, the spectacularly un-wholesome things they'd been up to.

"I've got it," he'd said. "You sure that's the whole list?"

"And clowns," Amy said. "I don't particularly care for clowns."

He and Amy were often almost the only patrons at the Prytania, and Henry had felt the same restlessness there as he felt now, the same twitching in his legs. Amy had loved it, though. She had loved the theater's baroque gold doors and sticky concrete floor and dusty red-velvet curtains. She'd sworn that if she ever got rich she would buy an antique organ for the theater so they could play it during intermissions and on Tuesday nights when they showed silent movies, which Amy also loved.

Henry, of course, couldn't stand them. He could never follow their plots; he grew impatient with the black dialogue cards, or whatever they were called, that interrupted every scene; he was repulsed by the characters' jerky, exaggerated gestures and by their ghastly makeup, by the rake's shiny, twirling mustache and oily hair, by the virginal heroine's sparkling eyes ringed with dark mascara. They all looked like ghouls, he told Amy. Everything about these movies, in fact, made him feel tense, as if at any moment—and he hadn't meant the pun, though Amy had groaned and then laughed—something un-speakable might happen.

Eventually Henry stopped going to these Silent Tuesdays, as the theater called them, and Amy went alone or dragged along one of her friends, usually Renée Bergeron, a high-school buddy of Amy's who eventually married a much younger man, an Argentine tennis player she'd met when she was handling publicity for a tournament in New Orleans. Henry could never remember the player's name and so al-ways called him Sancho Panza, which made Amy roll her eyes. "Pablo Sanchez, then?" Henry would say. "Pancho Stanza?"

96

"Paulo Suarez," Amy would say, laughing. "You're such a jerk."

Suarez was ranked something like one hundred fifty-second in the world, but Henry had actually seen one of his matches on ESPN. He'd called Amy over, pointed him out, but she hadn't seemed impressed. "Look at that," she'd said. "Is he winning?" But she didn't say anything when Henry told her that he was up a service break in the third set, probably because his answer was inscrutable to her. She wandered away, left him to fight off the perverse impulse to cheer for the guy's opponent.

Amy didn't watch anything on television except for the same old movies they'd seen at the Prytania. Once, watching *Anna Karenina,* she'd begun crying as soon as Greta Garbo stepped off the train and her face emerged through the cloud of steam, and she cried practically the whole way through the rest of the movie. He couldn't bear to sit with Amy all the way to the end, when Anna threw herself beneath the train.

"It's just too awful," he'd said, and Amy had nodded and whispered, "It is, it is," sniffling and blowing her nose, but he'd meant watching Amy cry, seeing her splotched face, her tear-streaked cheeks, not Anna's fate. He'd never read *Anna Karenina,* of course, though he had read the Classics Illustrated comic-book version when he was a kid, Vronsky drawn to look just like Clark Gable, Anna like Lois Lane in a Victorian corset.

The only other thing Amy watched on TV was the Weather Channel, an inexplicable obsession to Henry but one that made Amy practically giddy, especially when the meteorologists were dispatched to dangerous locations, hoods pulled over their heads as they stood near crashing waves on North Carolina's Outer Banks or on the boardwalk in Atlantic City, a trailer park's tornado-strewn ruins in Ohio or Kansas, a giant snowdrift in Albany or Boston.

"This is supposed to be the Weather Channel," Henry once pointed out when he spotted a vexed reporter crouching amid the overturned shelves of a grocery store in California, encircled by dented cans and shattered jars. "Earthquakes aren't weather, are they?"

"They *cause* weather," Amy said matter-of-factly without taking her eyes from the screen, refusing to be distracted. But then she turned, smiled, and said, "You really don't know anything, do you?"

"I don't," he confessed yet again—how many times would he have to say it?—but now he knew she wasn't listening. She was watching the somber reporter poking his microphone through the rubble as though the dented cans and shattered bottles might miraculously begin to recount their evening of terror for the camera. "I don't know anything," he'd said.

Now he lay staring at the motel's ceiling. Why didn't he know anything? Why didn't anything except the random and inconsequential stick in his head? How was it that he remembered, word for word, the stories of an old man drinking gin and tonic in a run-down grocery store but not the things that mattered, the things that had happened to him, that had shaped his life, his one fuckup after another? He tried again to remember what he'd told Amy about buying the Fresh and Friendly, about why he'd moved out, about what he believed was wrong with his life, with their life together. But he could not reconstruct these conversations, could not remember a single thing he'd said. Instead, he remembered the way Amy pinched salt from a bowl when she was cooking, the imprint her heels left in her shoes, the crescent-shaped scar above her right knee, the red speck he'd once noticed in her left eye, at the edge of the iris, something she'd never noticed herself. He remembered the graceful arc of Pistol Pete Maravich's shots, his sagging gray socks, his jaw cocked to the side in concentration, the swan's neck his arm formed as the ball peeled off his fingertips; he remembered Mary singing in her bedroom, late one night, an Italian aria so beautiful he was sure that he understood the words, that he knew the story: a maiden's lament for a lover gone off to war and likely never to return. He remembered the ragged, uneven cuffs on his father's gray wool pants, the fancy script on the packs of Chesterfield he smoked, a girl named Elise whom Henry had slept with in college who had laughed derisively when she realized he hadn't taken off his socks (white tube socks with three red stripes at the top). He remembered old phone numbers; the taste of a high-school friend's mother's jambalaya; Melvin the butcher, lanky and slope-shouldered, wiping his hands on his apron and, looking past Henry to the blue sky outside the window, glumly declaring, "It'll probably go and rain tomorrow."

And the girl. Here was the girl's voice—no, not her voice but someone else's, someone speaking to him. *Clarissa Nash learned the peculiar entanglement of love and disappearance the summer she turned twelve.* Was this from a book he'd once read? Was that all it was, all *she* was—a character from a book?

He remembered Amy stepping out of the shower, her skin scalded pig's-ass pink, as she'd once called it, steam rising from her shoulders and breasts, hair wild and tangled, knotted and roped. He'd wanted to screw her then, had wanted to screw her every time he saw her naked or his hand happened to fall against her bare hip when he rolled over in bed or he spotted her pulling a stocking up her leg as she sat on the low pillow chair by the bed. She looked like a French model casually posing for erotic photographs that seductively imitated ordinary domestic life.

Oh God. What an idiot he was to have given up this life. He was a numskull, a blockhead, a dunderbutt, a jackass, and he remembered

Amy once lying in bed and compiling a hilarious list of all the names for penises, prodding him to do the same for—pointing between her legs—"here," she'd said, spreading her legs. "This."

He wouldn't.

"Come on!" she'd said, pinching him, making him swat her hand away again and again, the two of them rolling around on the bed. "Jackhammer," she said in a breathy whisper, her ridiculous imitation of seduction. "Cock," she said, running her tongue along her lips, "tallywhacker. Instrument"—she was laughing now, shouting— "dong, tool, rod, pole, prick!" And he held her arms as she squirmed beneath him, panting.

He pressed his weight down on her, pinned her legs, made her keep still. "Cunt?" she whispered into his ear. "Pussy? Snatch? Come on, Henry. *Please.*"

Had he heard it even then, when he was making love to Amy, fucking her? Had he heard his own voice speaking the name? It *was* his own voice, wasn't it? *Clarissa Nash,* it had said, *Clarissa Nash,* as if he were summoning this girl, as if he were not simply recount-ing her life but speaking it into being. His voice: *Everything Clarissa Nash knew emerged from the books she endlessly, passionately read: stories of orphans with inexplicable, nearly olive complexions, too dark for beauty; curly-haired and bone-thin waifs who were smart enough to know they deserved a kinder fate.* That must have been it, just some book he'd once read, some cheap trashy paperback, or worse—some-thing highbrow, something literary, something he'd come across in graduate school? Was he rummaging through his own head, leaching another pointless memory from his brain, simply to come up with a woman—this woman—to imagine, with her schoolgirl breasts and peppermint smile, a low-rent version of Lolita—no, not to just imagine, of course. To imagine *fucking.*

Oh God. It was all so pathetic. He couldn't sleep, couldn't shut down his despair, his disgust, his desire. He finally got up and tried to open the room's windows, but they were sealed shut. He got back into bed, where he drifted in and out of sleep, plagued by his utterly predictable dreams of wandering and dislocation, climbing winding narrow stairways of crumbling stone in a gloomy Spanish cathedral only to find himself again and again in the cathedral's dank crypt; hacking his way through a verdant forest filled with the stench of rotten fruit, the ground covered with a thick muck of bananas and mangoes and papayas; clinging to the listing prow of a sinking ship, the figurehead carved, like a garish Mardi Gras float, into the form of the elephant god Ganesh, the waves swelling again and again over his head, the roofs of houses bobbing up out of the water all around him. On one of these roofs sat Bob Dylan, black boot heels anchored against the shingles—and even in the midst of this dream Henry felt the urge to laugh at how idiotic it had all become, with the elephant-head prow and Dylan strumming a guitar, singing in his nasally whine Skip James's "Hard Time Killing Floor Blues."

Henry couldn't hear him, though. He couldn't hear anything. The monotonous voice that had accompanied these dreams was gone, replaced by an equally suffocating silence, and he found himself behind the wheel of his car, driving for hours and hours along some barren stretch of highway, unable to find a place to pull over but so tired he couldn't keep his eyes open. Then the old man, the prisoner with the frazzled gray hair and beard, appeared out of nowhere, standing with outstretched arms directly in front of his car. And now there *was* sound, as if a switch had been turned on: he heard the awful thud of impact and the old man's piercing, anguished scream and then his final groaning breath, blood bubbling from the corner of his mouth, spilling a jagged line down his chin and through his beard and along his throat until it had soaked his shirt. *Enough,* he heard someone say, a woman's voice, and the word began to echo as though it had become an incantation, the one voice multiplying into a dozen voices, a thousand, too many to count, though he could hear Amy's voice and Latangi's among the chorus and then his mother's voice and Mary's and then the girl's, of course, Clarissa Nash's, a child's voice, taunting, playful, seductive—but he didn't want to hear it. *A man is dead,* he said, and he said it over and over again until he managed to tear himself from the dream, make himself wake up.

He sat up in bed, panicked, still drenched in sweat. He was certain that when the sheriff arrived this morning he would tell Henry that he'd changed his mind, that he'd examined the evidence and found that Henry had been responsible after all, that he would have to be charged with the old man's murder. *Whose murder?* Henry thought, and he realized that he did not know, had not even asked, the old man's name. They must have told him, must have given Henry the man's name, but he couldn't remember it. He needed to call someone—Mary or Amy, it didn't matter. He needed to call someone and say, *I'm here. I'm alone. A man is dead. I don't even know his name.*

He didn't have a phone, though; he looked at the nightstand next to the bed. There wasn't a phone there. Didn't every motel, no matter how run down or lousy, have phones in the rooms? Wasn't there some law or regulation that required them for public safety? Or maybe he was the only person left in the world who didn't have a cell phone, who had never had one. He needed money, needed cash, but all he had left in his wallet were a couple of twenties and a few singles. No ATM card, no Visa or MasterCard or American Express—he'd gotten rid of them all when he moved out, one more idiotic step in his insane, relentless purging. He still had a checkbook, but that was in the glove compartment of his car, and his car was gone, towed away.

What in the hell was he going to do? He needed to get out of this fucked-up, cheap-shit, no-phone motel, out of Virginia.

He heard something outside, someone, and looked at the clock. It was just past eight a.m.; he had less than thirty minutes before the sheriff showed up. He got up and looked out the window but didn't see anything except a man standing by a pickup truck in the parking lot. The man was stroking the dirty, matted black dog sitting in the truck's bed. When Henry opened the door to his room, though, he saw that Latangi had left some food there for him, a blue-gray school-cafeteria lunch tray with a basket of rolls and a pot of tea wrapped in a lace cloth and a bowl of strawberries.

He carried the tray inside, ate a couple of the strawberries, sipped the tea, then took a shower. He remembered the key Latangi had given him, the story she'd told about her husband's poems. What did she expect of him? What was she hoping he would do or say? He assumed that the poems would be terrible, a lonely life spilled onto the page in the form of sentimental couplets or quatrains or whatever the Indian equivalent happened to be. Was it ghazals? Was that the name? He couldn't remember. Through the years people had asked him again and again to read the things they had written, their stories and poems and novels; he'd been asked by his students, by his students' parents, by doctors and car mechanics and barbers and social workers, all of it irredeemably, unspeakably bad—all except for the work of a stocky UPS deliveryman named Karl Palmer whom Henry had gotten to know simply from signing for the endless packages and correspondence Amy received from her publisher. Karl had written a bunch of stories, he explained, based on the people he'd met driving his route, an idea so singularly unpromising that it had taken Henry more than a month to summon the energy to even glance at the bulky manuscript Karl had handed over. He'd wound up, though, absolutely stunned by what he read, by the simple, quiet beauty of Karl's writing, by the way he managed to convey the longings and failures and triumphs of his characters through their smallest gestures—how they held open doors or knelt in their gardens or spoke to their pets or brushed aside gray wisps of hair from their eyes. Each of the stories revolved around the character getting something in the mail—a letter dispatched years earlier, a grown daughter's sweater in need of repair, a postcard without a signature, a shortwave radio shipped back from Vietnam, an invitation to a granddaughter's wedding. He'd told Karl how wonderful the stories were, how much they deserved to be read. He said he'd ask Amy to send them to someone at her publisher, see if anyone there liked them as much as he did. "I don't know," Karl had answered, taking the manuscript back from Henry and holding it against his chest as if he feared Henry would try to steal it. "I think I'll work on them some more, maybe write a few new ones." A couple of weeks later he quit his job or was transferred, and though Henry was certain that one day he'd come across Karl's stories in a bookstore, he never had.

Sometimes it seemed to Henry that everyone he met wanted to be a writer, and they all seemed to imagine that he too was secretly waiting to have his work discovered. But he had never wanted to be a writer; he could imagine no worse fate than the writer's ceaseless struggle for eloquence, for originality and cleverness and insight and grace. These were, it seemed to him, precisely the qualities he lacked: eloquence, insight, and grace. There had been only a few moments in all his years of teaching when, by sheer accident, in the midst of a rambling sermon on Whitman's "Song of Myself" or during a dissection of the final paragraphs of Kate Chopin's *The Awakening*—Edna Pontellier stepping into the water to drown herself, the broken-winged bird falling from the sky—he had managed

104

a kind of transcendent brilliance, as if an electric current were running through his body, spilling forth from him with every word he uttered, his students somehow aware that he was approaching some dangerous, fantastic revelation.

He never actually got there, though, never found for himself or provided his students with some final moment of indelible wisdom. He just wasn't much of a teacher; he'd become one because he had no idea what else to do. He saw what his gifted colleagues accomplished, how again and again they could transport their students, how they could effortlessly, ingeniously, compel them to learn.

When he got out of the shower, which was lined with beautiful blue tiles rather than the usual molded plastic, he hunted through his bag for his toothbrush but couldn't find it. He had nothing, not a fucking thing except a bag of dirty clothes and forty-something dollars, and until this moment, that had somehow been okay with him, but now, just like that, it wasn't. It wasn't okay. He finished getting dressed and sat on the edge of the bed and stared at the blank television screen. He imagined that the two prisoners who had been standing beside the man he'd hit had concocted some story about how they'd seen Henry's car swerve across the shoulder. They'd jumped away just in time, he imagined them saying, but their friend had been too old, too frail, to react so quickly. Henry had been speeding, they were certain. He'd been speeding and had stared straight through the windshield into their eyes like a crazy lunatic or a demon or someone sky-high on crystal meth. He had tried to get all three of them, that angry-white-man son of a bitch. He had tried for sure to kill them.

Henry sat on the bed until he heard a knock on the door. Instead of the sheriff, it was the same deputy who had shown up at the accident, asked him a few brief questions, and silently driven him into town. The deputy removed his hat and said, "Good morning, sir," and shook Henry's hand. Henry looked at him, at the pink scalp visible beneath his crew cut and the imprint his hat had left along his brow. Henry realized that yesterday he'd been wrong; he'd thought the man was cold and unflinching, a hard-ass ex-military type, but in fact, he was just a kid. The accident, the glass and blood and the man's body, must have scared him. Maybe here, in rural Virginia, in Marimore County, he'd never seen such a thing.

"I'm ready," Henry said, and he thought about putting his arms out, wrists together, as if he expected the deputy to handcuff him. But this kid wouldn't understand that Henry was joking. And what kind of person would joke at a time like this anyway? A man was dead. *Still dead,* Henry heard in his head. Could you be *still* dead?

Henry followed the deputy out to the patrol car and climbed into the backseat just as he had done yesterday. The front passenger seat was outfitted with some kind of computer equipment—to catch speeders, Henry guessed. Once they'd pulled out onto the highway, the deputy looked back over his shoulder and said, "I've got family there, sir." The car radio squawked, and the deputy turned it down.

"I'm sorry?" Henry said, leaning forward.

"In New Orleans, sir," he said. "Or nearby, on the Gulf Coast. Pass Christian?"

"Sure," Henry said. "I've been there. Are they okay?"

"They're okay. Yes, sir," the deputy said. "We didn't hear for a while, but then they called."

"I'm glad," Henry said.

"Yes, sir," the deputy said. "We were mighty relieved. It's my cousin and her husband and their girls. Two of them, six and nine."

"How are things down there?" Henry said. "I haven't been able to keep up."

"From everything I hear, it's not good, sir. As far as my cousin's place goes, it's all gone. Their house and every house for miles. The trees too. All of them snapped off like matchsticks, they said."

Henry tried to imagine it, tried to picture the ravaged landscape. Once, when Henry was a kid, his father had taken him for a drive along the Gulf Coast not long after it had been hit by a hurricane. He'd been amazed by how far the tugboats and barges had been carried inland and by the houses with their walls stripped away, some with everything still in place, beds and tables and chairs arranged as if inside a giant dollhouse. His father had liked driving among such ruins, Henry suspected; he had seemed to somehow seek out these places—old railroad stations and abandoned warehouses and overgrown cemeteries and, once, an empty lumber mill that still smelled of sawdust and pine. It was as if his father were secretly hoping to commune with whatever ghosts might be lingering there. He'd send Henry out to the car to fetch his camera, an old Leica he'd bought from one of his students at Tulane, but once the pictures were developed, he was always disappointed with them, as if they'd failed to capture whatever mystery or romance he'd felt.

Sometimes, on Saturday mornings, he'd hustle Henry out to the car, and they would head west out of the city on River Road, staying on that two-lane highway as it followed the curve of the Mississippi, the flames and smoke from the gasoline refineries alternately illuminating and darkening the sky. Eventually, his father would turn off, not at the grand plantation houses that had been converted into restaurants or museums but at the signs for towns like Maringouin, Wallace, St. Gabriel, and Killona, towns where his father would drive past ramshackle houses and junk-strewn lawns until he spotted someone sitting out on a front porch, an old man smoking a pipe or a woman snapping beans or shucking corn. He'd stop the car then, get out, and wave. If the person waved back and said hello, his father would approach, put a foot up on the porch step, wipe his forehead with a handkerchief, and engage the man or woman in conversation. Sometimes Henry would get out and stretch his legs, but usually he just stayed in the car. He knew his father was almost done when he pulled the small black notebook and pencil from his pocket, pointed up and down the street, and then began jotting down directions. Years later, when he and Amy went to see *To Kill a Mockingbird* at the Prytania—somehow he'd never seen the movie, despite the fact that for years he'd taught the book to the high-school kids—he was struck by how familiar it all seemed, how much it made him think of his father. Henry wondered if his father had intentionally crafted this role for himself, an imitation of Gregory Peck's assured and honorable Atticus Finch, the noble white man these poor black folks could trust.

Henry knew, of course, what his father was doing: he was conducting research, asking about the town's history and its current state of affairs, about the jobs people had and those they'd lost, about the local churches and bars. He'd once explained to Henry that churches and bars were the two places you could find out the most about how people lived and the music they made. "God and the devil at war for men's souls," he'd said, "and music is always the ammunition." Armed with whatever information he'd gathered, his father would go back to these towns on his own, without Henry, showing up at the bars on Saturday nights and at the churches on Sunday mornings. He kept a tape recorder, a bulky reel-to-reel machine, in the trunk of his car in case there was something worth recording.

He'd also told Henry that if they kept driving on River Road just about all the way to Baton Rouge, they'd end up at the Angola penitentiary, about the worst and most hateful prison in the entire country. There was music there too, he'd said, songs the men had sung to get themselves through all the years of hard labor they were forced to do, working in the prison's cotton fields all day in the hot sun. "You've heard Lead Belly," his father had said, and Henry had nodded. "Well, that's where John Lomax found him. He got him out of there and made him famous."

Henry had asked his father if he'd ever been inside the Angola penitentiary and he said he had been, once or twice. Then he'd gone on and on about the problem of conducting accurate research, of getting the true history of such music. "These are people who have learned to tell you what they think you want to hear. There are a lot of men like me wanting to hear this music and record it. So they'll sell you whatever it is you're buying. You understand?"

His father had looked over at him then, squinting, and Henry had nodded again. But he hadn't really been listening. He'd been trying to imagine his father inside the prison, behind barbed-wire fences and iron bars. How frightened had he been that someone might pull out a knife or a gun? Had he stood next to someone who had killed somebody, someone who might wind up being put to death in the electric chair?

His father was still talking, explaining how John Lomax wasn't the first to go hunting for songs at Angola, that a professor from Iowa named Harry Oster had made recordings of the prisoners years ago, of singers with names that made Henry want to laugh: Hogman Maxey and Guitar Welch and Butterbeans and Roosevelt Charles.

"What did they do to wind up there?" Henry had asked.

"All kinds of things," his father had said.

"Like killing people?"

"Some of them," his father answered. "Some just had the misfortune of being in the wrong place."

"Like where?"

"Well," his father said, "for some people, just about anywhere can wind up being the wrong place."

After his father disappeared, Henry had wondered if it was possible that his father had somehow wound up in prison, not as a visitor but as an inmate, that maybe he'd done something so violent and shameful that his mother wouldn't tell Henry or Mary that this was where he was—in prison, at Angola. But what crime could he have committed that was so awful and unforgivable?

Henry knew the answer, of course. He knew it from all those blues songs his father had played for him, about the stranger who steps into the barroom and lets his eyes rest on the beautiful woman who belongs to another man and then buys her a drink or puts his hand on the fine soft skin of her arm or at the curve of her hip or says something in her ear that makes her laugh or pretend she's going to slap him. And just that—a single look or touch or word—would be enough for clenched fists or flashing knives or a drawn gun and a bullet right between the eyes or square through the heart.

He could have killed a man, Henry thought. *He could have killed a man and then done the only thing there was left to do. Run.*

Seven

THE DEPUTY pulled up at the courthouse, got out, shook Henry's hand again, and told him where he needed to go. "Just ask for Judge Martin's office," he said. "I'm on patrol, sir, so I can't show you in, but let me know if there's anything else I can do." He started walking back to the car but then turned and said, "Sheriff Roland is arranging a call for relief supplies, for things we could bring down to the Gulf Coast. I told him that, on account of my cousin and all, I'd like to drive the truck down."

He seemed to be waiting for Henry to say something—maybe to thank him for his charity or offer to go down there with him. "Well, good luck," Henry said.

"Good luck to you too, sir," the deputy said, nodding toward the courthouse. "Judge Martin's a good man." Then the deputy laughed and said, "A little scatterbrained sometimes, though." He nodded again. "Just so you know."

"Thanks," Henry said, and he headed into the courthouse. Just inside the front door, in a glass-covered case, a tattered American flag was on display. A sign inside the case, printed in what looked like a child's sloping script, said that the flag was from World War II, that it had been to Europe and back. *Count the stars!* the sign said. *How many are there?*

Henry looked for someone who could tell him where the judge's office was, but all of the people congregated in the lobby looked haggard and forlorn, slumped in their chairs with their heads down as though they were simply waiting to hear the awful price they'd pay for whatever they'd done wrong. Henry wondered if he was supposed to join them, to just wait there until he was summoned. He imagined gathering every last one of them around him, announcing he was in possession of some good news they needed mightily to hear. *Whatever awful torment and troubles you've got,* he would tell them, his voice rising, radio-preacher-style, words spilling forth like a waterfall, crackling like a spitting fire, *they sure enough can't be nearly as great as mine. Maybe you are plagued by relentless nightmares. Maybe you can't turn your mind from desire. Maybe you've lost your wife and your home, but here is the good news, my friends. How many of you have just killed a man? You may have wanted to a thousand times or a thousand times times a thousand, but how many have gone and done it, seen the red blood and smelled the dead red smell of it?*

Then a door at the rear of the lobby opened, and a short, wiry man in a suit and bow tie stepped out and looked around. Henry knew it had to be the judge by the way the others in the lobby looked at him, straightening their shoulders and pulling their hands from their pockets. Henry walked toward him, and the man stretched out his hand. "Mr. Garrett?" he said.

"Judge Martin?" Henry said.

"I'm afraid so," the judge said, and he put a hand on Henry's shoulder and, squinting his eyes, looked around the lobby as if he were momentarily confused. "Thanks for coming in. Let's talk in my office."

He led Henry back through the door and down a long hall and then into the courtroom, which looked to Henry more like a church. There were rows of old wooden pews facing the judge's bench, the pews covered in dark red cushions. A gold disk hung on the wall behind the bench, some kind of official seal, Henry guessed, though it wasn't anything he'd ever seen before; it had a bear holding what looked like a sheaf of arrows with a scroll beneath it that said something in Latin. The judge walked so fast that Henry, his legs still sore, had trouble keeping up. Through a door on the other side of the courtroom was the judge's office, and Henry was greeted there by a woman seated at an old wooden desk on the side of which was stenciled *U.S. Coast Guard* followed by a series of numbers.

"This is Mr. Garrett," Judge Martin said to the woman, and Henry thought he detected some measure of impatience in his voice.

"Well, hello!" the woman said brightly as if Henry were a child who had gotten lost and mistakenly wandered into the office. She rolled forward in her chair and shook Henry's hand. "I'm Marge," she announced. "You just let me know if you need anything at all."

"Thank you," Henry said.

The judge led Henry through another door into his private office. "Here," he said, removing some books from a chair. "Have a seat." Henry sat and looked around. There were files everywhere, covering the judge's desk and stacked on the floor and perched on the windowsill; open leather-bound books were spread across a long table amid scattered papers and cassette tapes. In a corner of the office were piles of cardboard boxes. Did just about everyone live like this, Henry wondered, in this state of chaos and disorder, their lives on the verge of spinning out of control? His own mess at Endly's, Latangi's crowded apartment, this judge's office—there was so much stuff in the world. He imagined what it must look like in New Orleans, thousands and thousands of people's possessions, all of it now junk, floating in the water or, surely worse, buried beneath it.

Judge Martin rifled through the files on his desk until he found the one he was looking for. "Here," he said, opening it, and Henry figured that it was the report the sheriff had written. "Just a minute," he said, looking up at Henry and then continuing to read.

"I don't know why I'm here," Henry said, and he realized how pathetic he sounded, how lost.

The judge held up his hand and then finally, after another minute or two, set the report aside. "Well, it's just a shame, isn't it? Of all the folks he had to choose—as if you didn't have enough on your plate."

"I'm sorry," Henry said. "I don't understand."

"There's not a whole lot to understand, I'm afraid," the judge said, and he pushed himself back in his chair. "Sheriff Roland was able to determine that Mr. Hughes was hoping to receive the inmate death benefit for his family. That's why he did what he did. But it's only for an accidental death, not a suicide, and it's pretty clear, despite the unconventional means, that's what we've got here." The judge picked up the report again, sighed, and threw it back onto his desk. "You just happened to be the one driving by. It's just lucky you weren't hurt."

"I'm not hurt," Henry said. He looked down at the cut on his arm, already nothing more than a thin, jagged line. He had been right, after all. This man Hughes had stepped out onto the highway, had raised his arms—not to fly but to welcome the awful impact, to have it be done. "What do I need to do now?" he said, looking back up at Judge Martin.

"Nothing at all," the judge said. "It might take a few days, though. I've got to sign off on this, file it in Richmond. I'll meet with Mrs. Hughes and explain it to her. I'll try to determine what her circumstances are. There are a lot of poor folks in this county, Mr. Garrett.

Five thousand dollars would have gone a long way. She's got diabetes, I know that. And she gets dialysis. She's no doubt facing some medical bills."

"Is that what it would have been?" Henry asked. "Five thousand dollars?"

"It's awfully sad, isn't it?" the judge said. "Five thousand dollars."

"Can I ask why he was there?" Henry said.

"On the work crew?" the judge asked, squinting again.

"I mean in prison," Henry said. He wasn't sure why he wanted to know. Was it that if the man had killed or raped someone, he wouldn't have to feel as awful about it?

"This and that. Bad checks, this last time," the judge said. "He wasn't a rotten egg. In fact, all told, he was a pretty good one. He was in my court over and over, though, and it was just about always in regard to money. Theft or fraud, breaking and entering. This is a poor county, Mr. Garrett. There's lots of folks in about the same shape. I didn't have a choice but to incarcerate Mr. Hughes for a while this time. I'm sorry I did, of course. I'm terribly sorry I did. He lost a daughter a few years back. Quite a few years now, if I remember correctly. She left a child behind, a boy. I administer the family court as well, handling divorces and determining custody. They wanted to keep that boy. Mrs. Hughes sat there and cried and said no matter her infirmity and her husband's record, she'd raise him properly. And she has. I've never had him here in court. He's probably fifteen or so by now."

The judge looked at Henry, but Henry didn't know what to say. He wanted to ask about his car, about how he might get some money, about what he was supposed to do next. But it didn't seem right to ask any of that. This man Hughes was dead; he'd left a widow behind, and a grandson. What had made Henry think his circumstances were worse than anyone else's?

The judge stood up. "You have transportation back to the Spot-light?" he asked.

Henry had no idea what the judge was talking about, then he remembered seeing something with the words *The Spotlight* in the motel office. Out front, near the highway, the sign was just a generic one; all it said was *Motel.*

"I don't," Henry said. "My car was in bad shape. It had to be towed. I don't even know where it is."

"Where were you headed?" the judge asked. "The report said you were fleeing the hurricane. It said you'd lost your home."

"I've got a sister in Baltimore," he said, and his words sounded to him less like the truth than the lyrics to a song, some country-music tale of heartbreak and regret. He decided not to tell the judge that he thought Amy might be living somewhere nearby. "I was thinking of going up to Baltimore to see her."

"Well, let's see what we can do for you," the judge said, and he led Henry out of the office to his secretary. "I've got to prepare for a hearing, but Marge will help you out."

The woman looked up from her computer. "I sure will!" she said.

The judge shook Henry's hand. "Again, I'm sorry, Mr. Garrett. Would you mind checking back with us in a few days just to make sure it's all settled?"

"I will," Henry said. "I'm not sure I'll get very far without my car." He couldn't believe this was all there was to it. A man was dead, and all the judge had had to do was shake his hand and that was that.

"Well, Marge will see about your car and anything else you need," he said. "And I hope you get back home before too long, Mr. Garrett. It's a real mess down there. I can't believe how bad it is."

How bad is it? Henry wanted to ask, but he simply watched as the judge retreated into his office and shut the door. When he turned to the secretary, she was staring up at him. "Now, you tell me what I can do," she said. "That's my job. That's what I'm here for. We'll get you fixed up straightaway." And she smiled at Henry and reached over to pat his arm as if, once again, she were speaking to a child. He thought about Latangi touching his arm in the same kind, solicitous way.

What did he need? *A car. Some cash. A clear head. A telephone.*

"I need to call someone," he said. "Is there a phone I could use?"

"Yes, there is," the woman said, and she pointed to a chair next to her desk. "Sit yourself right here, now."

Henry picked up the receiver and closed his eyes. He could not remember Mary's number. He could not even remember the Baltimore area code. He opened his eyes and saw that Marge was looking at him. Her face seemed to be frozen into a smile, as if it were something she applied in the morning with her makeup, her lips a bright cherry red, her eyebrows penciled into perfect brown crescents. He put the receiver on the desk and slumped down in the chair. "I'm not—" he began, but he didn't know what to say, couldn't figure out what to do next. He ran a hand through his hair and rubbed his eyes.

"Never you mind, Mr. Garrett," Marge said, gently replacing the receiver. "You just take it slow, and we'll get right through this one step at a time."

"Yes," Henry said, nodding, closing his eyes again. "I just need to think."

"That's just what I do!" he heard Marge say, and he could hear her clicking her fingernails on the desk. "When I need to, it doesn't matter where I am, I just close my eyes and bring everything to a screeching halt. *You need to think, Marge,* I say to myself. *You need to think.* I was reading about it in *Reader's Digest,* about how doctors have gone and proved it's true. Closing the eyes really is the first step in clearing the mind and finding peace. I can't remember if they used monkeys or people or just what they did, but somehow they proved it."

Henry listened not to Marge's voice but to her clacking fingernails. He thought of Latangi, of her pale blue nails with their specks of glitter. He thought about the red speck in Amy's eye and the rhythm of his father's bass and the man, Mr. Hughes, bloody, dead, lying on the highway, and he thought about what he'd believed when his father first disappeared—that he knew exactly where his father had gone. His father had talked about it once with Henry. He'd told him that for nearly a decade, Thelonious Monk had been living not in New York but across the Hudson in New Jersey, at the home of the same rich white woman, a baroness, who had taken in Charlie Parker. All those years and the world had heard nothing from Monk, no music or concerts or interviews, and most people just assumed he was dead. But he wasn't dead. He was right there, across the river, and he wanted to go there sometime, see if he could just talk to Monk, find out what he had to say after all those years of silence. He wanted to see for himself if what people said was true—that Monk hadn't touched the piano in years, that he hardly ever spoke a word, even to his wife, Nellie, who was living there too, that he just lay in bed staring out the picture window at the lights of New York as if he were peering up at the stars in the night sky.

And so that's what Henry had thought he'd done. He figured his father had gotten into his car and headed north up I-95. He imagined him pulling up at the gates of the baroness's mansion, imagined him telling whoever it was who answered the door why he was there, starting out the same way he did when he pulled his handkerchief from his pocket, wiped his brow, and put his foot up on people's rotting porch steps: *Good morning to you. I'm Professor Joseph Henry Garrett from down the road at Tulane University.*

But he'd have to say something else, Henry knew. He'd have to say, *I'm here to speak to Mr. Monk.* He'd have to say, *I just want to shake Mr. Monk's hand.* Or, *I think maybe I can help him.*

About four years later, when Henry read in the newspaper that Monk had died—from a cerebral hemorrhage, it said—he had felt like he was reading not just about Monk's death but about his father's, that Monk's dying meant his father must now be dead. Mr. Monk had resided with his wife, Nellie, in the Weehawken, New Jersey, home of the Baroness Nica de Koenigswarter, the obituary said. He hadn't performed for a decade, hadn't spoken publicly for years. There was no indication that during this period he had produced any new compositions. And Henry had set down the newspaper and cried—not for Monk, not really even for his father. He was crying purely for himself, for the silence that only now, this very moment, he had come to understand would never be broken. It was 1982; he was eighteen years old. He would never see his father again, never learn why he had left, never think of him again as someone still alive and breathing, capable of showing up one day at the door of his own house just as Henry had imagined him showing up, tired and disheveled but elated, at the house where Monk lived, knocking on the door, smiling, announcing exactly why he was there.

"How can I help you?" Henry heard, and he opened his eyes and realized that he was crying now, weeping with exhaustion and from the interminable clatter in his head—the sounds and images there, the memories, the endless cacophony. He could hear his own voice reading out loud to his students, imploring them to grasp the awful allure of Kate Chopin's words in *The Awakening,* of blue-grass meadows with no beginning and no end, of the sensuous sea enfolding the body in a soft, close embrace. *Her arms and legs were growing tired,* he had read out loud to them, but what had he ever managed to say to his students, to these children, that contained even the tiniest shred of wisdom, of insight or eloquence or grace? What could he have possibly said? Shouldn't he have warned them that the shimmering, translucent pool in which a book like this bathed its heroine's longing and despair was a mirage, as ridiculous as the swooning women in the silent movies he and Amy had seen, as deliciously sordid as Clarissa Nash dangling her schoolgirl breasts above him, nipples just above his mouth, just beyond the reach of his blunt thick tongue? Shouldn't he have told them how ugly it all truly was? Shouldn't he have realized how ugly it was all going to be? Some of them, some of those children, might still be there now, floating in oily, shit-smeared water, unrescuable, dead.

Marge was holding out a box of tissues, and when he didn't take it from her, she set it on the corner of the desk. "You're just breaking my heart, Mr. Garrett," she said.

And Henry managed to tell this woman everything there was to say—that he'd fled the hurricane and wound up in Virginia, that his wife was here somewhere though he didn't know where or if she'd even want to see him, that his sister was in Baltimore but they hadn't spoken for more than a year, that he did not have a car now or money or a telephone, that he did not know what to do, that this man Hughes was dead, that hundreds and hundreds of people, maybe thousands and thousands, he didn't know how many, were dead in New Orleans, that maybe all the ones who had managed to survive had lost their homes, lost everything, that he felt helpless and angry and confused and sad. So terribly sad. *All the time,* he wanted to shout but didn't. *All the fucking time.*

And the woman was standing now. She stepped around the desk and stood behind him, her hands on his shoulders. "Mr. Garrett, Mr. Garrett," she said as though she were trying to quiet a wailing infant. "We've been praying on this, Mr. Garrett. The women's group at my church—every one of us has been praying on this. We've been talking and praying about how we might help with what's happened from this hurricane. And now here you are, Mr. Garrett. Here you are."

She took her hands off Henry's shoulders and stepped back around her desk. "We'll care for you," she said. Henry looked up and saw that she was smiling. "Don't you worry one bit. We'll care for you."

"I'm sorry," Henry said. "I didn't—"

"Listen, now," Marge said. "I'm going to attend to this just as soon as I can. You give me one day, and you won't know what hit you. We've got a phone tree, Mr. Garrett. We've got movers and shakers in our women's group the likes of which you've never seen." She leaned across her desk toward Henry and whispered, "Here's our official name in the church. It's the Marimore First Presbyterian Women's Auxiliary. But that doesn't exactly roll right off the tongue, does it? So we call ourselves the Hounds of Heaven. Reverend Timlin doesn't care for the name. He says it's a sacrilege and an abomination. But do you think we care, Mr. Garrett? Forgive me for saying so, but Reverend Timlin has a stick up his you-know-what. The women in our group are a different breed, Mr. Garrett. The Hounds of Heaven like to laugh and have a good time. That's what we do. And we take action. The men's group, I'll tell you, can't hold a candle to us when it comes to action."

"My sister," Henry said. "I need to call her."

"I'll take care of that too. You've got your own mending to do, so I'll start mending that fence for you. You just tell me her name, and I'll find her number."

"Mary Garrett," he said. "In Baltimore. There might be more than one." He thought about Latangi searching for his name on the Internet, finding out where he worked. "The Walters," he said. "It's an art museum. You could call her there. I should call her there."

"You're ready to do that?" Marge said. "She's worried sick, I'm sure. She'd be so relieved just to hear your voice."

"If you could just find the number," Henry said, "I'll call her. I'll call her later."

"Yes indeed," Marge said, and he closed his eyes again as she typed into her computer, her fingernails clacking on the keys. "Walters Art Museum. Baltimore, Maryland," she said. "Easy as store-bought apple pie."

Henry waited, eyes still closed. He imagined hearing Mary's voice, the censure in it, the relief. He thought about Latangi saying that her husband's words had been waiting for him, just as this woman now said her church group had been waiting for him. It seemed so absurd, this notion that some divine plan had been steering him here. Was this the same plan that had placed the man in the road as he drove by, the same plan that had covered New Orleans with water, that had plagued his sleep with endless dreams, his head with endless clatter? He could see Louise Hart, a sweet girl, dumb as a toad, standing up before the class. He could hear her voice, its desperate hope, its pleading: *Well, I just don't believe it, Mr. Garrett. It doesn't say Edna drowned. It doesn't. So how do you know for sure?*

"Here you go, Mr. Garrett."

Henry opened his eyes to see Marge's hand stretched out toward him. He took the sheet of paper. "Thank you," he said.

"What's next?" she said. "Let's move right on down the list."

What *was* next? Money. His car. But before he could answer, an old woman in a wheelchair appeared in the office doorway. Henry could see that her legs were gone, the hem of the black dress she was wearing tucked beneath her seat. Behind the woman, pushing the chair, was a boy. He looked taller than Henry, his hair carefully trimmed. Henry knew immediately who he was, who they both were. He could see the resemblance in the boy's eyes, in the shape of his head.

"I need to see him," the old woman said, and the boy, maybe fifteen or so, looked apologetically at Henry and then at Marge. "They told me I can't see him, but I need to," the woman said, and she slapped her bony hands on the wheelchair's armrests. "I need to say my good-byes."

She had been looking at Marge as she spoke, but now she turned to Henry. "Can you please help me, sir?" she said. "Can you please, mister, sir, make them let me see my husband?"

Eight

A NARROW metal cot, sagging as though someone had slept on it for years, stood in the corner of the room, a tattered white blanket on top. By one window was a desk with a green banker's lamp, a wooden stool tucked beneath it. Below the other window were shelves filled with books so worn that the titles on the spines were illegible. The walls were bare, the floor covered with a cane rug. Henry pulled out the stool, sat down, and switched on the lamp. There was nothing else on the desktop, its surface polished to a smooth sheen, but beneath were two wide drawers, one on each side of the desk, and Henry assumed that they held Latangi's husband's poems. He gripped the brass handles and gently tugged at them. He wanted to test the weight of the drawers, to be certain that they weren't empty, but he did not yet want to face the task of reading. Her husband had devoted his entire life to writing, Latangi had told him, but Henry was afraid that a single poem, even a single line, might be enough for him to conclude that all that devotion and effort had been wasted, just as Henry had learned that all he had to do every fall was read a sentence or two of a first assignment and he would know just about everything he needed to know about its author: whether the student possessed enough imagination to appreciate the books the class would be reading and, if by some stroke of luck this was the case, whether he or she already knew how to give that imagination a persuasive, distinctive voice.

That first assignment was a simple one: What is your favorite word? Most of the answers were predictably uninspired. The girls would choose *love* or *family* or *faith,* the boys *truth* or *honor* or *responsibility,* their essays neatly packaged in the five-paragraph formula previous teachers had taught them, as if everything in the entire world, no matter how vast or sprawling, could be broken down into an introduction, points one, two, and three, and a conclusion.

But there were always a few students who understood the opportunity they had been offered. Asked to discuss their favorite word, they chose *seagrass* or *Natchitoches* or *whimsical* or *raspberry* or *willow.* They described the delicious taste of these words on their tongues; they rummaged through their memories, summoned moments from childhood they thought they'd forgotten; they moved forward one sentence to the next with the satisfying precision of a mower through tall dry grass. He felt an immense gratitude for such students, for the pleasure he knew they would offer him through their words; they nearly offset the helplessness and despair the rest of the students provoked in him, the awful knowledge that he faced nine months of prodding and poking them to understand—to truly feel—the books they read, how the whispering voice of the sea might indeed be seductive, how its touch might enfold the body in a soft, close embrace, how the words on a page might not simply describe the world but actually create it, make it more real than it had been before those words were written, before the writer had imagined them.

He had come here now to this room, though, with little hope—

with none, really—that he would find such a world in the words Latangi's husband had written. He had come simply because he did not want to sleep, did not want to be visited by more dreams. He no longer had the strength for them, for their absurd horror, the endless wandering and violence and desire. He had not known what to say this morning to the old woman who'd asked to see her husband, but he knew that she would find her way into his dreams—the bony hands with their crooked arthritic fingers, the blunt stumps of her legs, the worn black dress with its rust-stained white lace collar, the awful entreaty that she be allowed to see her husband's body, say good-bye to him.

Helpless, mute, he had looked away—had looked to Marge, who had quickly rescued him, walking over to the old woman, taking her hand, and telling her that she would do what she could.

"Where is he, Mrs. Hughes?" Marge had said. "You just tell me where he is."

"Out Madison Heights," the old woman answered, and she turned her head to look up at the boy, her grandson, who was still holding her wheelchair. He nodded.

"At Pearlman?" Marge asked the boy, and he nodded again.

"That's fine," Marge said, and she went back to her desk, quickly hunted through the phone book, and then called the funeral home. Henry listened as Marge explained the old woman's request. She tapped her fingernails on the desk and then said quietly, with the slightest suggestion of impatience, "Well, Mrs. Hughes is right here at Judge Martin's office, and Judge Martin has just now asked me to tell you to do what you need to do so Mrs. Hughes can see her husband."

She looked up at Henry and winked, acknowledging the lie she'd just told.

126

"That would be just fine, then," she said. "I'll ask them to wait until three."

Marge hung up the phone, walked back to the old woman, and took her hand again. "They'll let you see him, Mrs. Hughes," she said. "They've just got to tend to him a little first." Henry listened as Marge comforted the old woman, making sure that she and her grandson had transportation out to the funeral home and asking if there was anything else they needed.

"I suppose we're all right," the old woman said, and she lowered her head to hide her weeping.

Henry wanted to say something to this woman, to acknowledge that he was the one who had been driving the car that struck and killed her husband. When she looked up and slowly turned her gaze from Marge to Henry, he could see, from her pronounced cheekbones and high forehead, in the oddly delicate grace of her eyes and mouth, that she had once been striking, that even now, despite her wasted, ruined body and missing teeth, despite her horror and grief, some faint trace of that quality remained. He remembered how he had once stepped into his mother's bedroom to find her sitting with Mary beside her, art books scattered across the bed, each of them open to a different painting depicting Saint Sebastian, his stomach and arms and legs pierced with arrows. In all of them, Saint Sebastian's back was arched in a posture that looked less like agony than exquisite pleasure, long hair swept back from his face, cascading across his bare shoulders. Henry had stared at the paintings, embarrassed that they reminded him not of anything having to do with religion or art but of the pictures of naked women he'd once seen taped to a bathroom wall in a barbershop he'd gone to with his father, women whose backs were arched in precisely the same way, whose long hair was swept back across their shoulders, their bodies

127

the same voluptuous shape as his father's bass. His mother had smiled at him and said, "We're deciding if we agree with what Lorca said about Sebastian," but Henry hadn't let her explain. He'd made some excuse and left them there. He had not known who Lorca was; he hadn't cared what this person had said about Saint Sebastian. He'd remembered the dumb stirrings of desire he'd felt in the barbershop bathroom, the uncomfortable swell of his penis, the sickening sweetness of cologne and hair tonic in which the room seemed drenched, the rank scent of urine.

It was me, Henry wanted to say now to the old woman. *It was my car.* But he knew that this admission was not what the woman needed right now. She needed comfort; she needed relief.

She looked at Henry, seemed to study his face despite the cloudiness of her eyes. Marge stepped forward and led the old woman and her grandson out. "Who's driving you, Mrs. Hughes?" she said. "Are they waiting?"

"Pastor Rose," the boy said, and for the first time he looked at Henry. "He's out front."

"Then let's get you to him," Marge said, and she called to Henry, "Sit tight, Mr. Garrett. I'll be right back."

While Marge was gone, Henry looked at the piece of paper she had handed him, the number for Mary written on it. At the top of the sheet was a bloated orange cartoon cat—Garfield—curled up in a ball and sleeping, the bubble over his head depicting the dream he was having, which was simply the same image of a cat curled up and sleeping. He knew that he should call Mary now, let her know that he was alive, that he'd gotten out of New Orleans. He imagined her watching the news reports on TV, desperately searching every image for a glimpse of him. Was he trying to punish her with his silence? Was this his means of retribution for the fuck-you sunset card, for her failure to understand why he couldn't deal with the funeral and the estate? That's exactly what his mother had done; she'd punished him with her silence when his father left, refusing to talk about it, refusing to acknowledge a moment's pain or grief or regret. But Mary had been punished as well, of course. Why was she okay and he wasn't? It was all so stupid. In class he'd always pushed his students to analyze every character's motivation. Why had a character done what he'd done? What about him had led him to do it?

"He just felt like it," at least one student would always say. "It's just what he felt like doing."

And Henry would comically, exaggeratedly stomp his feet and throw his hands up in the air. He'd pace the classroom, weaving between the desks. He'd explain that this kind of response to literature, to life, was inadequate, that it displayed a failure of insight or imagination. "It's just lazy," he would say, glaring at the offending student until the class laughed and the student, embarrassed, squirming, tried to formulate a better answer.

Maybe, though, Henry had been wrong. Maybe there wasn't, after all, a clear motivation for any of the things that people did. Maybe they just did them for no reason at all or because of stupidity or selfishness or cowardice or anger or for reasons that made no rational sense — because the clouds happened to be a particularly gloomy shade of gray that day, because the barking of an old dog chained to a sycamore tree just happened to sound exactly like the crunch of soldiers' boots on gravel or the hum of bees like an engine in the head driving you mad.

He didn't know. Again, always, and forever, he didn't know. He couldn't think, couldn't decide whether he should run out of the office, throw himself in front of a car just as the old man Hughes had done, or sit here and wait for whatever mercy or further punishment was headed his way.

So he'd waited, or he simply hadn't moved yet, hadn't managed to organize the chaos in his head, before Marge returned. She walked right past him into Judge Martin's office, then she stepped out a moment later and announced that the good and kind judge had agreed she could go ahead and make a day of it.

"Of what?" Henry said.

"We're going to start setting things straight, Mr. Garrett," Marge said. "Lord knows you deserve it."

He could have told her, of course, that this—that *he*—was a lost cause, that he deserved nothing, but he watched her retrieve her purse from her desk drawer and then rifle through it. When she found what she was looking for—her car keys—she nodded triumphantly and said, "Just wait until you see my baby, Mr. Garrett. It's brand-new."

Marge's *baby* was a red Mustang convertible.

"I know, *I know,*" she said to Henry when he climbed in next to her, "this is not a good Christian woman's car, but I'll tell you what, it sure is fun." She started the car and revved the engine. "My husband bought it for me. I had a health scare last winter. The big C." She looked over at Henry as she tied a scarf over her head, and it occurred to him that maybe Marge's hair, with its tight blond curls, was actually a wig. "In my ovaries," she said. "Charlie was all torn up and he cried and said he wanted me to have anything I ever wanted in this world and then he went out and got me this."

She ran her hands along the steering wheel and laughed. Henry smiled at her. There was nothing in her face, with its pudgy cheeks and too-thick makeup and weak chin, that was pleasing, but she was—what? She was *buoyant.* He pictured her stepping out into the sea. She would simply float. The warm water would embrace her as though she were a swaddled child left among the rushes; it would carry her safely back to shore.

"Turns out it was nothing at all. It was just a cyst," Marge said as if she were still surprised, as if she'd just now been handed this good news. "When he's doing the bills, Charlie swears he's bringing her back to the dealer, but he won't. And he knows I know he won't, and that makes him even madder." She laughed and shot out of the parking lot, the car's tires screeching. "You just hold on, Mr. Garrett," she said. "We're going to have us some fun."

And Marge seemed to have a grand time despite the obstacles they faced. The mechanic at the repair shop where Henry's car had been towed didn't want to let Henry touch the car without orders from the sheriff, but once again Marge said Judge Martin had sent them over. She delivered this lie with an air of disinterested authority, as if she were a deputy on official business, but Henry was nonetheless surprised when the mechanic—*Gregory* was sewn in red script above the pocket of his gray shirt, though for some reason Henry doubted that was his name—shrugged and wiped his hands on a towel that was already black with oil and then led them out to the lot behind the shop, every bit of it covered with cars that had been smashed or crunched or dismembered, stripped down to grotesque-looking rusted skeletons.

When he spotted his car, Henry was shocked by how bad the damage was, the front hood folded like an accordion, the front wheels flat, turned nearly sideways. It couldn't have been the man's body that had caused such ruin; Henry must have struck the guardrail. He didn't want to look, but he pointed and the mechanic nodded and took them over. Something about this guy's manner, a kind of lassitude or silent resentment, made Henry wonder if the man had previously encountered Marge and the judge in their professional capacity—for marijuana possession or failing to pay child support, or maybe for assault charges after a particularly nasty barroom fight.

Henry opened the passenger door, which groaned as though it had rusted shut, as though the car had been out on the lot for months, but he wasn't able to retrieve his checkbook because the whole dashboard was dented and the glove compartment was stuck. The mechanic pulled a screwdriver from the belt at his waist like a cowboy whipping out a six-gun for a shoot-out, said, "Try this," and handed it over. Henry still wasn't able to open it, so the mechanic leaned in, took the screwdriver from Henry, and with a quick flick of his wrist pried it open. *Breaking and entering,* Henry decided. *That's how he met the judge.*

Once Henry had his checkbook, Marge drove him over to the bank, but the teller told him they couldn't cash his check because his bank was offline and wasn't allowing any transactions. "It doesn't say why," the teller said. He was a young man with pitch-black greasy hair tucked behind his ears and an acne-scarred face, and as he stared at his computer screen and shook his head, Marge stepped up to the counter, leaned across it, and whispered, "Could you please just call the manager over?" She looked back at Henry and rolled her eyes. "If you take a look at Mr. Garrett's check, you'll see it's from a bank in New Orleans. You know all what's happening down there? The hurricane?"

The teller looked up at Marge and then at Henry. He nodded hesitantly, as though he wasn't exactly sure what Marge was talking about.

"Well, Mr. Garrett here is from New Orleans," she said.

When the teller continued to stare blankly at Marge, she said, "He's a refugee. He needs our help."

The boy picked up his phone and, turning away from them, mumbled into the receiver. A moment later a large man wearing a red-and-white-striped shirt stepped out of his glass-enclosed office. "Come on over," he said, waving to Henry and Marge. "Let's see what we can do for you, my friend."

Seated behind his desk, the manager listened as Henry recounted his flight from New Orleans, his three days of driving, and then the accident. "Sure," the manager said, nodding, hands resting on his broad stomach. "Heard all about it." Henry wasn't sure if he meant the hurricane or the accident, but he didn't ask. The manager agreed to give Henry two hundred dollars, holding on to the check until his bank was up and running.

"Where can I get ahold of you if I need to?" he asked.

"The Spotlight," Henry said, and the manager nodded as though this confirmed some vague suspicion he'd had about Henry's character.

"We're going to find him something better," Marge said. "We're just getting started."

Once they were done at the bank, Marge drove Henry through town, pointing out every landmark they passed as though she were conducting an official tour: the local veterinarian's office, which was on the first floor of the largest house in Marimore, the second and third floors occupied by the veterinarian's investment-banker ex-wife and their three children; the coin laundromat, which had all sorts of plumbing problems, or so Charlie had told her, and he would know since he'd made a bundle trying to sort things out; the Elkwood Salon, which used to be the sheriff's office; the pharmacy and the new Catholic church, which hadn't yet had its grand opening or christening or whatever they were going to call the celebration; the Marimore Historical Society and the post office and the library. When they passed a restaurant named the Briar Patch, Marge turned into the parking lot. "I don't know about you, Mr. Garrett, but I'm hungry. And I'd like to get the branches of that phone tree shaking, so we're going to have to make a list of whatever you're going to need."

"I really don't think I need anything," Henry said. "You've already done enough."

"Just hush up now, Mr. Garrett," Marge said. "You could hardly be expected to know what you need, poor thing." She waved Henry out of the car and then pushed a button on her key ring to close the canvas top. "And don't you worry," she said. "This isn't charity. This is our mission. That's what it says on the sign above the door at our church as you walk out, and I believe it. *Welcome to the Mission Field,* it says. That's what my health scare did for me. Charlie says it got me not one but two new leases. One on life, and one"—she patted the canvas top of her car—"on this baby. And he's right."

Henry followed Marge inside the restaurant and then to a booth in the corner. The walls were covered with amateurish cartoonlike paintings of wide-eyed rabbits engaged in various activities—throwing a football, hanging laundry on a clothesline, dancing in circles on a hillside, peeling carrots in a kitchen. The paintings made Henry think of Latangi's apartment, of all the Hindu deities on her wall, and he felt as if they had just stepped into the temple of some bizarre rabbit-worshipping cult.

Marge didn't seem to notice the paintings. She glanced at the laminated menu, set it aside, hunted through her purse, and pulled out a notebook and pen. "Okay," she said, looking up at Henry. "Let's start with the basics and we'll go from there. No offense, but I'm going to guess you're in need of some clothes."

Henry looked at Marge. She reached forward to touch his hand. Henry smiled, tried to suggest he didn't understand why she thought he might need clothes. Marge took her hand away.

"I've got this feeling you're a real character, Mr. Garrett," she said. "You surely are."

So Marge had put together her list and, while picking her way through a chef's salad, used her cell phone to start making calls. Then she'd taken Henry to a Walmart a few miles down the highway and said she'd just wait in the car for him. "A man needs some privacy," she said. "And excuse me for saying so, Mr. Garrett, but I've learned from so many years with Charlie that there's nothing worse than watching a man shop, especially for clothes. Worse than women. You'd think they'd stepped into a lion's den, the way they're just frozen there like they're afraid to touch anything or even move. I can't stand it."

"Not me," Henry said, closing the car door. "I'll be back in a flash."

"All the same," Marge said, "I'll stay right here. You take your time."

Inside, Henry had indeed felt as though he'd stepped into a lion's den — or, more accurately, into one of his absurd dreams. The fluorescent lights cast a ghoulish purple-green glow onto everyone's skin, and the high shelves — crammed with food and clothes and children's toys and carpet-lined cat gymnasiums and kitchen appliances and bed linens — seemed as though any minute they might suddenly topple over and crush everyone beneath them. He imagined the Weather Channel reporter poking through the damage, imagined him saying that the local authorities had speculated that the shaking had started when a hurricane refugee, already responsible for one highway fatality, not to mention a ruined marriage and an altogether fucked-up life, stepped into the store.

He thought about Endly's and tried to picture the ruin there, the shelves overturned, water lapping against the storefront windows.

Would anyone have thought to check, before leaving town or digging in to ride out the storm, if Henry had stayed behind? Had any of the homeless men in the neighborhood sought shelter there after discovering that Henry hadn't bothered to lock the door?

He needed underwear and T-shirts, another pair of jeans, some socks, toothpaste, a razor—what else had Marge written on her list? He wandered through the Walmart's aisles and wound up at the back of the store in front of a long row of televisions, almost all of them playing the same cartoon—a veiled princess and an almond-eyed prince darting through narrow alleys and a busy street market atop a wildly flying carpet—except for one, a portable TV about the size of a paperback book, that was showing the news. There was no sound, or perhaps the cartoon's noise, the zip and swoosh of the flying carpet and the blaring music, were drowning out anything on the tiny flip-top TV. It was showing a report from New Orleans, the camera panning across thousands of people gathered outside the convention center in a sea of trash. None of them seemed to notice the camera; they appeared too exhausted, their clothes stained with sweat, their eyes swollen, their hair disheveled. They slumped on the ground or sat on plastic milk crates or stood leaning against one another. Mothers held limp infants in their arms; children lay asleep on dirty blankets spread on the ground. They were all brown-skinned, every one of them, their faces ashen, dusty. Henry imagined his father moving through the crowd, notebook in hand, fishing for information: *What songs have you been singing for comfort? What prayers have you been praying?*

Just outside the doors leading into the convention center, a woman in a wheelchair slumped forward, her head nearly to her knees. Henry could see, even on the tiny screen, that she was dead. He thought about Mrs. Hughes, heard her call out again to be allowed to see her husband. What in God's name was going on there? Henry couldn't imagine what they were all waiting for, what would happen to them. Where were the police or the army or the National Guard, anyone who could rescue them? Had someone told these people to stand outside and wait? Had they been told someone was on the way? Then the image shifted to a dusty roadway with armored vehicles and, in the background, a burning car, and Henry was confused for a moment, thought that this was somewhere else in New Orleans, one of the highways leading into the city, the army moving in to finally save everyone, but then he realized that the news had switched to another report, from Afghanistan or Iraq.

"A real beauty," Henry heard someone say, and he turned and saw a short, barrel-chested man standing next to him, his blue Walmart vest cinched tight at his waist and adorned with an oversize yellow smiley-face pin that announced *I'm Here to Help!*

"Price is a little steep, but it's worth it," the man said. "You can take it anywhere."

"What?" Henry said, and he turned back to the television. "I don't need this."

He hadn't meant to be rude, but clearly the man had been offended. "Any questions, you just let me know," he said.

When the man walked off, Henry tipped the TV screen down and turned away. *A real beauty,* the Here to Help man had said. *A real beauty.* On the store's booming loudspeaker, Henry heard what sounded like his own voice saying, *Clarissa Nash? Clarissa Nash?*—as if he were the store manager summoning a child who had wandered away from her parents. Yes. Clarissa Nash. He imagined her weaving through the aisles, lightly running her hands along the gleaming objects on the shelves, laughing when she caught her distorted reflection in the shiny surface of a waffle iron or mixing bowl or fog-free shower mirror. Soon, he was sure, she would turn into this aisle, into the lone row of television screens.

Where have you been? he would ask.

No. Not that. *Why are you here?*

No. What did he want to say? What did he want?

He was waiting for her. He would wait for her, and she would explain.

He would go find her.

But she wasn't there. There wasn't anything there. There hadn't been anything, of course—just the clatter in his head, Amy saying, *This time you've really fucking lost it, Henry.* And he wanted to scream back at her, make his voice echo through the Lucky Caverns: *Yes! Goddamn it, yes!* Which meant "help," he knew, and how is it that she didn't know this? It meant "help." Everything meant "help."

And Marge had finally come inside, had found him sitting in the pet-supplies aisle on a low stack of dog food, one of the bags torn, the dry food spilling out as if he'd been kicking at it with his heel. Behind Marge were a handful of Walmart employees, pressed up against one another in their blue vests as if they were a SWAT team responding to a hostage situation or a sniper, two of them brandishing their brooms as if they were rifles, and Henry actually laughed at the sight before him, at the idea of bumbling, blue-vested, broom-toting soldiers, but then he remembered something he hadn't thought about in years: the guy, a former naval seaman who had become a Black Panther, who'd entered the Howard Johnson's in downtown New Orleans, shot some guests and employees, set fires throughout the building, then barricaded himself on the rooftop and shot at the people down below, the police officers across the street at city hall, and anyone else he could find in his rifle's scope. Henry had been little, maybe seven or eight, but he remembered his father watching it all on their black-

and-white TV. He remembered his father talking about the Black Panthers, about their angry protests, their violent demonstrations, but also the free breakfasts they offered to those who lived in the Desire housing project, their calls for racial equality, their demands for justice. Henry wasn't sure if his father was telling him that he should admire the Black Panthers or fear them.

What Henry had felt, though, when he saw the smoke pouring from the Howard Johnson's and the ghostly shadow of the man the television cameras caught in the stairwell outside the building, what he had felt was an awful, sickening fear—the same thing he'd felt a few minutes ago looking at the images from New Orleans, watching the sea of weary brown-skinned bodies crowded together, spotting the dead woman slumped forward in her wheelchair.

He looked up at Marge. She seemed on the verge of tears, and he felt sorry for scaring her. He'd thought for a moment—for who knows how long—that he was at Endly's, the saccharine pop song swimming in his head something one of the scraggly artists had put on ironically (Olivia Newton-John? Celine Dion?), Tomas Otxoa sitting next to him in the La-Z-Boy and telling another story about his brother, the one about him calling home from his university in Bilbao and trying to speak to his mother in Basque as the Spanish operator listening in repeated again and again, *You must use a Christian language.*

"Poor, poor you, Mr. Garrett," Marge said, taking his elbow, helping him stand. Henry could feel her hands shaking as they held his arm.

Poor poor pitiful me, he thought, and he heard the music, heard Linda Ronstadt singing, though it was someone else's song first, he was sure, and he tried to remember exactly how old he had been when he heard this version and he was sure this was the album that showed her sitting before a mirror, her pink silk robe draped open, her hair up like Amy's.

"I should have known it," he heard Marge say, and Henry looked at her.

"Oh, it's my fault," she said, "thinking I'm a superwoman and all."

"What?" he said. He didn't understand her. He looked over at the Walmart employees, who were still standing there, though they had spread out, had organized themselves into an orderly row. "Oh, he's fine," Marge said, waving them away. "He's just diabetic. He needs a little fruit juice, is all. I'll take care of it."

She turned back to Henry. "We need to get you some real help," she whispered. "I should have known." And she led Henry slowly through the store, aisle by aisle, filling his arms with shirts and socks and jeans. She didn't ask him anything, didn't say anything more than "This will do" or "That's the ticket" as she pulled items off metal racks or plucked them from the shelves. When she found an empty cart, she took everything from Henry's arms as if she were gathering up an infant and she filled the cart with that and whatever else she decided he needed.

At the register, she'd paid for everything herself, insisting that Henry keep the two hundred dollars he'd gotten at the bank, then she'd driven him somewhere, he wasn't sure where—a real estate office, it seemed, the walls covered with plastic-framed pictures of sad brick ranch houses ringed by shrubs pruned into perfect squares. She introduced him to Rusty Campbell, a thin man with a sunken chest and a scraggly blond beard covering his pockmarked face. He'd been a doctor, Marge had told Henry, and was a doctor still but now sold property in the county. Henry shook the man's hand, and he led Henry back into his office, just as much a mess—no, even worse a mess—than the judge's had been, notebooks and files and magazines everywhere, but he found a place for Henry to sit.

"It's Henry, right?" he said, and Henry nodded.

"Marge has told me about all that's happening," he went on, and Henry thought, *When? When could she have told you?* But the man didn't wait—no one ever seemed to wait—for him to speak. "Let me tell you something about Marimore, Henry," he said, and he pulled out a pack of cigarettes and an ashtray from his desk drawer. He lit a cigarette and leaned back in his chair. "I'm speaking from first-hand experience," he said. "I'm speaking straight from my heart." He pointed at his sunken chest with the two fingers holding the cigarette. "Here in this part of Virginia is near about the worst place in the world for holding on to your reputation." He paused and turned his head away, as if he were looking for some particular detail in one of the framed pictures on the wall. "The worst place in the world," he said again, and now he looked back at Henry, "but I'll tell you what. It's about the best place to be once you've gone ahead and lost it."

Henry nodded and tried to grasp what Rusty Campbell was telling him. Was he suggesting that Henry had lost his reputation? Was he suggesting he was lucky to have wound up here? "I'm sorry," Henry said. "I'm not sure I understand."

Henry listened as Rusty Campbell began talking about forgiveness and humility. He sounded as if he were beginning a sermon. What he was doing, though, was relating to Henry the story of his life—how he'd been the local physician, just a regular country doctor like you'd see on TV, but had struggled more than a little—and for more than a short time—with drinking. "The drinking," he said, "was on account of all I'd seen and done a hundred years ago in Vietnam. I was in reconnaissance and, if you don't know what that really means, I'll tell you. It means striking out on your own or with at most one or two buddies and you better not be squeamish about the prospect of slitting somebody's throat—man or woman or child—before they can so much as cough or sneeze or whistle. You know what I'm saying?"

Henry nodded, and Rusty Campbell lit another cigarette.

"That's exactly what they'd do to you if they could," he went on. "The women and children too, sometimes. Of course, that's the very kind of thing that causes, once you get back, what we've taken to calling by the nice-sounding name of post-traumatic stress disorder. But that wasn't a word or even an idea back then. It doesn't take nearly so much to trigger this PTSD as what you've been through already, Henry, fleeing that wet-dog carcass of a city and leaving everything behind. You lost your whole life, and now there's this car accident. That's like getting a second incoming a minute or two after getting the first."

"It didn't—" Henry started, but he was hearing Tomas Otxoa's voice, *You must speak in a Christian language,* and the purr of a girl's voice and then his own saying, *A man is dead,* his own calling out the name Clarissa Nash and then saying, *Can I tell you about her? Can I tell you how she learned the peculiar entanglement of love and disappearance the summer she turned twelve?* But he finally managed to speak out loud, to say, "It didn't start with the hurricane."

And he heard Rusty Campbell laugh quietly, heard him drum his fingers on the desk before leaning toward Henry. "It never does," he said. "It never does, my friend."

Henry looked at him. "You're a doctor?" he said.

"Still got my license," he said. "Family medicine. I don't exactly do much doctoring anymore. Except, you know, when folks need some help."

He walked over to a closet, hunted around inside it, and then came back to Henry with sample packets of some kind of drug. "This is something just to calm your nerves and help you sleep," he said, setting the packets down on the desk.

Henry left them there. "I'm fine for now," he said.

"Okay," Rusty Campbell said. "But you come back if you need to. We'll just go from there. Right now, though, my friend, I've got some houses to sell."

He led Henry out to Marge, who was talking on her phone, and she waved Henry out to her car and then she got in too and began driving, still talking away. "Fine, fine, fine," he heard her say, "I understand. You can call Sally, and I'll call Elaine."

Henry closed his eyes and waited.

"You okay now, Mr. Garrett?" Marge said, and he opened his eyes.

"I'm sorry," he said. "I'm sorry for this mess."

"Don't bother yourself with sorry," Marge said. "Rusty Campbell's the one who got me through my scare. Rusty will help you. He's as good a man as there is."

Henry saw, up ahead, just past a traffic light, a sign in front of a cream-colored brick building. *Pearlman,* it said.

"There," Henry said, pointing. "That's the funeral home?"

"That's it," Marge said.

Henry looked at the digital clock on Marge's dashboard. "Could we stop? Could we go inside?"

"Oh Lord, Mr. Garrett," Marge said. "That's not what you need."

"You told them three o'clock, right?" Henry said. "That's what you told them?"

"They'll be arranging a service, I'm sure," Marge said. He heard the panic in Marge's voice, the first time she'd seemed undone. "You could pay your respects then if you want to."

"No, please," Henry said, and Marge slowed the car, pulled over into the gas station next door. "Please," he said, "if you've got a few more minutes. I just want to—" What? What did he want to do? He just wanted to say again that he was sorry. To say it better somehow. To say it in a way that might actually help. *How could it help?*

"Please," he said.

And Marge sighed and said, "I don't know what there is to do, Mr. Garrett. There's nothing you can do."

"Please," he said again, and he knew what he sounded like—like a child begging for a toy or a piece of candy. But Marge nodded. "Okay, okay," she said. She drove up to the funeral home and parked in the circular drive.

"Let me walk you in," she said, but Henry told her he'd be fine.

"That's what you said at the Walmart," she told him, but she smiled and waved at him. "I know, I know. Charlie says it all the time. 'You're not my mama.'"

Henry smiled back at her. "My mother," he said, "never had a car like this."

He watched Marge laugh and wave him away. When he stepped inside, he felt the cold rush of air. The floor was covered with a dark purple carpet, nearly the same color as the one in his room at the motel. Two plastic palm trees stood side by side near the door. Henry could faintly hear music playing, a hymn on an organ— "Deep River," he thought, and then he was sure. His father had played recordings of it, and he remembered hearing it again as he ran around outside of a church somewhere, his father inside, the choir's voices rising and falling—*My home is over Jordan* and *Dear Lord, I want to cross over*—as he tried again and again to jump and pluck the figs from a tree at the side of the church. Was Mary with him that day? She was—she'd bet him he couldn't reach the figs. And it was Mary who had explained, as if she were a schoolteacher, that the ancient Romans had worn crowns of figs when paying tribute to the god Saturn. He figured this was something she'd seen in a painting their mother had shown her in one of her art books, but she acted as if this were information anyone would know.

At the funeral home, Henry took a few steps forward and saw, in a small room to the side, Mrs. Hughes and her grandson, her wheelchair pulled up next to her grandson's chair. The boy was holding his grandmother's hand.

Henry walked into the room, but they didn't notice him. "Mrs. Hughes," he said, and now the old woman looked up and squinted as if she couldn't really see him.

"It's Henry Garrett," he said, going over to her. "The judge's office?"

The boy stood up, and Henry shook his hand. "I just wanted to say again how sorry I am."

"Yes, sir," the boy said. He was wearing a white shirt with a dark blue tie tightly knotted at his throat.

"You're his grandson?" Henry said.

"Yes, sir," the boy said, stepping behind his grandmother's wheelchair and taking hold of the handles.

"Have you been able to see your grandfather?"

"She's seen him," the boy said. "They wouldn't let me. They said I maybe could at the service."

"You know when that will be?" Henry said.

"Pastor Rose is inside," the boy said. "With Mr. Pearlman. They're making the plans."

Henry looked at the old woman, tried to see if she was following their conversation. He leaned near, started to reach out and touch her arm but then didn't. "I'm staying at the Spotlight, Mrs. Hughes," he said. "If you need anything, could you let me know? I don't know what I can do, but I'm very sorry. Please just tell me if there's anything."

The old woman nodded, and Henry shook the boy's hand again. "You'll do that?" Henry said. "You'll let me know if there's anything?"

"Yes, sir," the boy said, and Henry turned to go. Then he turned back.

"Would you tell me your name?" Henry said.

"Katrell," the boy said.

"Hughes?" Henry said.

The boy shook his head. "Katrell Sparrow," he said.

"I'm so sorry, Katrell," Henry said. He took the two hundred-dollar bills from his pocket and handed them to the boy. The boy held them and looked at his grandmother. She nodded, and he put the bills in his pocket. Did they already know, Henry wondered, who he was, what he had done?

"It's all I have right now," Henry said. "I'm sorry it's not more."

"Yes, sir," the boy said, and Henry saw now that the boy was shaking, that he was trying to hold himself still against all the grief and fear. He didn't want to cry, Henry knew. He didn't want to be seen crying. Henry raised a hand to say good-bye, turned away, and stepped out through the glass doors.

When Marge dropped him off back at the hotel, Henry sat on the bed and watched for hours the soundless television and all the pictures from New Orleans, the boats saving people from flooded homes and tree branches, the helicopters lifting men and women and children from shredded roofs, dead bodies floating facedown in black water, the crowd gathered outside the convention center somehow growing larger and larger, swelling until there seemed to be thousands and thousands there, all of them desperate and hungry and thirsty, burned by the sun, and he kept watching as he ate the food Latangi had left by his door, and he watched until he was worried he would fall asleep and wind up assaulted by his dreams, so he found the key Latangi had given him, and he walked down to the other end of the hotel, and suddenly here he was, sitting at Latangi's husband's desk.

A dead man's desk.

Yes, and all the clatter in his head: *A dead man's desk and a bright pink fig and "Poor Poor Pitiful Me" and Clarissa Nash and Tomas Otxoa and oh Lord, make a way out of no way, and oh Lord, blossom and blossom and ache.*

Quiet now, he whispered to himself, and he opened one of the desk drawers. Inside was a cardboard box and inside the box a manuscript bound with some kind of decorative string, a rainbow of colors woven and twisted together. He read the title page—*The Creator's Mistress* by Mohit Chakravarty—then the dedication to almighty Shiva and Parvati and to the beloved son Ganesha and to the princess of all earthly princesses, Latangi Chakravarty, beloved wife, and with prayers and gratitude to the esteemed Rabindranath, and Henry turned the page and—though he was desperately afraid to add yet another voice to all the wretched others clanging and swarming in his head—he began to read.

II

Last of all it was loss
he sang, how like a vine
it climbs the wall,
sends roots and tendrils
inward,
bringing to the heart
of the hardest stone
the deep bursting emptiness of song.

—Gregory Orr,
"The Ghosts Listen to Orpheus Sing"

Nine

FINALLY HE slept. He lay down on the metal cot and pulled the worn white blanket over him. He did not know what time it was or how long he had read, but he did not want to step outside and face the fluorescent glow of the parking lot, the desolate highway, the ghostly gray sky. He did not want to see or hear anything. He wanted Mohit's words to stay with him, wanted everything about the poem—the manuscript was, he quickly discovered, not a collection of separate poems but a single work, hundreds and hundreds of pages, thousands and thousands of lines long, vast and sprawling and sometimes for pages and pages almost incomprehensible to him, filled with allusions he did not understand, words that Latangi had left untranslated, a crazy impossible quilt, but all of it beautiful, devastatingly beautiful, even the manuscript pages so delicate and fine that the typed letters of each word seemed to have been embossed there—he wanted the lines, the images, the music of the poem to echo in his head. He wanted to continue hearing the strange and majestic cadences, the ordinary and the magical woven together into a seamless whole: a childless couple—the man with a withered leg, leaning on a crutch, the woman carrying agati blossoms—silently circling the temple at Madurai for forty-eight days, speaking only at night, once the moon had risen; a child perched beneath a palm tree playing some instrument called a *mridanga,* the rhythm summoning the barking deer from the forest, the red-tailed hawks from the sky; jealous gods churning heaven's oceans into powerful storms; a flower snake making its way room by room through a dark house and wrapping itself around the waist of a sleeping child; a young bride gently placing her feet atop those of her new husband.

Henry lay on the cot and tried to untangle the thread of the poem's story—the poet or God or both speaking to his beloved, the beloved asleep or absent or dead, the narrative a recounting of an arduous journey undertaken to rescue the beloved from her wretched state and return her to her rightful place at the poet's side.

This was, Henry knew, the story of every epic—a hero's death-defying voyage, a series of agonizing trials and tribulations, a final conquest that restored order to the universe, a city gleaming like gold in the sun, a funeral pyre's flames extinguished with drafts of glistening wine, love itself and nothing more steering the sun across the sky. But this single secret poem, hidden away in a drawer, with its baroque, antiquated language, its preposterously grand ambition, made it seem as though Mohit had not merely adopted this poetic form but had somehow invented it, as though he believed he was telling such a story for the very first time, the poet and his beloved reunited after years apart, once again bathing as they had as children in the Ganges, silver-finned fish rising from the water around them in graceful arcs, sun-blackened boys with long crooked cane staffs steering herds of buffalo through the dusty fields beyond the river-bank, broad-shouldered fishermen casting their nets into the water, pilgrims molding lingams on the muddy shore, old men squatting in the shade of the pipal trees and reciting holy verses, the lovers now standing in the middle of the wide river, garlands of marigolds on their heads, constellations of stars appearing in the sky one by one, each depicting some aspect of the poet's journey, night falling as the poet and his beloved embrace, as they sink down into the dark water, their fingers entwined and then their limbs and then their very souls as they descend slowly through the water until there is only darkness and they are no longer falling but rising, not back to the surface but to another realm, to a new life free of all suffering, the man's withered leg healed, the agati blossoms transformed in the woman's arms into a child.

When he had finished reading, when he had retied the manuscript with the colored thread and returned it to the drawer, Henry lay down on the metal cot. He felt that something new had overtaken him, something that he could taste on his tongue, that he could feel running through his arms and legs, an electric current or rushing river—he was not a poet; he couldn't think of anything but clichés. Somehow, though, by some trick of grace, Latangi had been right. Mohit's words had been, as she had claimed, waiting for him; it was as though he had been destined to step into this room and open this drawer and untie this colored thread. How had she known? How could she have known?

He thought of the scene late in the poem in which a haggard old woman has cast a spell upon the poet; left to wander in a thick mangrove forest, he can no longer remember his beloved's name, can no longer construct in his head even a single feature of her face or hands. He knows that he is racked with loneliness but can't remember who it is he longs to be with, so when his beloved finally discovers him resting by the bank where three rivers meet, he runs away despite her protestations of love, believing she is the old woman in disguise. He

153

later discovers that the old woman had in fact been his beloved, that she had been under her own miserable spell, one that stripped from her both her youth and her beauty until the poet returned, as indeed he would, to forgive her for stealing his memory.

Was there not a message in this for Henry? It now seemed possible to him—he was now willing to believe—that some divine, inscrutable force had been guiding him, that the life he had wrecked and then abandoned could, if he somehow managed to discern a proper path, if he could figure out exactly what he should do next, be restored to him. Was that what all his dreams of wandering had been about? Was it possible that he had been meant all along to undertake this journey, to rid himself of his every possession just as the young Buddha had done before achieving enlightenment?

Amy, he thought, *where are you now?*

And he imagined her magically hearing his voice, following the echo of his words across the mountains, through the woods, down below the earth. He imagined her following the echo and finding this motel, stepping into this dark room, kneeling before this cot, whispering, *I'm here, Henry, I'm here.*

Why couldn't his life, his story, be as triumphant as the work Latangi's husband had created? Why couldn't he and Amy, hero and heroine, be reunited through the wonders of mystery and magic and improbable grace? *Oh, Amy, where are you now?* he would say, and she would answer, *I am here, Henry. I have been here all along. You simply had to call for me. You simply had to remember.*

Oh God. What a lousy hero he was, the lousiest anyone could ever imagine: a coward and a lunatic and a fool. He was no hero at all, in fact; he was a man who had left his wife, who had thrown his money away on nothing, on an abandoned grocery store, who had endlessly dreamed not of peace or grace or redemption but of wandering and seduction, who had conjured a girl from thin air, molded her purely from the coarsest clay, an adolescent boy's version of mystery and allure: peppermint breath and petite pointy breasts and tiny hands to wrap around his cock and guide him up between her legs and shove him inside her, a girl with dark curly hair cascading across her face as she whispered and moaned with seductive schoolgirl pleasure.

What girl, what woman, would ever want such a man?

He thought of Don Quixote, but of course he hadn't actually read *Don Quixote,* so what he saw was not whatever figure Miguel de Cervantes had created but the gaunt and craggy Peter O'Toole in *Man of La Mancha,* sword in hand, proudly perched on his old mare. Henry had seen the movie with Amy at the Prytania. She'd leaned her head on his shoulder as Peter O'Toole, face caked with absurd makeup to create the illusion of age, sang "Dulcinea," as Sophia Loren spit and cursed at the old lecher but then, moved by his strange, sad protestations of love, by his pathetic romantic ardor, listened to the words: *I have sought thee, sung thee, dreamed thee, Dulcinea.* And Amy had held his hand as if they were teenagers, as if he were the one singing to her.

But no matter his infirmity, his delusions, his foolishness, Don Quixote possessed a noble and loving heart, a regal bearing. Henry did not. He possessed nothing.

No. He now possessed this manuscript, this beautiful remarkable epic entitled *The Creator's Mistress.* Couldn't he deliver this work to Amy, offering it as it had been offered to him: by sheer chance, by blind good fortune? Had he ever believed until now that a life could be changed by a story? Wasn't that what the English teacher guiding his students through a novel was supposed to believe? And the hysterical pastor, the ecstatic congregation, they believed it as well—that a story, a single story, could possess such power that as a result of its telling, of its words being pronounced, a life would be transformed.

How absurd to imagine that in a single empty room of a rural Virginia motel, such a story, a manuscript wrapped in colored thread, would be waiting in a drawer for a sad and lonely and pathetic man to discover it. But isn't that precisely how such extraordinary stories always unfolded, a great work rescued from oblivion, salvaged by a wayfarer, a nomad, a hermit?

Couldn't he just find Amy and say again that he was sorry? Couldn't he tell her that now, finally, once and for all, he understood how very much he had hurt her, how much he had given up when he'd left?

Couldn't he offer to her Mohit's poem? *Read this,* he could say. *It is the story of my love, of love itself, of a love lost and regained, of a life restored.*

The words had been waiting for him. Could they not, then, be waiting for Amy as well?

Our story, he could say to her.

And what would she say to him? How would she answer? Would she declare, once again, that he was a fool?

And his sister? How desperate Mary must be. By now, she had to be certain that he was dead, that he had failed to leave and had drowned, alone. Had she already begun to grieve, to forgive him, to think back over their strange, sad childhood? He thought of the time she had stayed out late one Saturday night and come home to discover her mother, still awake, sitting up in bed. Angry, threatening, she had said, "Where were you, Mary Claire? Tell me this very minute where you were."

"You know where I was, Mama. I told you," Mary said. "I was babysitting. I was at the Broussards'."

"You were *not* at the Broussards'!" her mother shouted with such certainty, such anger, that Henry, overhearing this exchange from his bedroom, had rushed to his mother's room and stood in the doorway, sure that Mary's lie had finally been discovered.

"I *was*," Mary said quietly, and Henry could hear the fear in her voice, the same pleading tone she'd used when he'd first learned what she was doing. She did not turn around, so he did not know if she even realized he was there.

"Well, I'll tell you this. Mr. Broussard called the house," her mother said to Mary. "He called here tonight. He said he hadn't seen you in weeks."

Oh God, Henry thought, confused. *He called. How could he have called?*

But he saw Mary's shoulders relax, saw her step toward her mother and climb next to her on the bed. "He didn't call, Mama," she said, running her hand through her mother's graying hair, tucking the loose strands behind her ear. "You know he didn't call. I was there tonight. They went out." She sat up now and held her mother's hand. "They went to a dinner party. Some politician's birthday, I think. There might be something about it tomorrow in the paper. It was at the Peristyle in City Park. Mrs. Broussard said there was a lovely string quartet and paper lanterns. She said she and Mr. Broussard danced and danced all night until their feet were sore."

Mary continued to stroke her mother's hair but looked over at Henry. He nodded and stepped away from the door without saying anything. How was it, he wondered, that even though he knew this family did not exist, he had nevertheless believed for a moment that Mr. Broussard had called, had spoken to his mother? She had sounded so angry, so certain. Had she suspected that Mary had been lying about something but had no idea what the lie was and so had tried this bluff? Or had she truly believed that Mr. Broussard had called? Had she been swept up into the lie simply because she had wanted to believe that lives like the Broussards' were possible, that her daughter could indeed enter the constellation of such shimmering stars?

It was only a few weekends later, though, that Mary came home and told her mother that the Broussards were moving away, that Mr. Broussard had gotten word that he was being transferred. She said that he couldn't tell her where they were going, that they would return to New Orleans someday but didn't know when that would be. And Mary had pretended to cry and had let herself be comforted by her mother. "You're going to miss them so," her mother had said, holding on to Mary, and Mary had nodded and continued to cry, an act so convincing that her mother had begun to cry as well.

He hadn't understood what Mary was doing, why she had devised an end to her story, but now, so many years later, lying on this metal cot, with the images from Mohit's poem racing through his head, Henry believed that he did finally understand. Mary had no doubt become afraid of the story she had invented, afraid of the power it had gained over not just her mother but her own mind, her own imagination. She hadn't *pretended* to be sad that the Broussards were leaving, he now realized; her tears, her weeping, had not been a performance. They were real; it had all become real to her.

His eyes were closed, but he heard the rumble of thunder outside, and then, a few moments later, the rain begin to fall. He heard it striking the low, flat roof of the motel and the parking-lot pavement. He heard the metallic ringing of the gutters, the rainwater rushing down, spilling out. He imagined the storm—perhaps the final vestiges of the hurricane—sweeping up from the South, the clouds stretched across the mountains like a dark sheet. He opened his eyes, and he felt the emptiness of the room. The girl Clarissa Nash was gone, and she would not, he now understood, come back, just as the ghost of his father playing the bass had not come back.

No, this was different. He had called out for his father, had lain in bed and closed his eyes and prayed that he would return. The girl, though, would not come back because he would not summon her again, would not ask again for that absurd, ghostly seduction. He wanted Amy, wanted his wife here at his side—no one else. Nothing else. Could it be that simple?

Then he slept. He slept and, for the first time in months and months, did not dream, did not have to fend off desire, did not have to wander aimlessly from one place to another, did not have to listen to his own voice spouting nonsense. He slept and woke up feeling restored to himself, clearheaded. How could it be that it was all this simple?

And that very day, beginning in the morning and stretching out until late afternoon, he watched in dumb astonishment as there arrived at the motel, at the door to his room and inside the office and even out front near the highway, one gift after another: shirts and pants and jackets and shoes and ties, bags of razor blades and shampoo and cologne and toothpaste, a clock radio and a toaster oven, paperback books and a stack of yellow legal pads and a box of pencils, a miniature refrigerator stocked with cans of iced tea and ginger ale and Dr Pepper, boxes of cereal and granola bars, bags of potato chips, cans of soup and baked beans, three tall plastic plants in ceramic pots, a red toolbox with a hammer and screwdriver and wrench, a teddy bear with a note pinned to its chest that said *Get well soon!*, a fishing rod, a backpack, a reading lamp, a wooden rocking chair, two folding beach chairs, a folding TV table, a folding card table, three rolls of quarters rubber-banded together, a handwritten gift certificate for a meal at What a Blessing, all brought by men and women and children waving shyly at Henry, haltingly stepping toward him and handing over whatever they'd brought—an ice chest, a thermos, a twenty-dollar bill—the adults shaking his hand and wishing him good luck, saying they were truly sorry for his loss, saying they understood what it meant to be down on your luck, saying they were ashamed at what the government was allowing to happen down there in Louisiana and Mississippi and the whole Gulf Coast and couldn't they just send in every soldier or National Guardsman and rescue those poor starving and scalded and thirsty folks, and Henry saying, *Thank you, thank you so much for everything,* and *Yes, I wish they would just do something soon, I'm sure they will, I'm sure it will end,* and *Thank you so very much for your generosity and kindness.*

And then, when Henry was sure there couldn't possibly be anything else, a final gift: an old, dusty, rusted, dented pale blue pickup truck, with Marge beaming in the driver's seat, honking the horn to summon Henry from his room, a Baltimore Orioles baseball cap perched ridiculously on her mop of tight blond curls.

"For you, Henry," Marge said, leaning out the window, giddily banging her hand against the door. "It's not a beauty, I know, but it hasn't been stolen either."

Marge jumped out like she was leaping from a horse and handed the keys to Henry. "Now, you can't go too far with it," she said, and she walked Henry around to the back of the truck. She pointed to the license plate, which said *Farm Use Only.* "It's a thirty-mile limit or something like that, Jim Ponton said. But maybe that'll be far enough for now. He said you could use it as long as you like." She led Henry to the front of the truck and patted the hood as if she were coaxing a nervous dog not to bark. "Maybe it will be good anyway for you to have a few days more before deciding what, where, and when."

"Maybe it will," Henry said. "And all these gifts, Marge. The food and clothes and everything."

"Folks just want to help," she said, and she looked out to the high-way as a white van turned into the parking lot. "I know it's too much. I know it is. But that's what folks here do."

The van pulled into a spot. The man driving put the window down and stretched his arm out and waved.

"That's Charlie," Marge said.

Henry waved and called out hello. Charlie waved back and then looked away, leaning forward as if he were busy searching for a station on the radio.

"He won't get out," Marge said. "He'll just sit there like a bump on a log till we're done talking, but he won't get out."

"That's fine," Henry said.

"Usually, I'd just make him wait awhile, stew in his own juices." She looked over at her husband and held up a finger to let him know she'd be there in a minute. He saw her and nodded. "But he drove all the way out to the Pontons and then followed me back here. He's lost half a day's work."

"You go ahead," Henry said. "I don't know what to say."

Marge held her arms out, and Henry stepped into her embrace. "You're going to get yourself better," she said, "then you're going to set about fixing all that's gone awry."

"I don't know about that," Henry said, feeling Marge release him from her grip.

"Oh, yes, you will," Marge said. "Like it or not, I've made you my own personal project."

Henry laughed. "A reclamation project."

"That's right," Marge said. "One hundred percent."

"That's a big job."

"Oh, it's nothing," Marge said. She looked over at her husband again.

"Will you thank him for me?" Henry said.

"I will," Marge said, and she took Henry's hand. "I'll check back with you tomorrow, but if you need something before then, I left my number in Jim Ponton's truck. And a little more cash—it's from Charlie's wallet—to tide you over until this bank thing is straightened out." She patted Henry's hand, then turned and headed toward her husband's van.

"Marge," Henry said, "you've done too much."

"Oh, just cut it out," she called over her shoulder to him, opening the van door. Her husband backed out but stopped in front of Henry. Marge had rolled her window down. "You think I don't have my own failings to make amends for?" she said in a kind of stage whisper, as if her husband somehow wouldn't hear her. "You're not the only one with a soul that needs saving."

"I think yours is well saved by now," Henry said.

Marge laughed. "I'm not so sure. You don't know how bad I once was." She turned to her husband. "He doesn't know, does he, Charlie?"

The man shook his head and smiled. "He don't know." Then he pulled away and Henry caught a glimpse of Marge throwing her head back and laughing.

Henry had not yet had a moment to speak to Latangi, to tell her that he had read Mohit's manuscript, to explain that she had been right about it somehow waiting for him. She had stepped outside of the office when the gifts began to arrive, and she had helped Henry store them—first in his room and then in the room adjoining it, unlocking the two interior doors between them. Henry had almost said something then about Mohit's poem, but she'd explained that she had an appointment—"A small business matter with an attorney," she had said, shaking her head but smiling—and he had watched her drive off in her car, a small blue Honda in which she seemed comically large. She leaned forward with both hands clutching the steering wheel, her wrists adorned with dozens of golden bracelets and bangles encrusted with colored stones, costume jewelry Henry had seen overflowing in bamboo baskets on the floor when he'd had dinner in her apartment.

He had wanted to say something to Latangi before she left to convey his gratitude. He imagined kneeling before her, touching the hem of her sari with his forehead, and proclaiming the beauty of Mohit's poem, explaining the great gift this work had bestowed upon him, the transformation he believed it had brought about. But it was as if Latangi knew what he wanted to say but was not prepared to hear it. She greeted with great enthusiasm those who arrived with gifts, bowing and repeating, *"Shuprobhat, shuprobhat, dhonnobad,"* and then "Good morning and thank you, yes, for your charitable offerings." It sounded to Henry as if Latangi was speaking with a stronger accent and in more halting English than she had spoken to him, as if she were an actress performing a role. Some of the people bowed back at Latangi, smiling but clearly feeling awkward and uncomfortable. He wondered what they'd thought when Mohit and Latangi purchased the motel, if they had greeted these foreigners with kindness and friendly curiosity or with suspicion and distrust.

Henry went back into his room and then over into the adjoining room to begin sorting through everything he'd been given. Most of it he didn't need, of course, and he began to separate those items from the rest—the toaster oven and teddy bear and fishing rod and beach chairs and card table—figuring there must be a Goodwill store nearby that would take them. He pictured the neon Endly's sign magically transported here to Virginia. But what if the folks who had given him these items saw them at the Goodwill and realized what he'd done, saw that he'd quickly discarded what they'd meant as heartfelt gifts? He'd have to keep everything for now, he realized, and he sat down on the bed and turned on the television. Unlike the one in his room, this TV started up immediately. Henry turned up the volume and punched the channel button until he found what he was looking for. At first a female reporter was interviewing a government official or soldier, a large balding man in khaki fatigues whose skin had been burned bright red, both the reporter and the official dirty and drenched in sweat as they stood on what appeared to be a runway, but as the man spoke about efforts to get drinking water and food to those who were dehydrated and starving, the same sorts of images Henry had seen earlier began to appear on the screen: the sea of people crowded outside the Superdome, everyone now sitting or lying down, boxes and trash strewn everywhere around them; a small flat-bottom boat motoring through a ravaged neighborhood, the men on board calling out to those who might still be trapped in their homes; a barefoot woman kneeling outside the convention center, her hands clasped together and her eyes closed, her face anguished as she cried out that her baby needed her medicine; armed officers patrolling somewhere downtown where the streets were dry—it looked to Henry like Poydras or maybe even Canal—the officers wielding rifles, pistols holstered at their waists. Another picture showed rows and rows of men and women lying on narrow brown cots at the airport's baggage claim, some of them with their hands weakly raised in the air as if trying to summon help, and then the scene switched to a helicopter hovering above the blacktop of a school playground, boxes of bottled water lowered from the helicopter into the arms of those gathered below.

When the scene cut back to the female reporter, she was speaking to a police officer, who explained that he'd been at work in New Orleans East when his mother was trapped in her house just two blocks from the London Avenue canal. "I told her," the officer said quietly, "but she was some stubborn. She refused to go."

"What did she say?" the reporter asked.

"She said she'd owned that home forty-three years and wasn't leaving. When we saw what was going on, I tried to get a unit out there but there was no way." He paused and then began to sob. "The levee was already gone. There was no way."

Oh God, Henry thought, and watching this officer sob, watching the reporter raise her hand and place it on the officer's shoulder, which shook and shook from his weeping, he now understood that his failure to call Mary, to let her know he was okay, had been unspeakably cruel. And Amy too. He'd failed them both, failed everyone. He turned the TV off and went outside. Latangi wasn't back, and the office was locked, so he couldn't get to the phone there. He knocked on the doors of other rooms, hoping he'd find someone with a cell phone he could borrow. But there was no one around. He went back to his room and hunted around until he found the rolls of quarters he'd been given. He figured he'd drive into town, locate a pay phone somewhere, use 411 to get Mary's number. And Amy? He didn't know exactly how he'd find her, but he knew he would. He thought about the description at the end of Mohit's poem of a ketaki tree, its leaves as sharp as swords but its white blossoms delicate and richly scented. Nectar from the tree's flowers, the poem asserted, would always relieve the prick of its leaves, just as life's salves would always assuage its sorrows. He was not sure he was prepared to believe this, but now he would at least try to see if it was true. He could do that, he figured. He could find out for himself.

Ten

HE FOUND Amy. Of course he found her. She had not, after all, been hiding, had not done what he had done—disappear. First, though, he spoke to his sister, Mary, who told him that she had been in touch with Amy ever since Amy returned home from Central America to discover that Henry had moved out. He didn't know what those conversations had been like, what Amy and Mary had found to say to each other, but he could imagine now, as he could not before, their shared confusion, the frustration and anger they both must have felt. And the sorrow, the despair, the sense of betrayal—he understood all of that as well. *She weeps at the feet of the lotus, a river of unseen tears,* he had read in Mohit's poem, a forsaken maiden crying for her beloved, *the dark wind thrashing in her tresses and the trellised branches overhead.* How had he not attended to Amy's tears, not felt the awful pain he had caused?

It was all related, he knew, to the clatter, to the endless wandering in his dreams, to the girl he'd conjured up in his head, but he didn't know why or how—just as this end to it, the silence and peace, the calm in which he suddenly felt himself immersed, was somehow related to reading Mohit's beautiful poem, of his living inside it from beginning to end. What a strange place the world had become, Mohit's words now woven into his thoughts as though they had been spun there in golden thread, *a blooming pipal tree and a bright moon painted against an ink-strewn sky.*

Even so, the old man Hughes was dead, his widow and grandson left alone, and the city of New Orleans, Henry's home, gone now, washed away, thousands left behind, dying. At what cost was such redemption as he now felt?

And he was still, as he had been before, alone.

He had spoken to Mary, called her, because, finally, he simply remembered her number, the ten digits appearing to float into view in the air before his eyes, as familiar and obvious as the simplest mathematical equation. He walked down to the motel office, quarters in his pocket, and looked inside. Latangi sat there behind the front desk, peering at the computer monitor. He stepped in and asked if there was a phone somewhere he could use.

"Yes, yes, Mr. Garrett, no problem, no problem," she said, lifting an old black phone and placing it on the counter next to the Ganesh lamp and the basket of green mints. "Some privacy," she said then, and she walked toward the door that led to her apartment.

"Latangi," he said. She turned before stepping through the door. He wanted to tell her that he'd spent the night reading Mohit's poem, that he believed it a work of great genius, a masterpiece that must be shared with the world. But was this what she longed to hear—of the work's greatness? Of Henry's admiration? Of his conviction that others would recognize that greatness as well? Or might it matter more to her to know that reading the poem had somehow cured him? What an absurd notion that was, though—the idea that one could be cured by a poem, that confusion and despair could be swept away simply by holding those delicate pages in one's hand and reading the words written on them. Was such a claim not further evidence of his lunacy? He thought again about the end of *The Awakening*, when Edna Pontellier strips off her bathing suit and stands naked beside the sea, absolutely alone, feeling the strange deliciousness of her own body beneath the blindingly bright sky. In that moment, perhaps for the first time in her life, she is free—but then, of course, immediately afterward, she is gone, swimming herself out from the shore, delirious and exhausted, hearing the barking of an old dog and the humming of bees, smelling the scent not of briny water but of flowers.

What could he possibly say to Latangi? That Mohit's poem had stripped his soul bare? How ridiculous, how absurd. That the words had washed over him like a pastor's sermon over an enthralled congregation? *Sit at His feet and be blessed! Expect to be landed upon the shore!*

"It's Henry, please," he said to Latangi. "Won't you please call me Henry?"

"Yes, yes, Mr. Henry," she said, just as she had the last time. "So sorry." And she left him there, quietly closing the door behind her.

He dialed the number, heard the phone ringing, heard the ringing stop. "Mary?" he said.

As soon as she heard his voice, she knew. She began crying.

"No, no," Henry said, listening to her cry, then he thought to say, "I'm okay, I'm okay."

He heard the crying stop, heard Mary catch her breath, sniffle. "Henry," she said, barely a whisper. "Where are you? Not New Orleans?"

"Not New Orleans, no," he said. "In Virginia. I'm—" He was going to say *I'm nowhere,* but he understood how he would sound: lost, adrift, unmoored.

"I'm in Virginia, not far from Lynchburg. A town called Mari-more."

Henry heard Mary take a deep breath; he held his own breath in against the silence, the empty crackle of the line.

"I'm sure you can imagine," Mary said quietly, "what I thought, Henry, what I've been sick with worry about."

He waited, listened for what she would say next.

"You can imagine," she said, and he heard the anger now. "You can imagine, right?"

"I know, I know," he said. "But things—" How was he going to explain it? Well, he needed to do it. He needed to get it all said. "Listen," he began, "there was an accident. I was in an accident."

Mary listened. Then he heard her saying "Oh God, oh God," but he kept talking. He wanted to tell her the whole story, as much of it as he understood how to tell, the three days of wandering north in his car, stopping at this motel in Virginia, maybe—*probably*—because he knew Amy was somewhere nearby though he couldn't remember where, and then the prisoners on the side of the highway and then, out of nowhere, one of them, an old man named Hughes, crossing the yellow line and stepping right in front of his car, throwing his arms out.

Only at this point, after telling her how the old man had died, right there on the highway, did he find himself unable to go on, despair rushing back over him. He saw the old man's body on the highway, arms thrown out at his sides the way he'd seen people, on TV, in New Orleans, in the water. "I just don't know," he said into the phone, and now he was the one sobbing. "I just don't know, Mary."

"Oh, Henry," she said, "I'm so sorry."

He didn't know what else to say. The line crackled again.

"It wasn't your fault, right?" he heard Mary say. "There wasn't anything you could have done?"

"No," he said. And whatever else might not be true, whatever doubts he harbored, he understood that this was not one of them—there was nothing he could have done.

"Okay," she said. "Okay. You want to come here, stay with me?"

"I don't know," he said again.

"You need to do that, Henry. I think you do."

"I can't," he said. "My car. It's—"

"No, of course, of course. I'll come get you."

"I don't know. I'm—" What could he say to her? That he thought he might stay here awhile, that there were things he needed to do? Of course, he didn't know what those things were, had no fucking idea. Finally, he just said her name. *Amy.*

"You called her, right?" Mary said. "She knows?"

"I don't—"

"Oh God, Henry," Mary said. "Listen to me. You need to call her now. Hang up and call her. I don't know if she'll talk to you. But she's your wife, Henry. Or she was. She needs to know you're alive. She doesn't even fucking know you're alive. Oh God, you can be a real shit, Henry."

"I know, I know," he said. He thought about the card Mary had sent with the inheritance check, the *Fuck you* she'd written on it, then he thought again about the Broussards. Why was it that this story, this thing that was not even real, this secret they had kept between them—they'd never, even as adults, told their mother that the Broussards were a fabrication—had lived so long in their imaginations? Did it have something to do with—*everything* to do with—what had been wrong with them, not their father leaving, but the silence about it afterward, how nobody seemed to think this truth was something that needed to be talked about? Art, literature, music, his mother's paintings, Mary's singing—all of this was fine. But the abandonment? The loss and grief? Why had no one—not Mary, not him, not their mother—talked about it?

"I don't know where she is," he said now to Mary. He meant Amy, of course, but in his own head it sounded like he was talking about their mother, as if she were the one he'd lost. "I don't have her number."

"Oh Jesus, Henry," Mary said. "Her number? You don't know her number?"

"I can't remember it. I've had trouble remembering."

"I've got her number, Henry. She's in a place called Lovingston. I don't know exactly where that is, but it's somewhere around Lynchburg. It's near Charlottesville too, I think."

"In Lovingston? You've talked to her?" He looked out at the motel parking lot. A man and a woman in a tiny black sports car had pulled up in front of the office. They squinted as if trying to see inside. Henry raised his hand to wave, and they drove away.

"That's what people do, Henry," Mary was saying. "Family and all that. They talk to one another."

Did we? he wanted to say but didn't, knew he should not. *We didn't.*

"Get something to write with, Henry," Mary said, and Henry leaned over the counter, found a pen with a blue plastic flower taped to it.

"Okay," he said, and Mary gave Henry Amy's number, speaking slowly as if to a child. Henry looked for something to write on. He grabbed one of the Lucky Caverns brochures, but the waxy paper wouldn't absorb the ink. So he did what he'd seen his students do countless times: he wrote the number on the back of his hand. He looked at the digits. Yes, of course. He remembered it now.

"You've got it?" Mary said.

"Yes."

"Right now, Henry. Call her right now. You understand?"

"Yes."

He understood that he deserved this, her talking to him this way. He deserved much worse than this. Even so—

"Call her right now, Henry," Mary said. "Then call me back. I'll come get you, you can stay with me, but you need to call Amy first."

He looked at his left hand, at the number there. "Listen, Mary," he said. "I want you to know something. I'm better. Or I'm getting better."

"I'm glad to hear that, Henry. Really. Amy will be glad to hear it too. Call her."

"I will," Henry said. "It's just—"

"What, Henry? What is it *just?* It's always just *something.*"

He wondered what he could say that would make any sense. He thought about the scene in Mohit's poem in which an old man reaches down and touches the soft brow of the newborn baby calf he has rescued from a thorny thicket. The old man discovers that simply from this touch, his youth is returned to him. The man is overjoyed until he looks down at a basin of water and doesn't recognize himself. Now he feels unsettled, unsure that this transformation has been a welcome one. Then a girl—a young princess or goddess—appears and beckons to him. *Come with me into the dark trees,* she says, *where we will invite trembling raptures and crystalline tears.* The man doesn't know whether or not he should follow her, take her hand. He doesn't know if ecstasy or anguish awaits him in the dark woods.

Should he tell Mary about Mohit's poem? He pictured Mary and their mother sitting up in bed, poring through the books with the images of Saint Sebastian, arms raised above his head, the beautiful arced torso impaled by arrows. Again he wanted to say to Mary, *Do you remember the Broussards?* And what would that accomplish? Anything at all? Maybe he was the only one who remembered this story; maybe even Mary had forgotten it. "I'll call her, Mary," he said quietly. "I will."

"And you'll call me back?"

Henry nodded as if Mary could actually see him, as if he didn't need to speak.

"Call me back, Henry," he heard her say again—a warning? a plea?—and then she hung up. He could tell that she'd spoken with hope, with trust, but also with only a small measure of faith. She didn't fully believe that he would call her back.

He deserved such doubt, he knew. He deserved much worse—a hundred arrows, a thousand, impaling his ribs and thighs, his shoulders and neck, piercing his chest, piercing his bloody, bloody heart. He looked down at the telephone as if it were something unrecognizable.

He did not call Amy—not immediately. He didn't know exactly why, but it had something to do with wanting to make sure first that he was, as he'd claimed to Mary, getting better. He knocked on the door to Latangi's apartment to say that he was finished with his call.

He planned to tell her now that he had read the poem, but when she stepped back out into the office, she was holding a teetering stack of small rugs, each the size of a doormat, the stack awkwardly cradled against her chest, held in place at the top by her chin. "Perhaps, Mr. Henry," she managed to say, "you could lend me some assistance?" The rugs nearly slipped from her hands as she spoke.

"Here," Henry said, taking the rugs from her.

She turned and walked back to her apartment and emerged with another stack of rugs. "Would you follow me, Mr. Henry?" she said, and she led him out to the parking lot and over to the blue truck Marge had delivered. She dropped the stack in the cab of the truck, then she looked at Henry and signaled that he should do so as well.

"Now," she said, raising her hand to her chest as if she were having trouble breathing. Henry looked at her, waited.

"So sorry, Mr. Henry. A moment, please." She smiled. "Perhaps I should have mentioned another request for assistance?"

"Yes, of course," Henry said. "Anything. You've been so kind."

"No, no, Mr. Henry. Only what is necessary."

Necessary. Henry remembered how he'd used that word, all the things he'd believed were necessary.

"Yes?" he said, and Latangi explained that the rugs had been purchased by a nearby school, which planned to use them in the entrance to each classroom. "All those muddy children's feet," Latangi said. "But do they ask these children to remove their shoes before they walk inside? They do not." She laughed. "Bad for them. Good for me."

"They're beautiful rugs," Henry said.

"Yes?" Latangi said, as if it were a question. She pulled from the sleeve of her sari a yellow Post-it note with an address printed on it. The address was in Lovingston, where Mary had told him Amy was living.

"Lovingston?" Henry said, and Latangi nodded. She smiled at Henry, and again he had to suspect that she knew much more than she acknowledged—if not by some strange mystical power, then simply by eavesdropping on his conversation with Mary. What were the odds that she would be sending him on this particular errand to this particular place?

"You just happen to need these delivered to Lovingston?" Henry said.

"Yes, yes, to Lovingston, Mr. Henry. Just up the U.S. Route 29 highway road." She pointed as if that would make it clearer.

Henry looked at her, tried to signal his reluctance. "I'm not supposed to drive farther than thirty miles with this."

"Seventeen miles, Mr. Henry," Latangi said triumphantly. "Seventeen miles there. Seventeen miles back. Google map. Directly north on the U.S. Route 29 highway road." She smiled. "I would be very grateful for this assistance, please."

"Seventeen miles," Henry said. He nodded at Latangi. "Okay."

"Yes, okay, Mr. Henry," she said, and she left him standing there by the blue truck. He could hear her singing as she walked away.

Lovingston, it turned out, was an even smaller town than Marimore, its Main Street veering off the highway and running for less than a mile, a few residential lanes sprouting from that one central branch, small businesses gathered along Main Street between large but generally dilapidated clapboard homes with wide porches, many of them rotted out. Henry had felt anxious about driving for the first time since the accident, but as soon as he figured out how to shift using the hand-operated gears on the steering wheel, he relaxed a bit and was able to look around as he drove. Just outside of Lovingston he passed a school named Briarwood Women's College, and Henry tried to imagine what kind of girl would attend such a place—in the middle of rural Virginia, where there was nowhere to go and nothing much to do. Maybe that was precisely why parents sent their daughters there, in the vain hope of keeping them out of trouble, of preserving what was no doubt in most cases an illusory virginity. If they learned a few things while they were tucked away, so be it. The school to which Henry was to deliver the rugs, though, was a Montessori school. It was situated behind an old red hay barn that now housed a restaurant or bar called Rumpelstiltskin's, the name painted on the barn's roof in a childlike scrawl. *No ethanol!* was painted beneath that, though Henry figured this part was obsolete, that there had once been a gas station out front—or perhaps an angry farmer had simply felt it necessary to proclaim his particular views in the same manner as others had on various farms he'd passed, *Jesus Saves* or *Repent* printed on barn roofs and silos, giant white crosses erected at the edge of overgrown fields.

Henry carried the rugs into the school and spoke with the friendly secretary in the front office. She seemed surprised by the delivery but didn't object to Henry's leaving the stacks of rugs in the hall. "You go right ahead," she said. "I'll let Principal Stevens know they're here just as soon as she returns." And the woman smiled at Henry as if she knew exactly who he was—which maybe she did. Maybe she'd been part of Marge's phone tree, a fellow soldier in her church's mission field.

He then drove up and down Lovingston's Main Street, turning onto each of the side lanes he encountered. He knew what he was doing—checking to see if any of the houses looked like the sort of place he'd imagined Amy living, some beautifully appointed bungalow shaded by old oaks, the front path leading to a lush trellised garden. Latangi might have known this as well, that he wanted to find Amy before speaking to her, that he wanted all the information that seeing her would provide: how she looked at him when he first appeared to her, how she stood, how she was dressed, what her hair was like—anything that might restore their familiarity. Or maybe she would keep her distance, study him as she would some unfamiliar or dangerous animal. But he was hoping she'd look at him some other way—with relief, with joy, with expectation that he might be better.

When he actually saw her, she did not look at him at all; she did not even see him. She was sitting inside her car, which was parked in the driveway of a small, ugly plum-colored brick ranch house. In the car with her was a man—stocky, red-haired, bearded, wearing round tortoiseshell glasses—and Henry simply watched as this man leaned slowly toward Amy, put his hand behind her neck, and kissed her.

When they both stepped out of the car and the man adjusted the cuffs of his sleeves and squinted toward the blue truck, Henry did the only thing he could think to do: he drove away.

Later that day, Henry would find out from Marge who the man was—a music professor from the women's college he'd driven past. Later, from a friend of Latangi's who was one of the man's colleagues, Henry learned more: He was a composer primarily of sonatas for bassoon, the instrument upon which he was considered something of a virtuoso, but also of cantatas for women's chorus and percussion. He was a dandy who dressed in fine suits, a bow tie at his neck below his absurdly well-sculpted red beard, and he drove a sleek silver sports car, a BMW convertible, which he parked ostentatiously around the small campus. His name was Hunter McClellan, and though the women of Briarwood—not merely students but colleagues and secretaries as well—swooned at his very presence, he had been, practically since the first day of her arrival in Virginia, pursuing Amy.

Henry had learned this when he asked Marge about him—he figured, correctly, she'd know who he was. Marge had shown up at the Spotlight to check in on Henry but also to get his signature on some documents that would officially declare him free of any responsibility in Marion Hughes's death. The rest he learned later, when he met the chair of the English Department at Briarwood, a woman named Rebecca Douglas who had become friends with Latangi while Latangi was enrolled in one of her evening continuing-education courses at the college.

Marge hadn't known, of course, why Henry was asking about this man. Standing among all the items that he'd been given by members of Marge's congregation, he simply told her he'd run across him in his silver BMW and wondered who he might be. All he had to do was describe him for Marge: the red beard, the stocky build, the tortoise-shell glasses, the cuffed sleeves he'd carefully adjusted as he squinted toward Henry.

"Oh, that's Hunter McClellan, I bet," Marge said. "You met him?"

"I didn't exactly meet him," Henry said. "I saw him. With Amy."

Marge looked confused, then she nearly leaped into the air. "Oh, I think I know your Amy!" she said, excited. "I'm sure I do!" But then Henry watched her fold her arms across her chest and grow quiet. "But Hunter McClellan," she said. "That's trouble."

She and Amy had spoken once or twice in the Food Lion, Marge told him, just about this or that—the produce or salad dressing or something—but then she'd seen her again at the annual garlic festival, where Amy had a booth to sell her books, and that was when Marge discovered that Amy wasn't just anybody but a real live *book writer,* as Marge called her. "She should be on the Food Channel," Marge said. "She knows everything and then some. More than Emeril, I bet. Oh, but Hunter McClellan," she said again, and she shook her head.

"I should be worried, then," Henry said, trying to sound light-hearted.

"Not *worried,* Henry," Marge said, patting his arm. "*Determined.* That's what I tell Charlie. *Worry* can't be put to good use, but *determined* always can."

"That's good to know," Henry said, nodding, again trying to sound lighthearted. What he felt, though, was that determination was—had always been—the central missing ingredient in his life. What had he ever been determined to do? Even the ruin he'd caused, as great as it had been, had been equivocal and half-assed, accidental. He hadn't had a grand plan for ruin, as he'd tried to tell himself; he simply had the ability to squander every last thing. *A squanderer. A coward. A louse.*

When Marge told him that she was headed next to see Mrs. Hughes and have her sign the document as well, he decided he ought to go with her.

"I don't think that's proper," Marge said.

"Well, I'd like to set things in order as much as I can," Henry said. "I'm trying to change course somehow, and that's part of it."

"It was not your doing," Marge said. "You don't need to set that right. You *can't* set that right." She quickly shook her head. "Oh Lord, that sounds just awful. But you know what I mean."

"I do," Henry said. "But maybe there's something I can do. We'll see. Please let me go along, Marge. I'm *determined*," Henry said, and he smiled.

Marge cocked her head to the side. "My, my, my," she said. "Determined, huh? Then I guess the two of us are going for another ride."

As he and Marge walked toward Marge's car, Henry spotted Latangi inside one of the rooms. "One minute," he said to Marge. He went over and stepped inside the room. Latangi whipped a clean sheet in the air as if she were a magician performing a magic trick. She leaned forward to stretch the sheet across the mattress.

"Latangi," Henry said. "I'm sorry to interrupt, but I was wondering if we might have dinner again tonight. I'd like to speak with you, if I could. I've read the poem, Mohit's poem. I've read it, and I want to speak with you about it."

Latangi looked at him, letting go of the sheet and gathering the skirt of her sari in her hand.

"It's very special," Henry said. "You were right to think so, to ask me to read it. I'd like to speak with you tonight." He tried to suggest by his tone the reverence he felt, the gratitude.

Latangi let go of her sari and stretched out her arms to once again take hold of the sheet. She whipped it up into the air. "No problem, Mr. Henry," she said. "It would be my honor."

"Thank you," Henry said, and as he stepped from the room, he saw Latangi lower her head. He saw her tears dot the white sheet.

The squalor was unimaginable. Marge had driven out into the county, turned off onto a narrow dirt road, and then turned again at a gravel drive. Henry listened to the loud crunching of the gravel underneath the tires; they pulled up to a trailer so run down that it seemed in danger of collapsing. Torn sheets and towels covered the windows, most of which were shattered or completely missing their glass panes. Broken furniture—rusted lawn chairs, a tattered sofa, a cracked rocking chair—stood in a circle near the trailer's metal door, which looked as though it had been repeatedly kicked in. A wooden ramp—for Mrs. Hughes's wheelchair, Henry assumed—led down from the door to a row of garbage cans overflowing with plastic bottles and trash bags.

"Oh Lord," Marge said, turning off her car and leaning her head against the steering wheel. "Jesus said how the poor would always be with us, but I just don't think He meant this. This makes regular poor look rich, don't it?"

"Yes, it does," Henry said, and he thought of all the items Marge's church had just delivered to him. He already had more than this. Why did he deserve such kindness and this family did not? Were they somehow responsible for their fate in a way that he was not? He understood now how much the five-thousand-dollar payment would have meant to this family, how much that must have seemed to Marion Hughes as he stood waiting for Henry's car to strike him.

As Marge and Henry stepped from the convertible, a young boy walked out of the trailer. One of the boy's arms hung limply at his side at a strange angle, as if the shoulder had been dislocated and never properly fixed. He raised his other hand to wave hello and then stepped back inside. When no one else emerged from the trailer, Marge called, "Mrs. Hughes?"

There was no answer, so Marge tried again. "Mrs. Hughes? Can you hear me?"

"I'll be right out," they heard Mrs. Hughes say.

"We could come in," Marge said. "It's Marge Brockman from Judge Martin's office. I've just got some papers for you to sign."

Marge waited, but Mrs. Hughes didn't respond.

"Mrs. Hughes?" she said, a little louder.

"Yes?" they heard her say.

"Can I come in?" Marge asked, and she started up the ramp.

"I'm coming out," Mrs. Hughes said again, and they saw her wheel her way into the open doorway. "Who is it, now?" she said, and Marge turned to Henry and shook her head.

When Mrs. Hughes understood who was there and why, she invited them inside, and Henry was shocked to discover how tidy the trailer was. The furniture was not much better than what was outside, but there were shawls and blankets laid across the chairs, and there were family pictures in frames on the end tables and hung on the walls. A vase of plastic flowers stood in the middle of a folding table near the kitchen, and Henry saw the open Bible there, one of those King James Versions with gold-tipped pages and Jesus's words printed in bold red ink.

"I was immersed in my reading," she said, looking for the first time at Henry. "The Lord's word is such a comfort, isn't it?" she said. "Even in the hardest of times."

"Yes, ma'am," Henry said. "Again, I'm so sorry."

"I got to see him," she said. "They did fine. They did real fine."

"I'm glad to hear it," Marge said. "I've heard they do good work."

"Yes, they did," Mrs. Hughes said. She continued to look at Henry, though he was not sure she could see him. He now wondered if she was blind—she seemed to be, her eyes turned toward him but clearly not focused, not seeing him. Then how would she have been reading her Bible? And how would she know if the funeral home had done a fine job with her husband? Maybe she'd simply felt his face with her hands, the familiarity of it a comfort to her.

"Do you know who I am, Mrs. Hughes?" Henry said then, and Marge moved toward Henry, put a hand on his shoulder as if to stop him from saying any more.

"I don't believe I do," she said. "I'm forgetful."

"He's a new friend of mine," Marge said. "He's here from New Orleans. You heard what's happened in New Orleans, Mrs. Hughes."

"I'm not sure," she said.

"Well, don't you worry about it," Marge said. "We've just got some papers for you to sign."

"I don't know," Mrs. Hughes said to Marge. "My grandson helps me with those."

"Katrell?" Henry said. "Your grandson Katrell?"

"That's right," she said, and she turned again toward Henry. "He's a good child. Helpful and upright. He walks with the Lord."

"I'm sure he does," Marge said. "But if he's not here, well, we just need these signed and we'll be on our way."

"There's only the little one here," she said. "Katrell's walked up to the convenience store."

"Yes, Mrs. Hughes," Marge said, and Henry heard the frustration in her tone. She walked over to the folding table and turned to the last page. "I'll show you right where you sign."

"Well, I guess I could do that," Mrs. Hughes said, and she wheeled her chair over to the table. "I'm not much for writing," she said, and Marge held her hand and guided it on the page.

"What's that I signed again?" Mrs. Hughes asked, and before Marge could speak, Henry said, "It's so you'll get your five thousand dollars, Mrs. Hughes."

Marge glared at Henry and began to say that this wasn't what the document was for, but Henry waved and made Marge look at him. He pointed toward his own chest—*I'll pay it,* he meant. *I'll find that money.* And though Marge glared at him again, she remained silent.

He'd done nothing with his inheritance but squander it, Henry thought; he should have given it to this woman instead. How much better to have simply given it away.

"Well, that would be something," Mrs. Hughes said. "Five thousand dollars. That would surely be something." And she lowered her head as if she wanted only to sleep.

Eleven

IT WOULD be weeks, maybe even months, before anyone could return to New Orleans, if in fact the city even could be saved. That's what Henry heard on the news when he went back to the Spotlight. They showed the buses arriving from out of town to take folks off to dry land, to places with enough beds to accommodate them, to Atlanta and Houston and Baton Rouge, to Shreveport and Monroe, to Little Rock and Jackson. By now those waiting to be rescued could barely stand, their clothes stained and tattered, the ground beneath their feet covered in trash, a thick sea through which they shuffled. Others awaited rescue in flooded homes, sprawling across rooftops, leaning out of attic windows. Old men and women were carried to boats on stretchers by soldiers wading through dank water; children clung to police officers' backs. Helicopters hovered above crowds in parking lots, people waiting for boxes of food and water to be thrown down to them. Henry could not determine exactly which areas were still flooded and which were not. They showed maps, presented diagrams, but even the reporters often seemed confused about where they were. Again and again these reports cut to floating bodies and makeshift graves of gravel and brick, to the complicated hieroglyphs scrawled on buildings: how many dead, and where, and when. Buildings burned, the smoke and ash thick as mud, the news cameras lingering there, as if someone, something, might suddenly emerge from the flames.

Henry sat and watched. He was sorting through more of the things that had been delivered to him: shirts and shoes, cereal boxes and shaving cream, slippers and safety pins, cans of tuna and a flashlight and a baseball cap. He wanted to talk to Latangi about the poem, yes, but now he also wanted to ask her about a job. Maybe she would be willing to put him to work. There must be chores that Mohit had once taken care of that needed doing. He had promised Mrs. Hughes five thousand dollars, and he wanted to make good on that pledge somehow. Marge had insisted the moment they got back into her car that this promise was an out-and-out crazy one to have made, that he owed this family nothing, that he had nothing himself, but Henry told her he was glad he'd said it.

Exasperated, Marge sighed, the first time Henry had known her to express anything but optimism and faith. She slowly shook her head and started the car.

"It's a bottomless pit," she said. "That family—not just Mrs. Hughes but all her grandchildren and cousins and such. I've watched them make use of county services for years. There's not a moment someone from that family's not incarcerated or fighting with Social Services or claiming their WIC card didn't arrive."

Henry listened. Who was it who'd said that true charity was for the undeserving? Maybe he'd seen it on one of those signs out in front of a church.

"I just want to do something for them," Henry told Marge. "Just as you did for me."

"I understand," Marge said. She did not point out again that he didn't have five thousand dollars to give to Mrs. Hughes. But he could earn it, couldn't he? He believed that he could.

"You didn't ask that man to jump in front of your car," Marge said. "I know he was trying to do something for his family, but he wasn't thinking one moment, was he, about what he was doing to you."

Henry let Marge talk, let her go on and on about it. He figured he could propose to Latangi that he clean the rooms and do whatever gardening or grounds work needed to be done. He could deliver, as he had today, the import items she managed to sell. He could be the Spotlight's night watchman, its handyman or superintendent, though of course he recognized how ridiculous such a notion was. Before being of any use, he'd have to learn how to do practically every single task the job required—how to fix a leaky faucet, stop a running toilet, replace a cracked window, repair a flickering lamp or broken TV. He thought of Lacey Gaudet's father, the arm he'd thrown over Henry's shoulder.

He'd needed a father.

Maybe he still needed one, or at least still needed someone to say to him, *Here is what happened.* Why hadn't his father stepped forward in those dreams not to play Monk on the old bass but to say to him, *You didn't have me because I couldn't find my way home, because I was so overcome by the very same confusion and helplessness and despair, the same cacophony and clatter and calamity, that have been visited upon you that I stumbled into an endless desert or swam into the widest sea or sharpened the sharpest blade* or—or what? That he had been so addled, so undone, so unmoored that he simply couldn't find his way back home? Wouldn't he have at least *wanted* to come home?

Someone was knocking on the door to Henry's room. He assumed it was Latangi, there to deliver more towels or confirm a time for dinner. He crossed through from the adjoining room and opened the door.

It was not Latangi; it was Amy.

Twelve

"Hello," Amy said, shyly, quietly, and she stepped forward and put her arms around Henry's back and then said into his chest, so quietly that he could barely hear her, "I didn't think you were alive. I really didn't." Then she stepped away, wiped the backs of her hands across her eyes the way he'd seen her do a hundred times, a gesture that declared that she would not cry.

"Well, I am," Henry said, palms out as if he were offering an apology, and he realized he was doing precisely what he'd imagined his father doing a thousand times—standing in a doorway and saying these words, knowing that they were not enough but that they were the only words with which to begin. *Well, I'm alive.*

Henry saw her look around the room at all the things stacked there. He figured she must think that he was doing it again, piling up junk everywhere around him. He didn't want her to think that he was still crazy.

"People gave me all of this," he said. "They felt—"

"Mary called me," Amy said, as if she hadn't heard him. "You didn't call me."

"I know," Henry said. "I didn't know—I didn't—"

"It doesn't matter, Henry," she said. "I'm glad you got out. That's all. I'm relieved. So many people—"

"Yes," Henry said. "Please," he said, "come in." And he stepped to the side, steered her past the boxes of stuff and into the adjoining room, where at least there was a chair she could sit in, near the television.

Amy shook her head at the TV screen, looked away.

"I know," he said. For a minute, they watched the images roll by, pictures of the ruin along the Gulf Coast, the shredded houses, the snapped trees. He turned the TV off and sat on the bed.

"I was going to call you," Henry said.

"Okay," Amy said.

"I saw you," he said. "That man. The red hair." He hadn't thought he would say this, but now he had. Amy looked at him. She'd cut her hair, arranged it in a different way. She was wearing blue jeans, a light blue shirt. She looked the same. Beautiful.

He didn't know what he wanted to say now. No, he knew what he wanted to say, everything he wanted to say. But how could he say it? "I saw him with you," he said instead. "At your house. The house where you're living."

"You came by the house?" Amy said.

"I didn't come by, exactly. I found it. By accident, sort of."

"Oh, Henry," Amy said. How did she say it? Disgusted? Despairing? Distraught?

"Please," he said. "Please listen."

Henry understood that he had this one chance, that maybe he wouldn't have another. He needed to tell her, to make her believe, that he understood the harm he'd done, that he had walked out, done exactly what his father had done, and hadn't even realized that he was doing it. He needed to say that he was sorry, say it a thousand times.

He needed to ask for forgiveness, ask for time to finish making himself whole. He needed to say that he had missed her and wanted her back and would do whatever it took, wait however long he must wait, to get her back. He needed to say that he was better, getting better, that he would not ever walk away again, could not even imagine it, would never again imagine it, world without end.

He thought of Mohit's poem, of the young bride placing her feet atop those of her husband, the gesture so particular, so tender, her arms crossed before her as though she were cradling their child.

Oh, there should have been a child.

"There's this book, Amy," he said. "I've found this book. You won't believe it. It's unbelievable, really. It's a poem, an amazing poem. A manuscript. In a drawer. You won't believe it."

She looked at him. He'd seen that expression before. Confusion? Fear? Anguish? Disgust? Which one was it?

"No, no," he said. "I'll tell you later about that." He reached forward to take her hand, but she didn't reach for him. He let his hand drop. "What I want to say is that I'm here. I'm not sure how I got here but somehow I know it was to find you, to see you. I want you to know—" But he stopped because now Amy had turned away. He followed her eyes and saw that standing there in the doorway between the two rooms was Katrell Sparrow.

"Mr. Garrett," he said.

"Yes?" Henry said.

"My grandma sent me. She wants to ask if you could help with some money now." He looked over at Amy and then back to Henry. "What you gave us before's gone and she says we need more."

"I don't—" Henry began. He turned to Amy, then back to the boy. "Wait," he said.

He looked at Amy. "Can we please talk later? I mean—" What

should he do here? "Amy, this is Katrell Sparrow," he said, and the boy stepped forward and shook Amy's hand. "Amy, it was Katrell's grandfather who passed away, who died in the accident."

"I'm so sorry," Amy said.

"Yes, ma'am," the boy answered, and he looked at Henry.

What could he do? What could he give the boy and his family? Then he realized that he could at least give them this, give them everything in these rooms. What did he need of what had been given to him? Nothing.

"You think you could help me load some things onto a truck?" Henry said to Katrell. The boy nodded. "I don't have money right now, but I've got this. I've got these things. Maybe some of this your grandmother might put to good use."

"Yes, sir," the boy said, looking around.

Henry turned to Amy. "I'm sorry. Can we—"

"No, no, it's fine," Amy said. "I'll help too."

So, together, they loaded as much as would fit into the bed of the blue truck—the rocking chair and lawn furniture, the cartons of food, the boxes of soda, the clothes—and Henry motioned for the boy to climb up front in the cab. Once he did, Henry went over to Amy. She was trying to cool down, standing in the doorway to his room and fanning her face with some paper. It was one of the Lucky Caverns brochures.

"I'm sorry," Henry said. "I know we need to talk. I want to talk, it's just—"

"It's fine," Amy said. "I'm glad you're safe."

"No, no," Henry said. "I mean, I'm sorry for everything. I want to talk about everything."

"Listen, Henry," Amy said, and she put her hand on his arm. "It's been a year. That's a long time."

"I know," he said. "I know. I was in a dark place. I know that."

Amy sighed. "Listen. We can talk. We can have coffee or something and talk. That's fine. But I'm not prepared to go down into that dark place with you. You understand? I'm not going to do that." Henry waited for her to say it, to say how much he had hurt her, but she didn't. Instead, she turned to look over at the truck. "It's nice what you're doing, Henry. It's good of you."

"Well—"

"Well, it is," Amy said, and she stepped forward, kissed his cheek, and turned to go. Then she looked back and said, "You wanted to give me something? A book? A manuscript?"

"Later," Henry said. "I'll give it to you later. Can I give it to you later?"

Amy looked at him. "I guess you know where I live," she said.

"Yes," Henry said.

"Okay, then."

And Henry watched as she got into her car and drove away.

The boy with the limp arm was Katrell's cousin, and his name was Stacey. He was eager to help unload the truck, cradling each soda bottle or cereal box or underwear pack against his chest as if it were a precious artifact unearthed during an archaeological dig. "He belongs to my aunt Celee," Katrell told Henry. "She had some trouble when he was born."

Mrs. Hughes stayed in the trailer in her wheelchair as Henry and Katrell carried everything inside. Looking at the things they'd brought stacked against the wall, Henry wondered what use they'd make of much of it, but Mrs. Hughes seemed pleased, nodding each time Henry set something down. "That's mighty kind," she said again and again.

When they were done, Henry walked over to the old woman. With her seated in the wheelchair, he felt as if he were looming over her, so he knelt. "Mrs. Hughes, I want you to understand that I'm going to have to earn that money I promised you."

"That's fine," she said, and Henry detected again the remarkable quality of the woman's features, as if her splotched, ravaged skin might simply peel away to reveal her true face. He thought of Mohit's poem, of the spells and curses that turned the young into the old, of the incantations and blessings that restored all that had been lost.

This woman had just lost her husband, but she'd lost a daughter, Katrell's mother, years before that. And how many others? How much else? What did he know, in the end, about such things? He'd lost a child. They, he and Amy, had lost a child. It—he? she?—had not even been born, had not ever lived. Even so.

"Mr. Hughes?" Henry said. "Your husband?"

The old woman nodded, as if she understood what Henry was asking: Who was this man with whom you spent all these years?

"A snake in the grass," she said. "Just a snake in the grass." But Henry saw that she was smiling, that her words, no matter how they sounded, were a testament of love.

"It might take a while, Mrs. Hughes," Henry said, "but I'll pay you what you're owed."

"I understand," the woman said, and Henry watched as she nodded and closed her eyes, not from weariness, it seemed, but as if she were watching something inside her, something Henry couldn't possibly see.

"I'll go, then," he said, and she nodded again, her eyes still closed.

Once he'd gotten into the car and prepared to pull away, the young boy with the limp arm, Stacey, appeared again in the doorway and, with his other arm, waved good-bye.

*   *   *

The prince—Henry believed he was a prince, though he seemed to be a god as well—was asleep in the forest beside a stream. Keeping watch over him was a lion, which was then joined by other creatures: a wolf, a bull, a deer, a lamb, a mouse. Birds—doves, swallows, hawks—began to swirl in the sky overhead; fish leaped again and again from the stream. One by one these animals pledged to forsake the actions of their past lives. The wolf would no longer pursue the lamb, nor the lion the wolf, nor the hawk the mouse. And one by one they realized that they would abide by these pledges not because they had evaded death but because they had not, that they had indeed already died but had now traveled beyond the realm in which death held dominion. They were in paradise, where death was forbidden to enter.

After his dinner with Latangi, Henry had returned to the room at the opposite end of the motel from his own to page again through *The Creator's Mistress*. He did not yet want to remove the manuscript from Mohit's study, vaguely fearing—as if he had himself been implanted in the magical world of the poem—that something terrible might happen to it should he do so: it might burst into flames or crumble into dust, or a sudden wind might whip the pages from his hands and scatter them across the earth. He imagined spending a lifetime hunting down each delicate page, imagined Amy joining him on such an impossible but noble quest.

At dinner he had told Latangi what he thought of Mohit's work—of the beauty and grace of the language, of the vast and magical world in which he had felt himself immersed, of the great power the poem seemed to possess, of how he had felt himself transformed even as he read. In the rush of his words he heard the echo of all those radio evangelists proclaiming what had always seemed to him absurd and theatrical and unconvincing—that lives of despair and defeat, of bitterness and regret, of toil and trial and tribulation could, in a single moment, be redeemed.

He told Latangi everything he'd done—leaving Amy, quitting his job, squandering every gift he had ever been granted, every fortune he had ever possessed—and he told her that he'd done it for no good reason, simply because of the chaos that had swirled inside his head, the noise and ruinous desire, the clamor and clatter, the cacophony. He did not have the words for it, had never had the words.

Now he did not need them, he said. He did not know, he told her, how Mohit's poem had quieted that torment, and he did not know for sure that one day it would not simply return. But he felt himself healed, felt himself able to be healed, and now what remained was to fix as much of what he had broken as he could fix.

"Your marriage, Mr. Henry?" Latangi asked, weeping for him that moment just as she had wept as he spoke of Mohit's poem, and Henry said that he did not know, just as he did not know when or if he would be able to return to New Orleans or if there would be a life for him there.

"So very much not knowing, Mr. Henry," Latangi said, wiping her eyes with a pale blue handkerchief.

Henry smiled and said, "Maybe that's okay. Maybe that's better."

"Yes, Mr. Henry," Latangi said, nodding. "Mohit would say, whenever we were unsure of what to do, 'We have reached a place too dark to see, so we shall go together.'"

And Henry had been certain then that, with those words, Latangi was making a pledge. She would, when he asked, agree to hire him so he could pay Mrs. Hughes the money he'd promised. She would allow him to continue to live at the Spotlight as long as he needed a place to stay. She would help him find his way.

When he left that night, she'd stood and hugged him, and Henry knew that Latangi had not actually spoken, that he had simply imagined it—*invented* it—but he heard her say, *My son, my son, my son.*

Now he lay down on the cot in Mohit's room and slept, certain as to what the morning would bring: this new life.

Thirteen

He did not see Amy for the next two weeks. He hadn't gone back to her house; he couldn't make himself do it, certain that she'd come out and say, unequivocally, what she had not had the chance to say when she'd shown up at the motel—that too much time had passed, that he had walked out on her and on their marriage, and that now, a year later, she was done; they were done. But he did not want to be done, had never wanted to be done. He had been ill, that was all. He had been ill and now he was cured, he wanted to tell her.

He was not cured, of course. He knew he was not. He was better; he *was* better. But the melancholy and despair, the clatter and chaos, swept over him now and again, particularly when he spent too much time watching the television, keeping track of what was happening in New Orleans—the city emptying out bit by bit until virtually nothing and no one remained except the giant piles of debris and the uprooted trees and dangling wires, the muddy, oil-and-shit-smeared streets and the gun-toting soldiers spread out across the Quarter and the Garden District in search of disoriented stragglers, of looters, of the forgotten. In search of the dead. Worst of all were these grim discoveries, dozens who had been left behind in hospitals and nursing homes and halfway houses, young mothers who had drowned cradling their newborn babies in their arms, the sick or elderly or disabled who'd died in their beds. It was not clear if their caretakers had abandoned them or if they had died as well.

How could it take so long to rescue the stranded, to recover the dead? How could there still be, after so many days, anyone left to save? Henry didn't want to watch any more but knew that he should, that he must—that for all the ways in which he had tried to flee his life, for all his efforts now to begin again here in Virginia, he still belonged to that city, was part of it in a way that could not be severed. He had been lucky; he understood that he had been lucky. He had been able to leave. He thought of all the folks who'd taken refuge in Endly's—the homeless, the crazy, the ancient, the infirm. Who would have taken them to safety? Why hadn't he thought to take them with him, as many as he could take? He'd had room in his car. What had saving his own small life been worth compared to all these others?

So he watched the news, looked for buildings he recognized, looked for the faces of those he knew. The city was now just a place of trash and ruin, of darkness and death, but even so, he searched for the familiar. Hundreds of thousands of others, spread out across the country, must be feeling the same way, watching the news too, reading the signs that the refugees in Houston and Atlanta held up before the news cameras, signs bearing the names of those they hoped to find amid all the chaos and loss.

When he couldn't stand it anymore, he would turn off the TV and step outside, watching the cars come and go in the parking lot, striking up conversations with those who looked his way. Many, though, seemed not to see him standing there, as if he had become part of the dreary display, his body undetectable against the background of the motel's dusty gray walls. But with those who did nod or wave hello, he discussed the heat, the clear sky, whatever destination the person was headed for: Monticello, Washington, DC, a business meeting, a family reunion, a new job. No one knew where Henry was from; none of them thought to ask, as if they had concluded that because he was already at the motel when they arrived, he had been there all along, simply waiting for these conversations. He listened to stories of aging parents and prodigal children, of just-born nephews and nieces; he learned what it was like to be a pharmaceutical-company representative, an itinerant youth pastor, an ambulance and fire-truck salesman.

Those who did not look over at him, Henry simply watched: couples drunkenly tumbling from their cars into the office and then, once they had acquired their keys, quickly shuffling to their rooms and drawing the curtains; exhausted parents carefully hoisting their sleepy children from minivans; men who looked exactly like he must have looked when he arrived: dirty and unshaven, a haunted look in their eyes, their clothes stuffed in rumpled duffel bags. What sad stories, he wondered, were they carrying with them? Wasn't it possible that, even this long after the storm, someone else fleeing New Orleans could show up at the motel, having exhausted the goodwill of relatives or friends?

Henry wanted to offer each of these guests—the furtive and the friendly, the content and the calamitous, the wretched and the blessed—a quiet benediction: that though they were unaware of its presence, Mohit's poem rested in the drawer of that one corner room, a light against the dark night, an anchor against all manner of stormy seas. *Sit at His feet and be blessed!* he wanted to tell them. *Make a way out of no way!*

A way out of no way. As simple and childish as that sermon's word-play seemed, wasn't that precisely what he was trying to do? He thought of the scene in Mohit's poem in which the young maiden doubts the prince's ardent expressions of his love.

Why do you speak so? the maiden asks the prince. *Aren't your words but a wracked ship?*

I am the wracked ship, the prince replies. *You are the sea into which I sink.*

No, she says, blushing. *Let me be your salvage. I will be your shore.*

Oh, Amy. He needed to photocopy the manuscript. He needed to give it to her, see if she might hear in the poem what he heard — that it spoke what he had never been able to speak. Maybe she'd think the poem was publishable; maybe she would pass it along to her editor or agent. He still had, though, the niggling suspicion — ridiculous, absurd — that doing this might break the poem's spell, that the delicate pages tied with the twined colored strings were part of the work's great power. Shouldn't it simply remain where it was, in this secret shrine?

He had even begun — not seriously, but still — to think of the Spotlight in precisely this way — as a shrine. Latangi had told Henry that when she and Mohit purchased the empty building, he had planned to call it the Ganesha Motel. Mohit had created the design for a sign he wanted to erect out front, the motel's name printed below a blue silhouette of the elephant-headed god, patron to both writers and travelers, their guardian and protector, steering both on their proper paths.

Latangi, though, had told Mohit the sign was a bad idea. She'd told him — and Henry figured she'd been right — that a sign saying *The Ganesha Motel* would keep customers away. It would confuse them. It would make them wonder if the place was not, despite its name, a motel but a Hindu temple, reserved for its own worshippers, just as the dozens of churches along the highway collected each Sunday morning only their own kind.

Mohit argued with her, Latangi told Henry. "But, yes, we know who wins these arguments," she said, laughing. "Always the slim girl, not the happy man." Though she triumphed in this instance, Mohit never acknowledged, she told Henry, the suspicion and judgment, even disgust, with which they were often regarded when they ventured out into, as she called it, *the Virginia world.* "Men and women look away and chitter-chatter," she said, motioning with her hands to suggest their gossiping. "I see their eyes grow thin, like the coin slots in soda vending machines." She squinted her eyes, then she shrugged.

Henry was reminded, with that peculiar image of the suspicious coin-slot eyes, what he had recognized when he first began to read *The Creator's Mistress*—that the poem was as much Latangi's as Mohit's, that the original Bengali work may have been his but that she was the one who had preserved its music, its beauty, in English. He thought then of Tomas Otxoa. Henry felt sickened at the thought that surely Tomas wouldn't have left New Orleans as the storm approached, that he wouldn't have known to leave. Such awful ruin.

Sit at His feet and be blessed!

I rest in your heart, bathe in your soul, find solace in your every word.

It was all the same everywhere, for everyone who believed, the prayer for relief from suffering, from pain and loss and grief and ruin.

"But not the children," Latangi had been saying, and Henry turned back to her. He hadn't been listening. "When children laugh at Mohit's dhoti kurta, they do not know to keep their thoughts to themselves. They have not yet learned this. They approach and ask why he is a man wearing a dress, and Mohit grabs the dhoti and pretends to be filled with surprise. 'Oh, what is this!' he cries out.

'I should not allow my bride to select my clothes!' and the children laugh with him. They want to touch the cloth. They want to learn its name. They want to know of the place where men wear dresses and women touch vermilion to their foreheads. I promise you, Mr. Henry, Mohit could gather as many children around him just by his words as the clowns with their painted faces and, *ayeee!*—" Latangi wrung her hands and made the screeching noise of a twisting balloon.

Henry smiled. "I'm so sorry I didn't get to meet him," Henry said.

"I am sorry too, Mr. Henry," Latangi said, and she placed a hand on his arm. "A great writer, you tell me, yes?"

"Yes," Henry said. "A great writer."

"A greater man," she said.

Though he hadn't seen Amy again in those two weeks, he had spoken once more to Mary. He had gone to the motel office and called her, told her he just wanted to check in. He thanked her for telling Amy where he was, for letting her know that he was okay. He said he was sorry that he hadn't done it himself.

"Yep," Mary said, unsurprised. She wasn't going to bother, he realized, to scold him.

"I saw her with that man," he said, "the professor. I couldn't make myself do it."

Mary didn't say anything, so Henry said, "You know about him?"

"I do," Mary said.

"Okay," Henry said. He didn't know what else to say, so he asked about New Orleans, if she was watching too.

"I am," Mary said. "It's hard to get out of your head, isn't it? Even here, in Baltimore, people are watching like they did after 9/11. Everybody's just waiting and waiting like there's a logical story being told, like there's going to be an ending to it and then everyone can finally turn their attention to something else."

"What's it going to be, you think? The ending?" Henry asked.

"I don't know," she said, and he heard the quaver in her voice. "Maybe *this* is the ending. Maybe it's already happened. Maybe it's just all gone."

"It can't be," Henry said. "They wouldn't let that happen." He realized that he was now trying to comfort Mary, that just that tremble in her voice had made him want to comfort her. He hoped that they could see each other before too long, he told her, that it would be great if she had the time to drive down from Baltimore. But he explained that he wouldn't need to stay with her, that Latangi had offered him a job—she hadn't exactly, but even so—and that he was hoping to help the family of the man who'd died in the accident, that this was something he wanted to do.

"Okay," she said, and he heard the wariness in her voice, the suspicion. "But you understand you can't make everything okay."

"I know," he said.

"That's what you've always figured you could do," Mary said, and Henry wondered why she'd say this, how she thought this could possibly be true. What had he ever done, really, to try to make everything okay? He couldn't think of a single thing.

"You need to choose, you know," Mary said.

"I'm trying to choose," he told her. "I'm choosing this."

"And Amy?"

"I don't know," Henry said. "I think she's already chosen." He'd learned more from Marge—who seemed to have as many sources of information as any private investigator could ever hope to acquire—and from Latangi's friend Rebecca Douglas, the English professor at Briarwood College whom he'd met when Latangi invited her over for dinner and introduced her to Henry. Hunter McClellan, it turned out, was not just a dandy in nice suits; he was a fine and decent man. He'd had a young wife, a former student, who had died from a rare cancer, and he'd cared for her with great love and attention. He'd been devastated by her death, but he'd eventually emerged from his mourning. He'd dated quite a few women before he met Amy. Once he'd met her, though—that was nearly a year ago, when she'd first arrived in Virginia—he'd had to pursue her quite a long time before she relented. *Relented.* That was the word Rebecca Douglas had used, and it had made Henry shudder in agony.

"Listen to me," Mary said on the phone to Henry. "She hasn't chosen. She doesn't love this guy. She doesn't."

"How do you know?"

"I just know," Mary said. "You just know these things."

Why, he wondered, didn't *he* ever just *know* something?

"I hope you're right," he said.

"I am. Hang in there."

How exactly was he supposed to hang in there? What did that mean? "How do I do that?" he said into the phone. "Hang in there?"

Mary paused, as if she didn't know whether or not she should say it. "It means don't be crazy," she said. "Do what you can to not be crazy."

"Okay," he said, and he thought again about what Amy had said to him even before he moved out: *See someone. See someone.*

"Can I ask you something?" he said.

Mary was silent, as if she sensed what was coming.

"Was she crazy too? Mama? I know Daddy was, but was she?" Just using those words, saying Mama and Daddy, brought everything back to him, took his breath out of his chest. He sounded like a child. But what other words for them were there?

"No," Mary said. "She wasn't crazy. She was injured. She was hurt."

"She didn't act hurt," he said, remembering how she'd made him send that gallery owner away, telling Henry that she was content, that all she wanted to do was paint.

"What do you mean?" Mary said. "Of course she acted hurt. How she lived, alone like that, all those paintings, all that art. That was all hurting. It was productive hurting, I guess, or at least the art part was. But the rest of it?"

"That's what I mean," Henry said. "It seems crazy to me."

"Listen," Mary said. "Everything she did—*everything* she did— was trying to find something to ward off the hurt."

"Why didn't we ask her what was wrong? Why didn't we say anything, you and me?"

"We were kids," Mary said.

"Then why didn't she?"

"I don't know," Mary said. "Maybe she knew even then we had it in us. Maybe we already knew."

"That we had what?"

"You know," Mary said. "Dad's craziness. His depression."

"I remember Dad talking about it, warning me. But I don't remember anything crazy."

"No, he just sank. That's what Mama said. She said he'd sink so low she couldn't find him."

"So she didn't talk about him leaving because she figured she knew what had happened, what he'd done?"

He couldn't make himself say it: *Killed himself. Committed suicide.*

"She knew," Mary said. "She knew what would happen when he went that low, when the weight was too great." He thought about how he'd skipped their mother's funeral, how he couldn't make himself go—*to ward off the hurt?* Was it all as simple as that?

"But you were fine," Henry said.

"I was *not* fine," Mary said. "You just didn't know me. I didn't let you, or anyone, know me. I'm fine now, it's true. I've got a career, and I love it. I've got friends. I see people. But it's not perfect. I haven't found the right person the way you did. But I talk about it. I take my meds. I do what needs doing."

He hadn't known, of course, that Mary took *meds.* He hadn't even known that she suffered from—*what?* What was the name for it? Was there a name? It was more than depression. He wanted to tell Mary that he heard things, that his head got filled with clatter. He wanted to ask her if her head did too. But how do you ask something like that?—*The noises? The memories? You hear them too? The song lyrics? The radio sermons?*

"What do I need to do?" Henry asked.

"That's the question," Mary said, and Henry could now hear the struggle, the hopelessness, the pain, in her voice. It had probably been there all along, all those years—when she kept their mother company, when she made up the story of the Broussards, when she left New Orleans for Baltimore and started her whole life over. He just hadn't known to look for it. Like their mother, she had always seemed to him content. He'd believed the face she'd shown him.

"I do know one thing," he said. "I know I've caused so much—" What was the right word? *Pain? Suffering? Hurt?* "Damage," he said. "I've caused so much damage."

Mary didn't even pretend to contradict him. "Yes, you have," she said. "That you've done."

"I'm sorry," he said. He didn't know what else he could say. "I'm really sorry."

"Well, a whole lot was done to you first. And maybe you can put an end to it. This family that you're trying to help, that's you trying to end it, I think."

"I don't know what it is," he said. "Maybe that's crazy too."

"No, it's a fine thing," Mary said. "What else can we do except help other people along? And maybe you'll succeed. Maybe you'll actually ease their pain a little. You will, I'm sure. But you're going to have to figure out what you should be doing. In regard to Amy, I mean. But staying sane is the first step. That's all the wisdom I've acquired through these years. First, you stay sane."

"Got it," Henry said, and he realized that he actually did get it now. He would talk to Marge about seeing her doctor friend again. If Rusty Campbell thought Henry needed medication, he would take it. If he thought Henry needed to talk with someone, go into therapy, he'd even do that. He hated the idea, and he didn't know how he'd pay for it, but he would do whatever he needed to do. After all this time, after so much damage, he finally understood that this was what it would take. He wasn't going to just figure this out on his own. Somehow he'd thought that Mohit's poem would do it, that giving the manuscript to Amy, having her read it, would put them both under the same enchanted spell. That was crazy—just as crazy as everything else he'd been thinking—that running away from his life would somehow make things better, that Amy would just wait and wait for him to get straightened out, that she wouldn't give up and find someone else. He needed to do something to win Amy back— he needed to be sane, yes, but what else?

He asked Marge what she thought. He asked Latangi as well. Both said more or less the same thing in their own very different ways— that he must simply *be,* that he must show Amy his true self. The problem, of course, was that most of the time he didn't feel as though he was in possession of a true self, something solid and predictable. Instead, he felt as though he were lost inside the clatter and chaos, the clutter and noise, the wreck and ruin.

Again and again, though, in the evenings when he could not settle his thoughts, when words and images and memories raced through his head, he went back to Mohit's study, to the quiet room with its bare white walls, the only movement a moth or two tapping against the windows, drawn by the fluorescent lights in the parking lot outside. He sat down at Mohit's desk, not a speck of dust on its surface, and he took the manuscript from the drawer. When he began to read Mohit's poem, he felt—what other word for it was there than *magic?*—he felt as though, by some strange magic, by some power of enchantment, his *self* had finally grown quiet, had become something certain and calm, something he did indeed in that moment possess.

Henry could not have found, had he been asked to do so, the precise words for this quiet, for the absolute peace he felt.

Henry took the blue truck and drove back to the real estate office—Marge had given him directions—only to catch Rusty Campbell walking out the door. "Mr. Garrett," he said, shaking Henry's hand. "Good to see you again, sir. I've got a nice A-frame heating up on Long Mountain. Two folks back to back want to see it. Care to take a drive?"

They drove west, toward the line of mountains.

"What's on your mind?" Rusty Campbell asked, lowering his window and pulling a pack of cigarettes from his shirt pocket. Henry tried to explain the way he'd felt in Mohit's study—the magic of Mohit's poem, the calm it had brought over him. He wanted to know if this seemed like another version of the craziness he'd been through before. "It seems different to me somehow," Henry said. "It feels more real, if that makes sense. It feels more like being okay than being sick."

Rusty Campbell leaned forward and squinted as if he were having trouble seeing. "I know doctors are supposed to believe in science," he said. "You know, cause and effect, treatment and cures. But I was never convinced that's all there is to it. And that motel where you're staying? I had my own kind of healing there. Spirits," he said, and shook his head, "and spirits—there's a world of difference, isn't there, between the two meanings one word can have."

"Spirits?" Henry said. "You mean, as in *haunted*?"

"I mean that too, I guess, but mostly I just mean liquor." He looked over at Henry and then back at the road. "I went to the Spotlight to dry out. More to the point, I was deposited there by my wife, who told me she was not letting me in the house again and would get a court order if necessary to keep me out. Well, the help I needed was losing every goddamn thing I ever had."

He threw his cigarette out his window. "I was visited by more than a ghost or two, and I figured my choices were being dead or being better. I finally chose better, or better finally chose me, and that happened in a month's time at the Spotlight."

They passed a lumber mill, pine trees heaped on one side of the property like giant matchsticks, neat stacks of two-by-fours on the other.

"I'm not saying there is or isn't something special about that place," Rusty Campbell went on, "but I tried church and I tried the hospital more than a few times without success and the one occasion when it worked was when I found myself waking up every morning in that one dark room at the Spotlight and wanting nothing really but to be a man who was sober enough to stand in front of his two boys again and look them square in the eye and say I was done with that past nonsense and I was ready if they were to start from scratch. I wanted nothing so much in this world as their forgiveness."

He looked over at Henry. "Which, by the way, is what I got."

"And your wife?" Henry said.

"Well, you win some and you lose some." They turned up a steep gravel driveway. "That's one I lost. Big-time. But this—" He stopped in front of a beautiful house looking out over the valley below. "This one I intend to win."

Henry waited outside while Rusty Campbell led one couple and then, fifteen minutes later, another through the house. He sat down on a bench at the top of a clear-cut and tried to figure out what he was seeing down below among all the trees, if he could indeed discern, as he thought he could, Main Street in Marimore and then Route 29 running north and south alongside it. He tried to find the stretch of 29 where the Spotlight stood, but he couldn't.

When Rusty Campbell was done and the second couple drove away, he walked over and sat down next to Henry. "Beautiful up here, ain't it?"

"It is," Henry said. "You make a sale?"

"We'll see," he said. "Here's something I didn't know: this real estate business takes patience. And patience is something I've always had to learn. I started out in the emergency room. A problem presents itself, you tackle it. Broken leg, ruptured appendix, stab wound, psychotic break. It can be rough and it can be scary, but at least you know what needs doing. But that's not how it worked when I came out here to practice."

"Why'd you stop working in the ER?" Henry said.

"Well, the hospital administrators decided—fairly enough, by the way—that they didn't want me working for them. That was one of the things my drinking cost me. Anyway, when you're a country doc, you've got folks' whole family history and all their good and bad affairs and money troubles and other worries to consider. Any one of those things might be the reason their head has been hurting or their leg has been twitching. Or it might be much worse, something that's going to get them in the end, but nine times out of ten, ninety-nine times out of a hundred, it isn't. The biggest lesson I learned was to just sit there with folks and wait them out. You wait long enough, they tell you what you need to know. Same in real estate. You just wait and it all becomes clear. But you've got to be willing to wait. If you don't wait, I've learned, you scare folks away."

Rusty Campbell pulled a cigarette from the pack in his pocket and lit it. He turned and looked back down the mountain, at the winding road and the gravel drive that had brought them up here to this house. Henry wondered if he was expecting someone else to come see the property. "Is that what you're doing now?" Henry said. "Waiting me out?"

"I'm resting is all," Rusty Campbell said. He coughed. "Anyway, I thought you said you were better."

"I feel better. I do," Henry said.

"That's something, then." He took another drag on his cigarette and then held it out and squinted at it, as if he were surprised to find it there. "But you want something more?"

Henry sighed. He noticed a deer and then another skitter in the woods. "Don't we always?"

"Yes, I guess we do," Rusty Campbell said. "I guess we do."

Rusty Campbell bent forward and coughed again, and Henry wondered if he might be truly sick. He thought again about *The Awakening*. Edna hadn't been sick the same way, but she also hadn't been well. She'd been depressed and miserable and one day she just swam out to sea and that was that. What if, though, there'd been someone to give her a pill?

There wouldn't have been a novel then, would there? There

wouldn't have been a story to tell. She'd have felt a little better, gone off for a swim, and then what? Would she just have returned to her life? It seemed impossible somehow. She couldn't have just gotten better.

Then it occurred to him: What about his father? Or his mother? How different would things have been?

Rusty Campbell seemed like he might be asleep; his eyes were closed, his chin resting on his chest. But he was just waiting, Henry knew. He was waiting to see where Henry's thoughts took him. Finally Rusty opened his eyes.

"I need to take something," Henry said. "Something, you know, to keep me sane. That's what my sister told me. I think she's right."

"That could help." Rusty Campbell nodded. "Given all you've said, I think it will. But even with all the stuff there is these days to take, it's not enough on its own. There's usually more to the story than that. There's still things to sort out. You understand?"

"I do," Henry said. "Yes, I do."

After they drove back to the real estate office, Rusty Campbell gave Henry some sample packs of something. "Prozac," he told Henry. "Pretty basic stuff. See what you think. If anything strange happens, call me. Don't expect to feel different right away. You won't. And don't expect any miracles."

"I won't," Henry said. "Thank you."

Rusty Campbell touched Henry's shoulder as he turned to go. "You know," he said, "my father worked with Marion Hughes's father for the railroad. It was Norfolk and Western then. My father was the station agent. His father was a fireman on one of the old coal engines. They both worked hard, but a fireman was as tough a job as there was. Dangerous as hell and about twice as hot. Marion and I played around outside the station sometimes when we were kids. I wasn't there the day an engine caught fire, but I soon learned his father was the one who'd died. I never saw him again until he was grown and his wife got diabetes and needed dialysis. She faced losing some fingers and then one leg and then another. That was a tough thing, telling them such news, but it was made a whole lot tougher just knowing what all those years had done to Marion Hughes, all those years since he'd just been a child who'd lost his father."

Henry nodded, and Rusty Campbell shook his hand. "You might take that into account," he said. "It's not the same, I know, but you went through a similar loss. Take it easy on yourself."

"I will," Henry said. "I'll try to."

In his room back at the Spotlight, Henry took out the sample packs that Rusty Campbell had given him and left them unopened on the vanity. He'd start taking them in the morning. He couldn't stop wondering, though, what it would mean, how he might be changing his own story. What if the path he was heading down was predetermined, the place where he was supposed to go? Wasn't it a good thing, though, to try to change it? Hadn't he done enough harm? Even so, he was worried there was some essential part of himself he'd lose. But looking around his room—at the stuff that he hadn't given to Mrs. Hughes, at the painting of the flying child and the worn purple carpet and the lamp with its paper shade—he couldn't imagine what it was he could possibly fear losing.

Fourteen

IT WAS only a moment, the briefest glimpse, but Henry was absolutely certain of what he'd seen. He could not possibly be mistaken. He had not imagined it or dreamed it or allowed memory and its accompanying ghosts to swirl through or obscure or alter his vision.

What had happened was this: That night, when he couldn't sleep, when the clatter had started up again in his head, he'd walked back down to Mohit's study, took the manuscript from the drawer, untied it, and began reading. The poem was so familiar to him now that he remembered long passages; he could easily conjure up in his head the images of the prince and princess, of the gods and goddesses.

He thought about what Mohit's hero had done, what all his years of reading had taught him every hero must do. He thought of Don Quixote, of Ulysses, of Ishmael setting out on impossible excursions that seemed destined to fail but in the end did not, would not, could not.

All along he'd thought his journey was leaving New Orleans, casting everything aside, escaping his life. What an idiot he'd been, he told Amy. The true journey—the journey that mattered—was to return.

He'd left Mohit's study and gone back to the room where he'd stored all the things he'd been given. He'd turned on the TV and watched a CNN report on how difficult rebuilding and recovery would be when residents were finally allowed to return. They'd showed Lakeview and Gentilly, Mid-City and the Garden District and the Marigny. They'd showed Bywater and Tremé and the Ninth Ward and up Esplanade all the way past Claiborne and the cemeteries to City Park. And when they showed Carrollton and then Uptown, he'd watched as the camera moved building to building along Magazine. The reporter was talking, explaining this and that, providing estimated costs—two hundred million here, fifty million there—but Henry had stopped listening when he realized he knew exactly where the camera was going, one block to the next and the next. He had leaned in, stared intently, was ready when the shot finally arrived: Endly's.

And there, right there, through one of the cracked, grimy plate-glass windows, clear as day, he could see him, inside, looking directly out: Tomas Otxoa.

"Who?" Amy said, sitting across from Henry in her kitchen at a small black lacquer table. She'd let him in, though it had already been well past midnight when he'd seen the news report. He'd gotten into the blue truck and made the drive to Lovingston, the truck's headlights again and again illuminating deer grazing along the side of the highway. He'd pulled into Amy's driveway as if he were a thief, coasting to a stop, engine switched off. He hadn't wanted to frighten her, though of course his knocking on the door until he woke her must have done so anyway. He hadn't thought to wonder if she would be alone until she'd opened the door, let him in. It was nearly three a.m.

"Right," Henry said, recognizing that he'd need to explain it all, that of course Amy didn't know who Tomas Otxoa was or about all the stories he'd told Henry or the fact that one day he had simply disappeared. She wouldn't know that Henry had searched for him, walked everywhere in the neighborhood for days and days, hunted for him in abandoned buildings and at the wharves along the river. She wouldn't know what it might mean that Henry had now seen with his own eyes that Tomas, after all this time, was alive and had wound up back at Endly's, that he had taken refuge in the old grocery store after the storm, maybe even during the storm, and—the most incredible, astounding thing of all—that Henry had seen in that brief camera shot not only that Tomas looked haggard and confused but also that he was holding against his chest a cardboard box, one precisely the size and shape of the cardboard boxes he'd seen Amy use again and again when she received or shipped off completed copyedits or page proofs, a manuscript box that, though he knew he couldn't be certain—how could he be certain, as impossible and crazy as it seemed?—he nevertheless believed was exactly and undeniably that: a box with a manuscript inside, a manuscript Tomas Otxoa, wherever he'd been, whatever he'd endured, had managed to keep safe during the storm. Maybe it was simply the manuscript of one of his brother's old novels. Or maybe it was a new one. Maybe he'd found his brother after all, or maybe all this time he'd been in possession of this one final novel and now he'd kept it safe, cradled in his arms, this one copy the only one and thus in danger of winding up, like everything else in the city had wound up, ruined and lost. Henry didn't know any of this for certain, of course, but he'd seen what he'd seen, and it might well be true; it was as likely to be true as not, wasn't it?

He stopped. He let the rush of his words become silence. He looked at Amy.

Yes, he knew what he sounded like. He knew what she was no

doubt thinking. And how could he—there was no way he could—convince her otherwise. Who would believe him, such an absurd coincidence—Mohit's manuscript here and Tomas's there, these two unknown works, singular, irreplaceable, finding their way somehow into his life, though, look, *look,* he had brought Mohit's poem with him. Here it was—and he pushed it, tied once again with the colored thread, across the table to Amy. At least she could read this, see for herself that this one manuscript, at least, was real, was what he claimed it to be, and maybe she would then be persuaded that he wasn't crazy or delusional or ill.

Amy's eyes were teary, her mouth pinched closed, her shoulders slumping forward. He saw in her expression the devastation, the pain, the damage he'd caused. He saw the exhaustion. Then he watched her run her hand through her hair and erase all of it, make her face go blank. "Okay, Henry. Okay," she said. "I'll read it. I need to get some sleep but I'll read it."

She waited.

"Yes, okay," he said, defeated. He must seem to her crazy, irresponsible, out of control. Not a person to be believed, not worthy of her forgiveness.

But he was not wrong; he wasn't. She would read Mohit's poem. She would encounter its grace, its great epic grace. She would be swept up in its story of refuge and redemption, of gods and princes, of the young couple longing for a child, bathing in the Ganges beneath the stars.

And he would find Tomas, save him, see what lay inside the box he held cradled against his chest.

He had no idea how he was going to manage it, just as he didn't know how he was going to pay Mrs. Hughes the money he'd promised. Maybe there was still money stuffed in the coffee cans at

Endly's. Maybe the insurance he'd been required to take out on the property would yield more, much more, than he alone needed.

But he didn't even have a car to get to New Orleans. And even if he did, how would he gain access to the city? It was still shut down, every news report repeated; it was still without electricity or running water. Bodies were still being discovered, dehydrated and delirious survivors found in collapsed homes or wandering among the wreckage. There were roadblocks on the interstate and on the causeway and on the bridges that hadn't been washed away.

He had to figure out how to get there, how to save Tomas.

He'd come here to ask Amy for—what? For her car? For her company? For her faith?

Amy led him back to the front door, quietly shut it behind him even before he'd reached the truck. He drove the winding road out to the highway in the awful darkness, and now the deer grazing on the side of the highway and the possums crouching in the median or slinking along the edge of the woods were all looking up as he passed, their pairs of eyes quick flashes of blinding light, twin matches being struck again and again and again, and he gripped the truck's steering wheel in his clenched fists and pressed his foot down on the accelerator until he could feel the truck's shuddering shoot up through his wrists and into his shoulders and, finally, into his chest.

He slept. And when he woke he realized the stupidity of what he'd done—he'd taken the only copy of *The Creator's Mistress* and left it with Amy. She wouldn't, in her disgust and despair, simply throw it away, would she? Even if she were filled with rage and grief at what he seemed to have become yet again—the delusional idiot who'd left her and moved into an empty grocery store—she cared enough about words and manuscripts and a man's lifelong devotion to poetry and his loving wife's faith in this improbably grand and romantic endeavor that she wouldn't just throw the whole thing away. Would she?

Oh God. He got dressed and walked down to the office. Latangi wasn't there, so he stepped behind the desk and knocked on the door to her apartment. "I'm so sorry," he said when she opened the door wearing a dark red nightdress, a gold-and-red-striped robe pulled over it, askew. She straightened the robe, pulled its gold belt tighter, pushed her hair away from her face. She smiled.

"Good morning to you, Mr. Henry."

"I'm so sorry," he said again. He hadn't even looked at the time.

"Yes, Mr. Henry?"

"I gave Mohit's poem to Amy. To read."

"Yes," Latangi said, smiling.

"I left it with her," he said.

"Yes," she said, nodding. "Okay. That is fine."

"I just thought I should tell you," he said. "I was worried. I didn't know if that was it, if there was another copy, if something happens to this one."

"No, no, Mr. Henry. Do not worry. It is all on the computer. One click and"—she made a whirring noise—"each page emerges from the printer. No problem at all."

Henry sighed in relief, in exhaustion. Of course it was on the computer. How ridiculous to have not figured this out.

"Yes," he said. "Of course."

Latangi looked at him a moment, then she stepped forward and spread her arms wide.

"Oh, Mr. Henry," she said. "Here, here. So many worries. I wish I could do something for you."

He heard the *rat-tat-tat* of Father Ferguson's pipe on the desk. *Your problem, Garrett.*

He stepped into Latangi's embrace.

Your problem, Garrett, is that you can't think straight.

He felt like a child, as though she were holding him as she would a child.

"Please, please, Mr. Henry," she said. "Inside. I would like my tea. And you—coffee, yes?"

"Yes. Thank you," he said, and he felt her let him go.

He followed her inside.

"Well, I have news for you, Mr. Henry. But it can wait a few moments—" She drifted off into the kitchen and left Henry in the living room, still crowded with stacks and stacks of import items: leather elephants and camels and giraffes, wicker baskets and wooden spoons and colored glass paperweights, tin cigar boxes painted with Hindu gods: Shiva and Parvati and Ganesh, dozens of others. Latangi had told him stories about so many of these gods that Henry had trouble separating one story from the next. He did remember her telling him that Shiva was the husband of Parvati and father to Ganesh and that he was usually depicted as being blue because in order to save the world from destruction, he had calmly swallowed all of the world's poisons. Parvati had feared the harm this would cause her husband, so she'd gripped his neck and squeezed his throat. He was saved, but his skin was forever stained.

"It's a beautiful color," Henry had said to Latangi, looking at a painting in her apartment of Shiva holding a trident, a cobra curled around his neck, another wrapped in his hair. "Aquamarine?" he said. "Turquoise?"

"Beautiful, yes," Latangi had said, "but only if you are one who is content to live this life with blue skin. I do not think I would be."

"Well, at least it's a great story," Henry had said.

"Yes, yes," Latangi had replied. "'It is the power of the story, not

its truth,' Mohit would tell me. 'A story's greatness,' he would say—
and, you see, he wags his finger like an old schoolteacher—'is measured by how wide and deep and far the earth shakes when words are
spoken.' Wise, yes, my Mohit?"

"Yes," Henry had agreed.

Now Latangi emerged from the kitchen with a tray—her teapot
and cup, his mug of coffee, some thick slices of bread. "So you have
visited your Amy?"

Henry nodded.

"That is good, yes?"

"Not so much," he said.

"It is only time," Latangi said. "You will see. She will return to
you." She set her teacup down, sat, and folded her hands in her lap.

"You have something to tell me," Henry said.

Latangi looked down at her hands.

"Something important," Henry said. "Yes?"

Latangi nodded but sat there quietly.

Henry had never seen her at a loss for words, and he wondered if
perhaps she was going to tell him that he must move out, that she
could no longer afford to have him occupying a room for no charge,
that the little bit of work he was doing for her—making deliveries, going to the grocery, hauling trash and broken furniture to the
landfill—wasn't enough. Or maybe she too had decided that he was
crazy—the hours and hours he spent reading in Mohit's study, the
promise he'd made to Mrs. Hughes about the money he'd get her.
Or maybe he'd frightened a guest; maybe he'd appeared to be lurking
in the parking lot. He thought then, for the first time in weeks, of
Clarissa Nash, the girl he'd imagined, the terrible desire he'd felt, the
awful dark raging conflagration of desire. Had he made some woman
feel as though he were dangerous, as though he might attack her?

Who, though, could it be? The guests at the Spotlight—the sales-men and utility workers, the illicit couples, the young families with their little children, the haunted men—there was no one to whom he would have signaled such a thing. Loneliness, maybe. Yes, loneli-ness. But not desire. He'd felt free of it. He'd wanted only peace; he felt he had been restored to himself, restored to wanting only Amy.

"So I will be leaving," he heard Latangi say. "This. The Spotlight. Virginia."

He didn't understand. He hadn't been listening. He'd been at-tending to his own thoughts, to the clamor inside his head, the cacophony: Tomas Otxoa through the cracked window; his father playing the bass; the parking lot's fluorescent light flickering; the car-pet's dark paisley design; Father Ferguson and cherry pipe smoke, the *rat-tat-tat* on the desk and his mother, in bed, paint-smeared; the scent of liniment, of linseed, of lilac.

Lilac. In Latin, *Syringa vulgaris.* Where, from whom, would he have learned such a thing? From Amy? One of her books?

"What?" he said. "I'm sorry. I was lost. Could you please start again?"

And so she did start again. She told him everything she'd already said—that Mohit's brother had followed the path that Mohit had forsaken. Iri was a physician, a neonatologist, one who cared for tiny babies in a Calcutta hospital, and he had a year ago been widowed and they, she and Iri, had seen one another at Mohit's funeral and then again at his daughter's wedding in Toronto, just three months ago, and he had made his proposition then and she had considered and considered it, had read and read Mohit's poem for the wisdom it might offer—Mohit, who had loved and respected his brother Iri, who had of course loved and respected her, who would have told her, she now believed, that it was good and just and proper that she

222

should be cared for by his brother, by blood of his blood, and that this union would be one of mournful joy, for his brother and his wife to share their loss and make this new life together.

Henry placed his hands over Latangi's hands.

"Thank you, Mr. Henry," she said. "Thank you. You cannot know this, but it is your presence here, your recognition of Mohit's wisdom in his poems, that has enabled me to feel certain in this decision. Thank you. Yes, thank you."

She lowered her head and began weeping, and Henry moved closer so that she could lean forward and place her head on his shoulder, so he might offer to her whatever little comfort he could simply by being there beside her. He continued to hold her hands in his own. He remembered the henna, the faint traces she'd had on her hands when he'd met her. Would they be painted again when she married?

"When?" he asked her, and she understood.

"Soon," she said. "Soon." And she rested her head against Henry's, her forehead against his cheek.

Back in his room he lay down, shut his eyes against the morning light. He must get to New Orleans, try to save Tomas Otxoa. But Latangi was leaving. *Soon,* she'd said. He would have nowhere to live, nowhere to which he might return. He had no car, no money. And Amy was certain again that he had lost his mind, and she wasn't wrong, was she? *Soon, soon.* How could he save Tomas when he could not save himself, when he could not offer Tomas or Amy or Mrs. Hughes or her grandson Katrell or her grandson with the withered arm—what was his name? He couldn't remember—he could not offer a single other person a moment's solace or comfort? Though he had at least offered some small morsel of it to Latangi, her head on his shoulder, weeping for all she had lost though she whispered to him that she was not sorrowful, she was not. *This Virginia,* she had said, *this Ganesha*—and she had wept and wept and finally raised her head, dried her eyes, and said, *Yes, this Ganesha Motel. What do I know of such things?*

The Ganesha Motel, Henry had said, nodding.

Let it be so for its final days, she had said, nodding with him.

He had comforted her, assured her that he would help however he could help. He did not tell her, though, that he, too, was leaving, that he must leave. He had meant to tell her, to say that he had seen a man who needed rescuing and that he knew no one else who could do it, who would even believe that he had seen what he'd seen and what it might mean: the manuscript, another manuscript perhaps like Mohit's, there in New Orleans, in all the wreck and ruin. A story's greatness, Mohit had asserted, was measured by how much the earth shook by its very presence. What did it mean that the earth seemed to shake and shake, to be opening now beneath his feet, as it must have opened beneath Mohit's as he wrote his great work, as it must have opened beneath Tomas's, this brave and desperate man clutching those pages to his chest?

Even if he was wrong, didn't he need to try to save this one man, though he could not save even himself?

Didn't he need to do this, at least this?

Well?

Yes.

Fifteen

HERE HE was. Let the soft eyes open.

It had taken nearly a week but here he was, in Marge's red convertible, her candy-red baby, and Marge there with him, behind the wheel, the two of them flying down Interstate 81, the top down, and with them, in the backseat, wind in his face, eyes wide at the wonder, Katrell Sparrow. Wasn't that the earth opening now before them? Wasn't it opening now like the newest flower?

Here they were.

Let the soft eyes open, he heard in his head. Were these Mohit's words? No, from another poet, from a poem he'd taught his students—forever ago. *If they have lived in a wood, it is a wood.* He let the words come. *If they have lived on plains, it is grass rolling under their feet forever.*

And the highway rolled by beneath them.

He was tired of resisting. Let the words come, the images. Let sound and music, clamor and clatter. Anything. The thump of the bass, his father's callused fingers; Mary singing to little children, her hips shimmying; Amy, in the kitchen, laughing, stirring, spoons

225

clanging, a dozen different scents: rosemary, basil, garlic, onion, thyme. *Sit at His feet and be blessed. Make a way out of no way.* He would welcome all of it, see it all as wonder. If he had managed all of this, wasn't anything possible?

Ulysses. Ishmael. Don Quixote. Gilgamesh. Lawrence of Arabia. The dogs and cat in that children's movie, *The Incredible Journey.* All the same story. There wasn't any other.

First had been Marge. She had wanted the chance to see it for herself. She wanted to get the word back to her congregation, see it firsthand and report on what they could do, why their help was so desperately needed, not just for Henry's sake now, she'd tell them, but for any and all others—*any and all others*—who found themselves in dire need, who found themselves lost or alone in this world, forlorn or forsaken.

Charlie had needed some convincing, Marge told Henry. He'd needed assurances she wasn't running off with a younger man—*Oh, how I wish!* Marge said she'd told him and then laughed her wicked laugh so Charlie would know she was just teasing—and once he'd given the trip his blessing, which meant rolling his eyes and then shaking his head, she'd started gathering contributions from her congregation lickety-split, ten- and twenty- and fifty-dollar bills, rolls of quarters, personal checks, a dozen Sacagawea coins taped to a piece of cardboard, jars of nickels and dimes. And not just from her church but from across the county. She knew *near everybody,* she told Henry. Rusty Campbell had made a gift—"a *significant* one, I'm here to tell you," she said—and Latangi Chakravarty had as well, and Judge Martin and Sheriff Roland and Wayne and Robert at the Elkwood Salon where she had her hair done every week and each one of the tellers at First Marimore Bank and from plenty of others, regular folks, and she'd given what she could give too.

She'd told everyone—*every last one of them,* she said—that she and Mr. Henry Garrett were going to find someone in need, whether near or far, and make this offering in the name of the good Lord's kindness and generosity and mercy, no matter who it was or where or when, for *whoever you feed or clothe or comfort you do as well unto the Lord.* So Henry should not have been surprised when, instead of heading straight out of town, she'd driven back to the trailer where Mrs. Hughes and her grandson lived and stopped the car and turned to look at Henry.

"Don't you make the same mistake Charlie made when he married me," she told him.

"And what was that?" Henry said.

"Don't you underestimate me," she said. She touched a long painted fingernail to her temple. "These wheels just turn and turn and keep on turning."

She reached into her purse and pulled out a cloth wallet and handed it to Henry. The wallet had a Japanese painting printed on it: a waterfall and rolling hills lined with flowering trees. Inside was all the money she'd raised, converted to hundred-dollar bills.

"There are those, I guess," she said, looking up at herself in the rearview mirror, "who'd say I deceived them, and I'm prepared to let the Lord be my judge and jury, but I did more than a little thinking since we last came here." She turned to Henry. "I decided you were right and I was wrong. It's the ones among us, no matter the cause of their suffering, who it's our business to look after first. I know folks meant this money to go to someone in New Orleans, someone hurt from this storm, but I know who I meant it for all along and I said as much, if not directly. It breaks my heart we've got this family—and who knows how many others—living right here in this county in such poverty and despair. And if this has the added bonus of releasing you from one of your own burdens, well, then, that's fine by me. You with me, Mr. Garrett?"

"I am," Henry said. "I'm with you." He handed the wallet back to Marge. "Thank you. I can't thank you enough."

"Let me tell you this just to be sure you understand," Marge said, putting the wallet in her purse. "I'm having fun, Henry Garrett. There's no two ways about it. I am. This is the mission I feel called to."

And when they stepped inside the trailer and Marge gave the cloth wallet to Mrs. Hughes, she leaned over and said straight into the old woman's ear to make sure she heard every word of it, "This is from Mr. Garrett, yes. It's about everything he promised. But I want you to know it's from folks across this county as well. We're all sorry for your loss. We are. It's not enough, I know. It can't ever be. But we'd like to offer this as a small comfort."

Henry watched Mrs. Hughes raise her splotched and skeletal hand and touch Marge's cheek. Her fingers trembled. *"Bring the full tithe into the storehouse,"* she said. She lowered her hand, let it rest against her sunken chest. "You know that verse?"

"I'm afraid I don't recall it just this moment, Mrs. Hughes," Marge said, and she looked over at Henry.

"I can't remember the whole of it myself," she said. She raised her hand and reached toward Marge. "But I'm full grateful. May the Lord bless you."

Marge took the outstretched hand in her own and said, "Now, Mr. Garrett and I are headed to New Orleans, Mrs. Hughes. We're going to look around."

"Yes," Mrs. Hughes said, nodding.

"And there's a man there Mr. Garrett hopes to help in his suffering just as he's tried to help you. I'm going to accompany him. And I'm going to keep you and your family in mind and ask the Lord for His blessings upon you. We'll be back, though, and I'll check in on you. You hear me?"

"Yes," Mrs. Hughes said, nodding again. She pulled at the blanket covering her lap and her missing legs, the cloth wallet resting there. At that moment, Katrell Sparrow stepped into the trailer holding two plastic Food Lion grocery bags. He set them on the folding table, the bags collapsing, items spilling out: milk, apples, a pack of gauze bandages, a loaf of bread, a soda bottle, a frozen pizza. Henry watched as the boy walked over to his grandmother and stood behind her, taking hold of the handles on her wheelchair as though she might want him to steer her somewhere.

"These folks have kindly provided for us," she said quietly, picking up the cloth wallet, then holding it to her chest.

The boy nodded. "Yes, ma'am," he said.

"They're headed down to where that storm hit, where so many folks lost their homes."

"Yes, ma'am," the boy said again.

"If they'll have you," she said, "I'd like you to go with them."

The boy looked at Marge and then at Henry. *Bring the full tithe into the storehouse.* The verse slipped into Henry's head, joined others there: *Except the Lord build the house. They tell me that city is made four-square.*

"You hear me?" Mrs. Hughes said.

"Yes, ma'am," the boy said.

"No, Mrs. Hughes," Marge said. "We couldn't."

I'm going to a city that's not made by hand.

"He's had some trouble in school," Mrs. Hughes said. "I don't believe it's his doing. He says it isn't. But he's had a suspension."

"We just can't," Marge said. "We don't even know if they'll allow us into the city. We might drive down and then have to turn right back around."

Marge again looked over at Henry, cocked her head to signal that he should say something. Why had the clatter started up now, here? Wouldn't it be fine for this boy to go with them?

Katrell stepped forward, around his grandmother's wheelchair. He looked at Marge and then at Henry. "I'd like to go," he said. "I'd like to go if I could."

"He might be of some service to you," Mrs. Hughes said. "He's got a suspension."

There had been a fig tree in that churchyard, he and Mary playing beneath it while their father was in the church. There was singing inside. He let the singing come to him, tried to remember the hymn being sung. "Ride on, King Jesus." And there had been a fig tree in Mohit's poem, a great tree offering shade to the lovers in a garden of *siuli*-flowers, jasmines, *jamrul*.

"Mr. Garrett?" Marge was saying. "Mr. Garrett?"

Henry closed his eyes, opened them again. He looked at Katrell Sparrow, the boy's lanky limbs, his long neck. Not a sparrow, not a hawk—what? An egret, maybe, or a flamingo. Couldn't they use a companion on this journey? Though he was a child, wouldn't he soon, in the blink of an eye, be a man? Henry thought of the story Rusty Campbell had told him about Marion Hughes, about him losing his father in the fire on the train. Didn't he have something he might offer this boy?

"If you can spare him, Mrs. Hughes," he said. "If you can spare him, we'd be honored to take him."

"Yes, sir," Mrs. Hughes said, nodding, taking hold of the boy's arm. "He's been good to me, a solace. The Lord's blessing."

"He'd be a blessing to us as well," Henry said, and he felt himself possessed by this language of belief, comforted by its certainty, its beseeching. *Make a way out of no way. Sit at His feet and be blessed. Expect to be landed upon the shore.*

"He'll be fine," Henry said to Marge.

"You'll care for him," Mrs. Hughes said.

"He'll be fine," Henry said again, his voice like a ringing bell sounding out across a wide clear lake. He felt the chill of his fear that he and Marge—and now this boy—would fail.

"He's never been nowhere," Mrs. Hughes said. "He needs to see what's out there."

"He'll be fine," Henry said again, and he turned to Marge, nodded.

Finally, Marge smiled. "All aboard, then, I guess. This train's about to leave the station."

For the first time, Henry saw the boy smile, saw him proudly pull his shoulders back as if he were a soldier who'd been called to attention.

Marge turned to Katrell. "You have a sleeping bag?" she asked.

"No, ma'am."

"Well, okay, we'll manage," she said. "Grab a few changes of clothes. We'll take care of the rest. We'll be gone a few days, a week at most, if—well, I don't know."

"Yes, ma'am," the boy said, and he emptied out the two Food Lion bags, walked over to a plastic basket in the corner of the room, pulled clothes from it, and then stuffed them into the grocery bags.

"That's all you need?" Marge said.

"Yes, ma'am." The boy walked over to his grandmother. "Call Aunt Celee, Mamaw," he said. "Call Aunt Celee to come on over with Stacey. They can stay with you."

His grandmother nodded. He leaned in and kissed her on the cheek. She waved him away. "Go on," she said. "Behave yourself."

Outside, Marge pointed to her car. "You ever had a ride in a convertible?" she asked him.

"No, ma'am," he said.

"Well, hold on to your hat," Marge said. "You're about to."

Henry watched Katrell settle into the backseat, the two plastic bags of clothes perched on his lap. What could he possibly be thinking? He was headed out into the world with two complete strangers, and he didn't seem the least bit worried or afraid. And Henry realized he was the one who felt comforted—by the boy's anticipation, by his faith.

Here they were then, the three of them, the car's top down, the wind in their faces. It was too loud for conversation. He thought about Amy. She'd come to see him again at the Spotlight to return Mohit's manuscript, to tell him that she had read the poem. "Beginning to end," she'd said. "It's beautiful."

Yes. Henry had nodded. *Yes, yes,* elated that he had not been wrong, that she had seen and felt its power.

"You were right," Amy said. "It's really truly something."

Henry led her down to Mohit's study. He wanted her to see the space, see and feel how it was like a monk's spartan cell: bare walls, a cot, a lamp, a desk. He carefully placed the manuscript back in the drawer just as Amy began to speak.

"I've got a theory," she said.

Henry looked at her. He could tell, just by those few words, by her tone, that she'd rehearsed what she wanted to say.

"I was thinking a lot about you as I was reading," she said. "I think, well, because of your history, because of how you grew up— and maybe it's not just that. Maybe it's something else. Maybe it's just who you are. But I think it's hard for you to navigate your own experience, your own way through things. And something like this—books, stories—they're the way you've always done it. Does that make sense?"

Henry looked at her, waiting, expecting more. This would be it, he figured; this would be how she told him that he'd lost her for good.

"That's all, really," Amy said. "I think you're forever relying on something else to explain how you're feeling, the way you see things. You've always had trouble saying it for yourself."

She was right, of course. He'd loved to teach, to talk about literature with his students, because it had given him a way to say all the things he otherwise couldn't figure out how to say—about longing and loneliness, about sorrow. It was not, though, just that they gave him a way to talk about these things. It was more than that. It was as if he couldn't even really see anything, couldn't see himself, without these stories. They'd given him the only sense he had of who he was.

He looked at Amy; how beautiful she was here before him. He thought about all those times they'd slept together and his silence, his inability to announce his own desire. An emptiness opened in him, too vast, too painful.

"This poem," Amy said, "it's a love story, Henry, I see that. I get it. I know that's why you wanted me to read it. You wanted to say to me that you still loved me. Maybe I'm wrong. Maybe that's not it—"

"No," Henry said. "That's it." He looked away.

"Okay, then," Amy said. "Look at me."

He turned to her, lifted his head.

"I hear you," she said. "I'm not ready to say that back, you understand? I'm not saying I won't ever be, but I'm not right now. Whatever reason you had, whatever history or illness made you do it, you left me. And I had to put another life together, or try to. I've lost a lot too. You, my husband. My parents. That's not the same, I know, as losing them when you're a kid. But it's still something."

Here I am now, he wanted to say but couldn't. It was still too difficult to speak. He was still too empty, too lost.

"And home. The house. The whole city. That too."

"Do you think—" Henry said. "Do you think you could go back?"

"I don't know," she said. "I can't think about that yet."

"I'm trying to go back," Henry said. He knew he shouldn't start talking again about Tomas Otxoa, about seeing him in the cracked window, trying to find him; he knew what she'd think, how irrational it would seem. But he needed to tell her something. "I want to see it. I want to be there. I feel like I need to."

"I understand," she said.

"I'm going to go soon. There's someone at the town hall trying to help me. A secretary. Marge Brockman. You know her, or she knows you. She ran into you at the grocery, I think. Anyway, she went when you were signing books. She's going too."

"Can you just go down there? I didn't think you could."

"I'm going to find out," Henry said.

Amy nodded.

"But I'll come back here," he said. "The motel's going to be sold, but I'll figure out something."

"Okay," she said.

"I know you're seeing this guy," Henry said. "I know that maybe that's something. So I understand I've got to wait."

"Yes," Amy said. "You've got to wait."

"Then I'll wait," he said. "I'm not sure how I tell you that, how I show you that I'm waiting."

Henry thought about what Mary had told him, how she knew Amy wasn't in love with Hunter McClellan.

234

"You could remind me, maybe," Amy said. "You could figure out, maybe, a way to remind me."

"I'll do that," Henry said. "I'll figure it out."

So here they were, the highway rolling away beneath them. A month ago, he'd wandered for three days before he'd wound up in Virginia. But now, with just one day of driving, they were already through Virginia and almost through Tennessee, night settling in as they approached Memphis.

After they'd stopped for dinner and put gas in the car, Marge asked Henry to drive, and she climbed into the backseat with Katrell. As he drove, Henry could hear her talking, asking the boy about his life. Again and again Henry looked in the rearview mirror. All he could see in the dark car was the outline of their two faces, with flashes of light every now and again from other cars. He'd see their eyes, then their profiles, rectangles of light scanning across them.

He kept his head cocked to try to hear Katrell's answers. He'd been only three, he said, when his mother died. He'd met his father once or twice—the name Sparrow was from him. For a long time his father had been incarcerated near Norfolk. He thought that was where he still was. He'd never had a bedroom of his own but had slept on the sofa in his grandparents' trailer, which was fine except when they had family over and everyone stayed up late laughing and playing cards and fussing. He was decent at basketball because he was tall but he liked football better, liked the contact, the hitting and getting hit.

"I know just what you mean," Henry heard Marge tell him. "My Charlie likes NASCAR, but I'd rather watch football any day. You like the Redskins?"

"No, ma'am," Katrell answered. "I like the Cowboys."

"Then we can't be friends, I guess," Marge said, and Henry heard both of them laughing.

There were fewer and fewer cars on the road. He heard Marge ask Katrell about being suspended from school, about what had happened, but he couldn't really hear Katrell's answer—something about a girl and a fight, it seemed, his tone of voice more resignation than anger.

What had Mrs. Hughes wanted, really, in asking them to take her grandson with them? Clearly he was the one who took care of her, but maybe she just wanted him to see that the world was a bigger place than that run-down trailer. Maybe she wanted to plant in him the idea that there was somewhere else he might go. But this trip? To New Orleans? Maybe she just believed in charity, in doing right by someone else, and she wanted Katrell to offer whatever help he could. Henry didn't know.

It was nearly midnight when he started looking for a place to stop; they were at least five or six hours from New Orleans. He had some money because Latangi had cashed another check for him even though his bank in New Orleans hadn't yet reopened. Their main office on Carondelet had *taken in water,* a recorded message announced when Henry first called. Later, that message was replaced by another apologizing for *circumstances beyond our control,* then another that referred him to a different number, a different bank, but by that point Henry had given up.

He'd driven through Memphis and then down I-55 into Mississippi. Jackson was a couple of hours ahead. Marge and Katrell had both fallen asleep. It was late—the clock on the dashboard said it was 1:35 a.m. Should he stop or just keep going? With each motel he passed, he thought about Latangi. She'd told him that she'd still be there when he got back but that she'd be leaving soon.

"How long is soon?" Henry had asked, and she'd looked away from him.

"Soon is soon, Mr. Henry," she'd said. "In Bengali, *soon* is *shiggiri*."

"Shiggiri," Henry said.

Latangi nodded, smiled. *"Shiggiri,"* she said again, correcting some error he'd made in pronouncing it that he couldn't detect.

"And this?" Henry had asked, indicating the motel. "What will happen to this?"

"It will be sold, Mr. Henry, if a buyer is located." She raised a finger in the air. "With one provision, though, Mr. Henry. If you would like to stay, you must be allowed to stay. Was this not my promise upon your arrival?"

"Yes," Henry said.

"Well, then," Latangi said. "This elephant is faithful one hundred percent."

Henry looked at Latangi. She laughed. "Dr. Seuss?" she said. *"Horton Hatches the Egg?"*

"Yes," Henry said.

"This is one of the books that taught me English."

"Me too, I'm sure." Henry laughed. "And if you can't sell the motel?" Henry said. "What then?"

"I am optimist," Latangi said.

"I'm afraid I'm not," Henry said.

"I don't agree, Mr. Henry. No. Pessimist does not go home to" — she waved her hand — "to such a place to save someone. That is not pessimist."

"No," Henry said. "It's crazy."

"Crazy, yes," Latangi said. "My Mohit was a poet. Do you think I do not know crazy? And I believe you are more like Mohit than you acknowledge."

"Thank you," Henry said.

"Bhalo thakben," Latangi said. "It means 'good-bye,' Mr. Henry. It means 'keep well.'"

"Keep well," Henry said.

Latangi wiped tears from her eyes and smiled. "You will keep well, Mr. Henry. I am certain. One hundred percent."

He was not well, of course, but he was better. He drove through the darkness, Katrell Sparrow and Marge asleep behind him, and he listened to the clatter in his head, the shouts and whispers: his mother, Amy, Father Ferguson, Mary. And strangers: Vietnamese children's voices, their singing sharp and metallic; black children's voices, spilling through an open church door, clear and joyous; the Alabama Sacred Harp Singers performing "Antioch," a recording his father had played again and again, the men's and women's voices stacked one upon the other like heavy bricks. He felt as though he were watching from the bank as men and women in white robes stood knee-deep in a stream, prepared to be baptized. *Expect to be landed upon the shore,* a preacher shouted, and music swirled through it all, koras and slide guitars, trumpets and drums. Henry did not know why he was no longer frightened, but he wasn't. *You will keep well,* Latangi had told him, and perhaps he believed her after all.

He realized that what he would miss most of all, after Latangi herself, was Mohit's study—the bare white walls, the desk, the cot in the corner with its simple blanket. All of that, yes, but not so much that as the spirit Henry had come to believe the room possessed, the hold that it could claim on him simply by his stepping into it, taking a seat at the desk, lying on the cot.

Three more hours until they reached New Orleans. Too many to finish the drive tonight. And what would they face when they arrived? Henry had no idea. A roadblock? A police interrogation? A sign demanding that they turn around? He thought about *The Wizard of Oz,* the door to the Emerald City slammed shut, a gruff voice behind it barking that the wizard would not see them, that they might as well go home.

He was too exhausted to be driving, too unsteady. The clatter had grown louder and louder. At the next motel he spotted, a Travelodge, he veered into the parking lot. Marge and Katrell stirred when the car stopped.

"I'll be right back," he said quietly, but Marge sat up quickly, as if he'd shouted.

"Sit tight," he said. "I'll get the rooms." And she nodded and fell back again against her seat, closed her eyes.

"Dear Lord," Henry heard her say just before he closed the car door, "the dream I was having."

Inside, Henry tapped the bell on the desk. When no one appeared, he tapped it again. The clock on the wall read 2:15. *Love not the world,* Henry heard in his head, *neither the things that are in the world.* Finally, a woman appeared. She looked Indian too, though much younger than Latangi, and she was wearing a T-shirt and jeans, black hair pulled back, knotted in a ponytail. *Ole Miss,* the T-shirt said in blue and red letters.

"Two rooms?" Henry asked. "Do you have two rooms?"

"Yes, yes," the woman said, nodding. She began typing on the computer keyboard. "License and credit card, please."

"I'll pay you cash," Henry said.

The woman stopped typing. She looked at him, suspicious.

"I'm from New Orleans," Henry said. "I'm going back there."

"Okay," the woman said and resumed typing. "Cash."

"Are you from India?" Henry asked.

The woman stopped typing again and stared at Henry. "No," she said, impatient. "I'm American. A citizen."

"So sorry," Henry said. "I just asked because, well, I have a friend in Virginia. She has a motel. She's Indian."

"Pakistan," the woman said, her tone softer now. "My parents came here from Pakistan."

"I see," Henry said. "For *this?*" He tapped on the counter to indicate that he meant the motel. "Why *this?*"

"That's exactly what I asked them. 'This is what we do,' my father said. 'This is the opportunity we are given. Motels. Convenience stores.' He said Americans didn't want them."

"Too much work, I guess," Henry said. "How old were you?"

"Thirteen," the woman said. "From Islamabad. To Mississippi," she said. "To Goodman, Mississippi."

"That's where we are?" Henry said.

"That's where we are," the young woman answered, shaking her head, the life she knew—however difficult it had been—suddenly pulled from under her feet. "Want to guess how many Pakistanis there are in all of Mississippi?" She placed two room keys on the counter, the key chains gold plastic triangles with numbers printed on them.

"Guess," she said, smiling now.

Henry picked up the keys. Rooms 27 and 28. He held them up. "Twenty-seven or twenty-eight?" he said.

"Close enough," she said, shaking her head. "Close enough. I hope you get some sleep."

The room had two beds. Katrell Sparrow sprawled out on one of them. He had not even gotten under the covers. Marge was next door. When they arrived, she'd opened the connecting door between the two rooms. She'd leaned in and, smiling, offered Katrell a toothbrush and toothpaste.

"Anything else you need?" she asked him.

"No, ma'am," he said.

"Then get some rest. We'll see what tomorrow brings."

Henry took a shower. When he stepped back out into the room, he found Katrell already asleep. It was after three a.m. The clatter in his head had quieted. He lay down and heard the room's air conditioner humming. He could see it stirring the heavy curtains in the window, a line of fluorescent light appearing and disappearing as the curtains fluttered. Eventually, his eyes adjusted to the dark, and he could see Katrell's long limbs, one of his arms dangling off the mattress. He could hear his breathing: smooth and deep and silent, no rattle or wheeze. *I write unto you, little children, because your sins are forgiven you.*

Quiet, quiet.

Shouldn't this boy, this young man, be afraid? Or at least thoroughly perplexed by this journey, by the people he had given himself over to? How had he come to be here? How had all the losses he'd endured, the poverty in which he had lived, led to this? Shouldn't he be blind with bitterness and rage?

Henry realized that *he,* of course, was the one who had been endlessly fearful and perplexed, endlessly injured, endlessly bitter. *She looked into the distance,* he heard in his head. He tried to stop himself from picturing Edna Pontellier standing there on the beach, stripping naked, stepping into the water. He tried to see, instead, the words, as though he were merely reading: *She looked into the distance, and the old terror flamed up for an instant, then sank again.* He listened to his own breathing. He set his own terror aside, let it slide away, let it sink.

Quiet, quiet.

He listened to the air conditioner's humming, watched how the breeze stirred the curtains, how it covered and uncovered the strip of light. Tomorrow, he thought, tomorrow—but he kept himself from thinking any more, any further. He closed his eyes and slept.

Sixteen

HE WOKE up to wind and rain. He could hear the wind rattling the room's windows, whistling beneath the door. He could hear the rain beating against the hoods of cars in the parking lot and against the squat motel's flat roof, pouring over the gutters, splashing onto the pavement. Katrell Sparrow was still asleep, one arm still dangling off the mattress.

Henry closed his eyes and listened; he imagined New Orleans filling up again, water pouring once more through the breached levees, running through the streets, battered houses washed away, more bodies floating facedown, shirts and dresses billowing out like tattered sails, like burial shrouds.

Keep well, Latangi had told him. *Bhalo thakben.*

On the TV he'd heard the reporters and anchors, the politicians and stranded residents—he'd heard them all say the same thing: *This doesn't look like America. How can this be America? Who could believe that we would allow this to happen here?*

Keep well, Latangi had said. He listened to the wind and rain. How was he going to keep well?

243

When Henry began taking the pills Rusty Campbell had given him, he'd been afraid that somehow he would lose his place in this life the way one lost one's place in a book, turning page after page in search of a familiar line or scene, unable to locate it. What if taking the pills left him wanting only peace and quiet, content to leave To-mas Otxoa to whatever fate might await him, content to forget Amy, to let his past—his mother, his father, Mary—slip away? The clamor and clatter, the music and voices, the passages from books, the lines from poems, the snatches of conversations and dreams—they were all part of his memory, the material from which, *of which,* his self was composed. But he understood now that he did not have to forsake that self, that he still remembered all of it: the sweat on his father's brow, the musty scent of his gray suit, the scratch and pop of the record in its groove before the music began, the hand clutching the steering wheel, the white crescents in his father's fingernails against the bass's black neck, the weariness in his voice. *Don't go looking for it. Don't.*

He had wanted to go looking. He had wanted to see that place where his father had gone. How dark it must be, a lightless cavern, an ocean of unimaginable depth, but was it empty as well, as empty as Mohit's monastic study? Or was it a place of swirling memory and sensation, of ceaseless clatter and clamor?

Yes, he had wanted to know, definitively, where exactly his father had gone, and how could he know unless he followed behind him, called out again and again for him, listened for an answer?

How easy it would be, really, to get up, open the door, and walk out right now into the wind and rain, to disappear down the bank of the highway, drenched and anonymous, into the brush and pine woods. And then? And then what? What would he have to do? Find some body of water—sea or lake or swamp—to step into? Find a rope? A gun? Could he not simply lie down and let sleep overtake him?

What courage would be required?

Not courage. No. *Cruelty.*

There was Marge and Katrell Sparrow. He couldn't just leave them here.

And Amy, Mary, Latangi.

He heard Katrell Sparrow stir. Henry opened his eyes and saw the boy sit up.

What was there to say to him, to this child who had not invited a moment of the loss and grief and sorrow into his life? And to the thousands and thousands of others visited, as this child had been visited, by wreck and ruin?

"It's raining," Katrell said quietly, barely a whisper, rubbing his eyes.

"It is," Henry said, sitting up as well so that he faced the boy, their feet nearly touching. "How did you sleep?"

"I don't know yet," Katrell said, shaking his head side to side. "I'm still too sleepy."

Henry thought about Marge, what she would do now. She would laugh at the boy, find pleasure in his grogginess, in his reply.

How did you sleep?

I don't know yet. I'm too sleepy.

A wonder. It's all a wonder, Amy had said.

A wonder. A wander. *That too,* she'd said.

God, how he missed her. Just like in a book, the lousiest of love stories, his heart ached and ached. How could he say good-bye to the dead, to the clatter, to the chaos inside him? He must say good-bye, but how?

Henry heard tapping on the door between the two rooms. Marge.

"We're awake," Henry said.

"Rise and shine!" he heard Marge call out.

"Just a few minutes," Henry said.

She rapped three more times on the door, a kind of salute. "See you in the lobby for breakfast!"

"Okay," Henry said. Like in a book, the rain had stopped. Marge had appeared, and the rain had stopped.

Just beyond Jackson, still three hours from New Orleans, the destruction was already apparent. The trees—long lines of pine beside the highway—had simply snapped in the ferocious winds. Power lines had been ripped down; metal towers had collapsed; houses sagged, roofless, blue tarps thrown over them. Marge was driving again, and Henry kept nodding, kept answering *Yes, yes,* as Katrell Sparrow pointed to anything that caught his eye. "Look," Katrell would say as they approached a sagging billboard stand or the twisted ruins of a gas station or a concrete slab covered by what had been a building but was now merely a crumbling pile of bricks. "You see that?"

Henry saw it all, of course, and began to worry about Katrell encountering what lay ahead. Surely by now there wouldn't be anything so horrible and grotesque that the boy should not be allowed to see it. Surely by now all the bodies had been discovered and removed, the dead animals carted away.

As they made their way closer and closer to New Orleans, past Ponchatoula, past Lake Maurepas, Katrell stopped pointing, stopped asking Henry if he too had seen this or that. There was too much now, too many snapped trees and dangling wires and damaged buildings, too many piles of rubble. They all simply looked out at the ruin. Even Marge seemed stunned into silence. She tapped her fingernails on the steering wheel and from time to time shook her head. But she didn't say anything; she didn't seem to know what to say. Nearly every tree was snapped in half or torn from the ground; nearly every structure had been leveled. Dirt and sand spilled across the highway; lining the road was an endless array of detritus: overturned boats, giant spools of black wire, crumbled cinder blocks, tree stumps, rusted refrigerators, abandoned cars, a backyard swing set, a microwave oven balanced atop a child's high chair, a row of saplings, their root balls knotted in burlap, lying on the ground like the bodies of executed soldiers. The sky was clear; the sun was shining. There were no birds anywhere.

Here was the land of the dead, Henry thought. There seemed to be no one anywhere. For miles and miles there were no other cars. He had expected—well, what had he expected? Activity and enterprise, recovery and rebuilding. He had expected *something*. Instead, there was nothing.

And then, up ahead, with the skyline of downtown now clearly visible in the distance, Henry saw what he'd figured they would see as they neared the city: a roadblock, bright red plastic barrels stretched across the highway, orange and white wooden sawhorses behind them, each displaying a sign that said *Do Not Enter*. Marge slowed as they approached.

What was the story they would tell? Henry had known all along that they would have to have a story to tell, that it would have to be a good one: why they were there, why they should be allowed to enter the city, why they *needed* to be allowed. And Henry knew what he planned to say; he'd known that since they left, though he'd not told Marge, though he'd not really even told himself. The words were just there, ready to be spoken, the only words he figured would be sufficiently compelling. *My father,* he would say. *My father was here for the storm, and I saw him, I saw him on the news, still here in the city, in a building I own, and I am here to get him because he is old and he is not well, is of course not well, because why else would he not have left, why else would he not have called out for rescue, for someone to save him, but we are here all the way from Virginia, and all we need is to get to this one small building, an old grocery store on Magazine Street, and find him if he is still, if he is still—*

But there was no one to whom he might tell this story, to whom he might beg to be allowed entrance. Beyond the red plastic barrels and the orange and white wooden sawhorses there was no one, not for as far as they could see ahead, so what were they to do? What else was there to do but drive past the roadblock, ignore it, drive until someone stopped them, asked what in the hell they thought they were doing, where in the hell they thought they were going.

"Here we are," Henry said as they stopped at the roadblock, and he turned to Marge.

"Well, I guess it *is* about noon," she said. "Must be lunch break." She looked over at Henry and laughed. She was afraid, though. Henry saw that for the first time—that for all her lighthearted banter, she was afraid of what they were going to find.

"Do we wait?" Henry asked her.

"I don't believe we wait," Marge said. "There's no hiding in any case. Sooner or later we'll be spotted. They want to turn us around, they can turn us then."

"Okay," Henry said. He motioned for Katrell to get out with him. The red barrels were weighted with concrete, but they managed to nudge two of them far enough to the side to create a path Marge could fit her car through. Then they moved three of the sawhorses and, once Marge had driven through, put everything back where it had been.

It felt strange to Henry—sickening and strange—to be standing there in the middle of the highway with this boy whose grandfather he'd struck and killed. What had he been thinking to allow Katrell to make this trip, to allow him to see all this? He put his arm around Katrell's shoulder. "Thank you," he said. "For the help with this."

"Yes, sir," Katrell said.

They got back into the car. "That's not all," Henry said to Marge. "That can't possibly be all."

"We'll just see," Marge said, and they drove on, slowly, debris piled everywhere, tree branches and torn carpets, refrigerators and sofas, dirty clothes spilling from garbage bags, tattered blankets and curtains, plastic children's toys. Henry thought about Endly's and all the discarded items people had left outside the door. How was there so much stuff in the world? And then again he saw Tomas, inside, looking out. Where would he have gone now, almost a week later? He could not still be there. What had he been thinking, that he could save Tomas?

After they'd driven a few more miles, Henry directed Marge toward the fork in the highway that would lead them downtown. They approached another roadblock with the same red barrels. Here, though, was a police car with flashing lights parked directly in the center of the road.

"Okay, now," Marge said, creeping forward, lowering her window. "Here we go."

An officer stepped from the police car, and Marge began rifling through her purse, no doubt searching for her license. Henry could see already, from the man's stern expression, that they would be turned around, denied entrance. This officer would not give a damn what story Henry told him.

Henry shut his eyes, just for a moment. He shut them not to quiet but to register—was that the right word, *register*?—the cacophony, the clatter and clamor: Latangi's lilting voice and Skip James singing, *Crow Jane, Crow Jane, hold your head up high*, and his mother, *I'm content, I'm content*, and Tomas Otxoa, *You must speak in a Christian language*, and pebbles blowing across his great-uncle's shoes high on the mountain and the car, his car, striking the old man, all the blood there, all the ruin before him.

He opened his eyes and turned to Marge. "I'm sorry," he said. "I've got to do this."

"What?" Marge said, still rifling through her purse, so nervous that her shoulders were shaking.

He looked back at Katrell. "Take care of her, you hear me?" he said, hearing Mrs. Hughes's voice in his own. *You behave yourself.*

He stepped from the car.

"No!" he heard Marge cry out, but he didn't turn to look at her.

"Get back in the vehicle," the officer said, clear and straightforward, and Henry saw him place his hand on the holster at his hip.

"Listen, man," Henry said, and he lurched to the side as though he were drunk and fumbled at his belt.

"Back in the vehicle!" the officer shouted again.

"We've been driving, you know, forever," Henry said, shaking his head. "I've just got—" He pointed down to the side of the highway and began walking.

He wouldn't shoot him—a staggering drunk—in the back, would he, just because he was heading off to pee? Henry kept walking.

"Officer! Officer!" he heard Marge calling, and he did look back now for just a second and saw Marge holding something—a sheet of paper—out of the car and shaking it, waving it for the officer to see. Henry kept walking, threw one arm up, one finger raised, to signal that he would just be a minute, he would be right back once he'd relieved himself.

"Fucking hell!" Henry heard the officer shout. He didn't turn around. Either the officer would shoot him or he wouldn't. He walked down the embankment toward the road below.

"Son of a bitch," the officer said. "Crazy drunk motherfucker."

Henry could see exactly where he was. City Park Avenue. Canal Street. St. Patrick Cemetery. He kept walking, waiting to hear the officer fire. Would he hear the shot before the bullet struck him? Or was it too quick, too small a slice of time to be heard?

He must be, he decided, out of sight by now. He must be.

So he started to run.

Seventeen

I'M GOIN' away, to a world unknown. Henry shook the words from his head. No. No. Not a world unknown. He was home. True, the ground beneath his feet was a mosaic of dried mud—amber, fragile as glass, cracking and then turning to dust with his every step. True, a thick gray film coated every oak leaf and branch, every fence post and street sign, every car roof and window and front porch and shrub. The air was thick with an oily septic stink. And every house, every building, was inscribed with the awful spray-painted hieroglyphs he'd seen on TV: who had entered and when and how many dead. Even so. He was home.

He could feel the entire city circling him, the clatter now tuned to a familiar pitch, not of the ruin around him but of memory—lines from Whitman he'd memorized at fifteen and the languid grace of Pistol Pete, his mother laughing with her friend Marianna Greco, the scent of magnolia and stench of skunk, algae-covered seawall steps, blazing New Year's Eve bonfires on the levee, the old stereo's glow, his father's eyes squinting behind his glasses, brow furrowed, the scrawled note left behind: *I'm worried now, but I won't be worried long.*

And the city wasn't empty. He'd been wrong. It was far from empty. There were people working—hauling scraps of metal and wood from warehouses and storefronts, repairing telephone and electric lines, steering backhoes through rubble—though Henry seemed to be a ghost among them, invisible and silent, even as the cacophony hammered away inside his head. He walked up Canal Street toward Carrollton. No one looked up from his work; no one even noticed him passing. Maybe eventually he'd come across the police or National Guard; he'd seen them on TV marching in a line through the French Quarter to prevent looting. He imagined them stopping him, pinning him facedown in the dirt, and hauling him off—but where would they take him? On the news, in that first week after the storm, he'd seen the shots of Parish Prison and its flooded cells. He'd seen the inmates herded onto the Broad Street overpass in their bright orange shirts and pants, heads slumped in the heat and humidity—not even handcuffed, merely waiting for rescue, waiting for the water to recede so they could be transported out of town to another prison. Or perhaps, Henry thought, they'd simply been set loose, left to wander on their own without food or water or shelter until they finally expired.

Henry was already thirsty; his clothes were already soaked with sweat. He'd hidden for a while in the St. Patrick Cemetery, resting his back against the cool marble of one of the larger family mausoleums. He'd looked over the damage in the cemetery, marble doors to crypts wedged open, stone vases upended, crumbling brick and concrete scattered across the narrow paths between the tombs. Two black wrought-iron gates, *Charity Hospital* inscribed in the iron trellis above them, had been pulled off their hinges and lay, still latched together, on the ground. Henry figured they marked the section where the indigent and anonymous who'd died at Charity were buried. The headstones inside the gates looked like giant books with tattered covers bleached white in the heat and rain and sun.

Henry soon realized that no one would be coming after him, that no officers had been dispatched to track him down. He wondered what the officer who'd approached the car had told Marge and Katrell, if he'd simply instructed them to turn around, to head back home, to forget about their drunken idiot of a friend who had wandered off alone.

What would Marge have told him? That Henry was not a drunken idiot but merely desperate, maybe a little unhinged, that he'd come all this way determined to find someone, an old man he'd seen on the television, an old man he knew who seemed to have wound up in an abandoned store? Okay, so yes, the idea was more than a little crazy, Marge would say—Henry could hear her saying it, could see the sweet knowing smile she'd present to the officer.

Yeah, well, give me a break, Henry imagined the man telling her. *Who's not alone here? Who's not crazy? Let's just hope for his sake he makes it.*

Yes, he was alone. He thought about the commerce he'd once had here—with Amy, with Amy's friends, with the folks at Endly's. He thought about the crowded halls at Ben Franklin, the crush of students between classes, his colleagues. He thought about the school building itself. What remained and what was gone? He remembered a Chekhov story he'd once taught, just a few pages long, about a carriage driver whose son had just died. On the evening the man returned to work, neither of his fares—an officer in a greatcoat and then three young men at the conclusion of a night of drinking—would listen when he spoke, when he told them that he had lost his son. No one would attend his grief. And so the story ended with the man alone in the stables speaking to his horse, a ragged old mare, recounting his son's funeral, his trip to the hospital to retrieve his son's clothes, the myriad small details that he was desperate for someone to hear.

Who would listen to all the grief—the loss and sorrow and despair—that needed to be spoken here? He felt the weight of that grief, so much heavier than his own, begin to settle inside him. He had not suffered the way so many thousands of others had suffered. He had not been left behind, had not had to climb to some rooftop, filthy and thirsty and starved, and wait day after day after day to be saved. He had not watched his home get washed away, had not wound up wading through—or, worse, floating facedown in—the oily stink. He did not lose a wife, a child—at least, he did not lose them in the storm. And all he *had* lost in his life—well, he had been given years, and he still had years now before him to recover, to pay his debts, to ask for forgiveness, to secure some reward.

He had years before him. He tried to imagine it, these years. He couldn't.

Had Marge and Katrell done what they had no doubt been ordered to do—turned around and begun the long trip back to Virginia? What else was there for them to do? There was nowhere they might wait for him, no way to know when he might return. He hoped that they were not frantic with worry, that Katrell had not been overwhelmed by what Henry had done, had not feared what Henry in those first few moments had feared—that the officer would remove his gun from its holster, raise it and aim and fire. He hoped Marge had said to the boy, *Oh, he'll be just fine. That Henry Garrett's a smart one. We'll see him back in Virginia before long.*

So this was it, then; he would make his way to Magazine Street, to Endly's, and then—what? What if he found Tomas Otxoa? What would he do then? He had no idea. He had no car, no way to save him, no way to save himself. *Walk with me,* he could say, wrapping his arms around the old man, steering him outside. *Walk with me until we are too weary to walk any farther. We'll lie here beside the road, close our eyes until morning, set off again.*

Make a way out of no way.

How absurd. They wouldn't even make it out of the city. How was it that he never thought anything through?

But there would be people in Virginia waiting for them, ready to help: Latangi, Marge, Rusty Campbell, Amy. All the others who'd given money. Imagine their surprise if Henry and Tomas simply appeared, as he had appeared a month ago, tired and dirty but prepared to be saved.

Henry turned at Carrollton Avenue and headed uptown. Here, in Mid-City, was the neighborhood where his father had been raised. Henry hadn't known his grandparents—they'd died young, his grandfather before Henry was born, his grandmother when he was three or four—but his father had once shown Henry and Mary the house where he'd grown up, a block off of Bienville Boulevard, a narrow white clapboard shotgun with green shutters, a statue of the Virgin Mary out front and plantain trees around back. About the only thing Henry had known about his grandparents was that his grandfather had worked as an engineer at the Dixie Brewery on Tulane Avenue, that his grandmother had been a secretary there when they met. He'd had no idea what his father's childhood had been like. *Maybe a brewery wasn't the best place for him to work,* his father had once told Henry, shaking his head, but Henry was too young to grasp what his father meant.

"That's it," his father had said when he'd pulled up in front of the house. "That one." He pointed.

Henry and Mary waited for whatever story might follow, but their

256

father just sat there in silence, staring at the house. One of the shutters in front was crooked, a few of the slats broken, the green paint chipped; it leaned away from the house.

"Does it look any different?" Mary finally asked, but their father didn't answer; he didn't seem to hear her question.

Henry watched him take off his glasses and wipe them on his shirt. Then he put the glasses back on, started the car, and drove off. He seemed to have forgotten about Henry and Mary in the backseat.

They'd looked at each other, bewildered, frightened. Somehow, they understood—from their father's posture? from the way he drove? maybe just from the silence itself?—not to ask any more questions. Even so, they were children. They could not have known what was going on with their father, what he had been thinking. What memories had seared their way into his head? What clatter and chaos, what confusion and sorrow, had he endured?

Where had he gone? Henry couldn't believe that he still didn't have an answer to this question. Even if he couldn't answer the thousands upon thousands of other questions he had, shouldn't he have been provided—*offered, granted, delivered*—this one answer, just this one?

He walked and walked, down Carrollton all the way to St. Charles, an hour of walking, maybe two, every familiar block and building made strange by the dirt and dust and stench, by the fallen trees and dangling power lines, by the shells of battered cars, by the thud and shuffle of his own feet, by the empty sky. He began to notice others walking as he walked, block to block, each of them wading through, as Henry waded, the debris scattered across the sidewalk—discarded surgical gloves, smashed water bottles, paper towels, cardboard boxes, broken pipes, upended furniture, rubber boots—as if they were all imprisoned in the same ceaseless dream, the very one he'd started having when the clatter and clamor and chaos began, a wandering phantom or mendicant or nomad or hermit, the whole world in ruins around him.

Could it be that he'd known, long before the storm, that this moment lay ahead, that so many would find themselves forsaken, left to wander these streets alone? No, he had thought the destruction would be merely his own, not the entire city's.

No, not the *entire* city's; the palaces on St. Charles Avenue—glorious homes with cut-glass windows and stone walls and trellised gardens—appeared to have been spared. The rusty waterlines marking the level to which the water had risen, etched across so many of the ruined houses he'd walked past, were nowhere in evidence here. A few windows were cracked, some trees torn from the ground. Otherwise, these grand houses had been spared. Even so, there might be dead inside them, Henry thought. Maybe there were hermits as well, survivors who had shut themselves away, subsisting on whatever had been stored in the mansions' bountiful cupboards, drinking wine for lack of water, beer for lack of bread.

And look, now, just as he'd imagined it: a figure, a young man, unshaven, hair unkempt, clothes gray with filth, emerged from a side door of one of these houses, a rust-colored stone mansion. Henry watched the man step out onto the side lawn, loosen his pants, and unleash a stream of piss into a long boxwood hedge. Did he belong there, Henry wondered, or had he broken in, found no one there, and decided to stay? When he noticed Henry looking, the young man solemnly waved, then headed back inside.

Henry continued walking. He noticed now that although here too gray dust covered the trees, the streetcar tracks along St. Charles Avenue were inexplicably shiny, almost golden in color, as if the force of the storm had miraculously scrubbed them clean. He thought of the story Tomas Otxoa had told him about the death of Bernardo Belaga, the drunk whom everyone in the town of Tolosa had believed was an idiot. One hot summer day, Tomas told Henry as he closed his eyes and sipped his gin, Bernardo had walked to the outskirts of Tolosa where there was a pig farm, and in the heat of the noon sun Bernardo climbed the metal rungs to the top of a grain silo. From there, he had fallen into the grain below and, buried beneath it, suffocated. The town's inhabitants lamented Bernardo's idiocy, certain that he had mistaken the silo for a cistern in which he would bathe and refresh himself, but Tomas said he and his brother, Joaquim, suspected a different explanation. They believed, actually, that only they possessed the truth of Bernardo's death—that he had been seduced by the golden ocean of grain beneath him, a beauty so bright and shimmering that he felt compelled to immerse himself in it, an immersion so complete that it would, of course, result in his death.

And Tomas had then opened his eyes, drained the last sip from his tumbler, and smiled sadly at Henry. "This would become one of Joaquim's best-loved stories. 'Our Icarus,' he named it. All Basque children read it in their schools."

"That's an awfully sad story for children," Henry had said, and Tomas had looked at him, clearly contemplating Henry's words.

"Well," Tomas had finally responded, "are children to be denied their sadness?"

Yes, Henry thought now, *I would spare every child, every single one, even a moment's sadness. I would spare them every loss, every disappointment, every misfortune, every grief.*

They will all—loss and misfortune and grief—arrive anyway, he thought. *They will all arrive unbidden, of their own accord. Why summon them?*

That was what his father had meant, what he had wanted to tell Henry: *Don't go looking for it.*

But he *had* gone looking, *had* summoned loss. He'd done exactly what his father had warned him not to do, had let himself succumb to the sorrow, the grief, the clatter and chaos, the awful storm inside him. But he had not summoned this—he had not wished for all this ruin.

As Henry approached Audubon Park, he spotted a dog wandering toward him down the allée of oaks at the park's entrance, the first animal he'd seen in the city. The dog was thin, with dark splotches—scabs or sores—scattered across its mangy fur. The dog didn't seem to see Henry; it moved past him without lifting its head. Henry wondered how it had survived all this time, what food it could have found. He thought about the animals in the park's zoo. Had they been saved or left to starve—or set free from their cages to roam the park and then head out beyond it, lions and leopards scavenging among the ruins like wolves, feeding on squirrels and rats and, when those were gone, trash? He imagined elephants rumbling down St. Charles, monkeys swinging through the oaks, a lion stepping out to block his path, *head held high and furious with hunger*—whose line was that? Mohit's?

Oh, Latangi. *You have lost everything, yes?* she had said to him. Now here he was, having lost it all again.

He turned at Upperline toward the river, toward Magazine Street. He was almost there.

He had imagined the sort of destruction he'd seen on TV, not simply the storm's damage—cracked windows and twisted aluminum siding and flooded floors—but damage from looters as well: overturned shelves, broken bottles, pried-open doors. But there had been, of course, nothing to loot at Endly's, and clearly Henry had not even remembered or bothered to lock the store's glass doors. He braced himself, took a breath, stepped inside.

Someone, someone, had been here. Someone had found the broom in back and swept into a small pile the bits of glass from the one window that had cracked, struck by a branch or a stone or a bottle perhaps, some object lifted in the wind and hurled against a corner of the window, a spiderweb of lines running through the glass, the corner fallen away but the rest of the window intact. The broom leaned now against one of the two checkout counters, the toy cash register there as well, its drawer closed. Henry pushed the button that opened the drawer. *Mary had a little lamb.* There was still money—a few ones, a five, some quarters—in the till. The store's shelves were undamaged, the floor unflooded, his father's bass still there, untouched, standing in a corner, leaning there as if waiting to be played. He walked to the middle of the store and first whispered—his voice felt unfamiliar—then called out.

"Tomas? Tomas?"

Inside his head, Henry saw him again, saw him peering out through that one cracked window, eyes blank or searching or wet with fear, the cardboard box tight against his chest.

"Tomas?"

He did not believe, not really, that there'd be an answer. Even so, he called out again.

"Tomas?"

He listened, waited.

What more, he wondered, *can this world have in store for me? What more can I, can anyone, expect?*

Eighteen

HENRY SAT at the front desk of the Ganesha Motel, head clear for the moment—and for the longest time now—of the clatter and chaos, the wreck and ruin. He did not know where precisely to cast his gratitude: to the heavens, to medicine, to those who had taken him in and cared for him for no other reason than that he had landed here. He looked out to the motel's parking lot. A year ago, alone and exhausted and undone, he had stopped his car and stepped into this office, and Latangi Chakravarty, in her red and orange sari, fingernails adorned with glitter, feet clad in golden sandals, had greeted him, refused his money, and offered him a room.

A year ago. And then the accident, the awful death of Marion Hughes, the discovery of Mohit's poem, the return to New Orleans, all the craziness, the loss and grief, the desperate rush toward—well, finally, ultimately, toward *this*.

Three days ago, on the anniversary of Katrina's landfall, he'd paid his quiet tribute by calling his sister in Baltimore. He'd told Mary he was just checking in, but she'd understood why he'd called, why he'd want to talk to her. Of course she'd understood, and she'd been grateful. She'd already decided to return to New Orleans, to be part of its rebuilding. The art museum there, in City Park, was looking for a new director; the previous one had decided to stay in San Francisco, where she'd gone after the storm to be near her daughter and son-in-law and their children. Mary had gotten the job. In a couple of weeks she'd be leaving Baltimore and moving to New Orleans.

When she first told Henry that she was going back, she'd asked if he remembered the time they'd ridden their bikes all the way to the park to see the King Tut exhibit, how the street that stretched from the edge of the park to the museum had been painted blue to suggest the Nile, golden-crested waves and golden-scaled fish scattered throughout the blue, golden stars and a golden crescent moon shining there as well as if the night sky were reflected in the water, and though Henry had not remembered it until that moment, until Mary had described it in such detail to him, he remembered it as she spoke—remembered the thick black wide-seated Schwinn he'd had and Mary's smaller sleeker red one, tassels on the handlebars, a silver thumb bell perched there too. He remembered crossing Bayou St. John and seeing the old men on the bridge hauling up crab nets, shaking the skittery crabs out into wooden baskets. He remembered their sad dark faces beneath their straw hats, their wide hands as they tied the chicken necks into the nets and lowered them back into the water.

All the art she'd encountered with their mother, she told Henry, all the canvases on the walls and all the pictures in books and all the galleries into which she'd been led, but it was that one day, riding along that bright blue street as if they were magically pedaling above the water, that she'd truly fallen in love with painting and art and museums, with the magic they were capable of creating.

"I remember," Henry told her. "I do." And it occurred to him that there were probably a million other things to remember from his childhood if he let Mary guide him, if he relied on her memory rather than his own.

"Maybe you'll come down once I'm settled in," Mary said.

"Sure," Henry told her, though he wasn't ready to go back just yet.

That morning he'd gotten up early and driven into Marimore and gone to breakfast at What a Blessing. He'd wanted to check in on Katrell Sparrow, see how he was doing. Katrell had been hired to help with the early-morning baking each day before school, a job Marge had gotten for him. She'd had some dealings with Maurice Rose, the owner, when one of his employees walked off with the entire contents of the store register. Rose had wanted Judge Martin to go easy on that young man, whose father was a fellow elder at Maurice Rose's church, and Marge had told him that she'd see to it that Judge Martin fully understood. And Judge Martin had done— as of course everyone did with anything Marge requested—exactly what she'd asked him to do, sentencing the young man to the time he'd served in the county jail directly after they'd caught him and he couldn't make bail. All the money he'd taken was still stashed in a plastic Food Lion bag in his car trunk. He'd felt too guilty, he told Judge Martin, to spend it.

Henry had gotten to know Maurice Rose and liked him. He was tough on Katrell, demanding he be there on time, insisting he keep his grades up if he wanted to continue working at the bakery, expecting him to show up at church Wednesday nights and Sunday mornings. Whenever Henry slipped away from the motel for breakfast or lunch at What a Blessing, Maurice Rose stepped from behind the counter, wiped his hands on his long apron, and shook Henry's hand. They talked about jazz and about the band that Maurice Rose had assembled, a few old guys from the Rivermont Senior Center, some who'd played in bands years ago, not jazz but blues and funk and Texas swing.

A week later Henry brought in his father's bass and offered it to Maurice Rose. "I've kept this for years and years," Henry told him. "It's about time somebody played it."

Maurice Rose admired the instrument, running his hand over the wide body, then he pulled it toward him. He plucked each of the four strings, played up and back down one scale—B-flat, Henry saw— and then another. "That's a mighty nice one," he said, nodding. "I couldn't take it."

"I'd like you to, though," Henry said.

Maurice Rose shook his head.

"What if Katrell Sparrow was interested in learning?" Henry said. "Would you take it then?"

"Well, I guess I'd hold on to it if he wanted to learn."

"I think he will," Henry said.

And Katrell had indeed agreed to the lessons, to coming back twice a week after school. He confessed to Henry it gave him a reason to quit football, which was proving to be a lot harder than he'd expected. "I'm just too skinny," he said. "One hit by those big dudes and I go flying."

Katrell had been living with his aunt Celee and his cousin Stacey the last six months, ever since his grandmother had passed away from kidney complications related to her diabetes. Henry had attended the funeral along with Marge, and they'd both been shocked to learn that Mrs. Hughes had been only fifty-seven. She'd looked thirty years older.

During his eulogy the minister mentioned Marion's death, the sudden tragedy of it and the pain that it had caused her, and Henry expected the gathering to turn to look at him sitting in the back row with Marge, but not a single person did. Instead they listened as the minister announced, "Here is a song of rising up, a song of degrees," and they all solemnly intoned *Amen*.

"The One Hundred Twenty-Seventh Psalm," the minister went on, his Bible open in one hand, the other raised above his head. *"Except the Lord build this house,"* he read, *"they labor in vain to build it."* Henry remembered seeing the first half of this verse on a sign outside of one of the churches along the highway. Maybe it had been this one.

The congregation responded: *Amen*.

"Except the Lord keep the city," the minister continued, *"the watchman waketh but in vain."* Amen.

"It is vain for you to rise up early, to sit up late, to eat the bread of sorrows: for so He giveth his beloved sleep." Amen.

"Lo, children are a heritage of the Lord: and the fruit of the womb is His reward." Here he looked down at Katrell seated in the front row. *Amen*.

"Happy is the man that hath his quiver full of them: they shall not be ashamed." He closed the Bible and raised both of his arms above his head. *"They shall not be ashamed,"* he repeated, *"but they shall speak with the enemies in the gate."*

Amen.

As usual, Henry couldn't follow the actual meaning of these verses, and he wondered if those around him could—or perhaps they'd heard them so many times they'd become a kind of comforting music, somber and beautiful.

Surely, Henry said to himself, hearing the minister's resonant baritone, *I have eaten the bread of sorrows.*

Yes indeed. He'd eaten his fill of the bread of sorrows. So many had.

A wire basket was passed around to collect the funds needed to pay what the minister called "Sister Hughes's final obligations." Then the service was over, and Henry and Marge stood as, row by row, the gathered mourners filed out behind the casket. Many shook his hand as they walked past, nearly half of them wearing gold ribbons on their dresses or jackets to signify that they were family.

When they arrived back at the motel, Henry thanked Marge for going with him to the funeral. "Not just that, of course," he said. "Thank you for everything."

"I'll tell you what," Marge said, switching off her car. "You don't know this because it all happened before you landed here, but I needed this. Charlie could tell you. Rusty Campbell could tell you too. I needed to do some good. I needed someone to help. I'd had the life kicked out of me in about a hundred different ways. Not just the cancer scare. That was just one part. There's so many others it'd take two weeks and a gallon of box wine to get through."

"I'd be happy to listen," Henry said. "All you've done for me."

"It's been something, hasn't it?" Marge said.

"Yes, it has," Henry said, and they sat there a moment in silence, both of them shaking their heads.

What Marge had managed, Henry knew, must have been an incredible performance, and he wished he'd been present to view it. The last he'd seen when he staggered away from the highway was Marge waving something out the car window. He learned later that it was a letter with Judge Martin's signature on it, a letter stamped and embossed with the official seal of Judge Martin's office. It stated that Marge was a sheriff's sworn deputy with the Commonwealth of Virginia's solemn and express permission to enter the city of New Orleans to locate a family member of one Henry Archer Garrett. Of course, Marge had made it all up, had forged Judge Martin's signature.

The police officer had been more than a little skeptical, even when Marge pulled out a badge, which she'd taken from Judge Martin's desk drawer.

"You know good and well Virginia law don't mean a goddamn thing here," the officer said.

"You got any local judges handy?" Marge said, smiling. "Or have they all run off?"

"Run off," the officer said.

"Not you," Marge said. "Not me either. We just keep doing our jobs. If I could tell you the half of it." And Marge turned then to look back at Katrell, as if he were part of the great mystery.

"Who the hell is this Henry Garrett guy anyway?" the officer said.

"If I told you that," Marge said, "I'd have to kill you. Or at least *kiss* you."

Now the officer smiled at Marge, shook his head, and laughed. "He's not dangerous?" he asked.

"No, no, no. Not by a long shot," Marge told him. "He's not drunk either, by the way. That was all an act."

"A goddamn stupid one," the officer said. "I could have shot him."

"He must have known you wouldn't," Marge said.

"Well, I didn't know it," the officer said. "You know where he's going, where you're trying to get?"

"I don't, not exactly," Marge said. "A store on Magazine Street."

"Then you're going to need someone to get you uptown. There's too many streets still blocked. You wouldn't make it. Let me see what I can do."

Marge said that when the officer went over to his car to make a call on his radio, she turned to Katrell, smiled, and said, "I'm freely confessing right here and now to all the lies I've been telling. You believe the Lord will forgive me on account of the good I'm trying to do?"

"Yes, ma'am," Katrell answered.

"I do too," Marge said.

The officer came back. "It may take a while for someone to get over here," he said. "Probably an hour or two. You mind waiting?"

"Not at all," Marge said she told him. "How much trouble can that man get himself into?"

"You'd be surprised," the officer said.

"No, *you* would," she told him, shaking her head. "*You* would."

Two weeks before Mrs. Hughes's death, Latangi had married Iri Chakravarty, Mohit's brother. They'd held the ceremony in Virginia rather than in India. Latangi had wanted to return to Calcutta as Iri's wife, she told Henry, not his betrothed. "I am an old woman, not a young virgin," she said. It had taken Mohit's brother a while to set work aside at the hospital in Calcutta and fly to America, and Latangi had used the time to teach Henry everything he needed to know to run the motel. She'd hired Rusty Campbell to find a buyer, but he'd confessed to Henry that she'd told him to ask for a price so high no one would ever pay it.

"She wants you to have it, you know," Rusty Campbell told him. "She says the man she's marrying has more money than they'll ever need. I tried to tell her it's the land that's valuable and not the motel, that Exxon or BP might want the lot for a station, but she said she didn't want the place torn down. I told her you can't stipulate such a thing in a sale, but she says, 'I believe I can do whatever I want if I do not actually accept an offer, yes?' And I laughed and told her, 'Well, you've got me there with that one.'"

Latangi had asked Henry if he'd serve as a witness at the wedding. She'd asked Amy as well. It was clear to both of them what Latangi was up to, getting them back together for such an occasion. Latangi had asked Henry if he'd read something from Mohit's poem, and Henry had spent hours and hours hunting for the right passage.

I have searched and searched for my beloved, he recited in Latangi's apartment, which had been strung with bright flags and twinkling lights and filled with the scent of the spectacular meal Amy had brought with her, Bengali dishes Latangi had taught her to prepare—enough recipes for Amy to begin another book, Latangi had suggested to Henry, one that could prompt them to pay a visit to Calcutta together.

Henry had looked at Latangi, pretending scorn.

"I am a devil, yes," she'd said, smiling, lightly slapping his arm.

I have searched and searched for my beloved, Henry recited at the wedding, *in the syama vines and the eyes of the gazelle, in the flowers of the kurinci and the skylark's breath, only to see now, as the dawn's mist clears, you are already here beside me, hand to my hand, breast to my breast, hearts not two drums but a call and echo, call and echo, two silkworms weaving a sturdy house from fragile thread.*

And when Henry looked at Amy, he saw that she was weeping— smiling and weeping, nodding at him, hands raised to her chest— offering another small moment of hope that in time he might be fully forgiven. He would remain here in Virginia, he'd decided. He would remain as long as Amy remained, until he knew for certain if she would choose him again. Meanwhile, he would keep well. He would do everything he could to keep well.

The insurance money from the damage at Endly's hadn't been nearly enough to buy the motel, but it had allowed Henry to make some desperately needed repairs and refurbishments and to erect a sign out by the highway, exactly what Mohit had wanted, the neon-blue outline of an elephant's head with *The Ganesha Motel* in bright red above it. He took a picture and sent it via e-mail to Latangi.

Ōyān?nāraphula! May Ganeshvara guide you in your every endeavor! Latangi responded. *Do not forget that although he is portly, mischievous, and merry, he is also Lord of Obstacles, Remover of Impediments. I eagerly await word of your every success.* And then as a postscript she'd added, *I am contented but miss you, Mr. Henry. My blessings.*

And so far things had gone well. The motel had begun to get more and more business, and Henry had been able to hire two women to clean the rooms and another to take care of the front desk in the evening. He'd cleared out the items that remained of Mohit's import business, donating most of it to the junk store in Marimore, which was more than happy to have it.

He'd left Mohit's study exactly as it was, and though now and again he'd go out to dinner with Amy, most evenings he spent there in that room. He had a project that he'd spoken to no one about, not even Amy. He was afraid of what she'd think, afraid it would be the thing to convince her he'd not fully straightened out his head.

But he wasn't crazy; he wasn't. It might take him forever to accomplish what he had set out to do, but look at what Mohit had done all those years, what Mohit and Latangi had done together. Look at what they'd made, what they'd brought into being.

Every time he sat down now at Mohit's desk he thought about what had happened, what he'd found in New Orleans, at Endly's. At first, of course, he hadn't seen it. He'd seen his father's bass in the corner; he'd seen the bent dusty shelves. He'd called out for Tomas; he'd called and called until he understood, finally, that there wouldn't be an answer.

But then he'd seen it. On a low shelf at the end of the aisle, left there as if it were nothing to notice, the cardboard box Tomas had been holding against his chest as he peered out through the cracked window.

Henry had walked over, sat down. He'd slid the box off the shelf, let it fall into his lap. It wasn't empty, he could tell by the weight of it. He felt the chill of his sweat-soaked shirt against his chest. He pulled the top off the box, and inside were pages, hundreds of them, a manuscript, damp and discolored but not obliterated, the ink smudged but not washed away.

The words were inscrutable, nothing Henry had ever seen. Basque, of course. He could simply look at them and see that they must be Basque. He'd heard Tomas recite enough of the language to recognize it, the *rat-a-tat-tat* of consonants, the string of *k*'s and *z*'s and *x*'s unlike any other language known to man—a language, Tomas had told him again and again, as old as stone and steel, as earth and sea and sky.

So Henry did not know what exactly he had in his possession. A manuscript, yes, but what was it? He turned from one page to the next as if he might come across a word or two he recognized, but of course he didn't. Only when he reached the final page did he see, scrawled in ink, a name and an address, the address in Bilbao, the city where Tomas had told Henry his brother's novels were sent to be published. Was this the manuscript of one of his brother's books, one Tomas had kept in his possession? Tomas had said that he did not know where his brother might be, that he had searched and searched but had never found him.

When Henry looked up from the manuscript, he saw Marge and Katrell outside, peering in through the front window. Next to them was a police officer. He imagined the officer taking out his gun. Did he imagine it or was that what the officer was doing? He tried to stand, realized he couldn't. He slipped the top back over the box and held it against his chest. He closed his eyes and, as soon as he did, felt water rising over his legs, reaching his waist; he felt the water cover his shoulders and neck. He gasped for breath, felt himself sink below the surface.

Then someone took hold of his arm, touched his shoulder, his chin. He opened his eyes and saw Marge leaning over him, her hands below one arm, trying to help him up, trying to lift him.

From the water? There was no water.

"Mr. Garrett, Mr. Garrett," he heard Marge saying, and he saw Katrell Sparrow, felt him take his other arm. "We're going to stand up now," Marge said. "Gentle, gentle."

"What are you doing?" Henry said.

"We've got to get you up. We've got to go now," Marge said. "You'll be just fine. Don't you worry. We've got you."

"Where are we going?" Henry asked. "Where are we going?" He heard a siren; he looked down at his feet, looked for the water he was sure he'd felt rising beneath him. He heard his father's voice and Mary's. He heard the humming of bees.

"We're going home," Marge said. "Back to Virginia."

Henry looked around, saw the officer through the window, saw his father's bass leaning against the wall in the corner.

"That," Henry said, pointing. "That needs to come with us."

"What?" Marge said, and Henry pointed again.

"I don't know," Marge said. "I don't know as it will fit."

"It will," Henry said. "It will. It will."

"Okay," he heard Marge say. "Okay. We'll give it a try."

She turned to Katrell, said to him, "You go fetch it. Haul it out there. We'll put the top down. I'll manage Mr. Garrett."

She turned back to Henry, steered him forward as if he were a frail old man.

"Now we need to get going," she told him, "or all three of us will wind up Lord knows where."

"We're there already," Henry said. He hadn't meant it as a joke—he wasn't exactly sure what he was saying—but Marge had laughed. "I guess we are," she said. "I guess that's right where we are. *Lord knows where.*"

"The end," Henry said, though what he'd meant to say was Endly's. "The end is..." But he was too exhausted to go on, to make sense of whatever it was he was thinking. He managed to climb into the car, into the backseat next to his father's bass, and Katrell sat up front with Marge. Before the officer had led them out of town, Henry was already asleep, the manuscript box in his lap, his arms folded across it.

Most nights now he sat in Mohit's study with the manuscript before him, books scattered everywhere, covering the floor. He'd made a copy to mail to the address in Bilbao; he'd kept the original in Mohit's desk drawer. He'd been afraid it might somehow get lost in the mail. Along with the manuscript he'd sent a letter explaining who he was, how he'd come to be in possession of these pages. He said he hoped to get news of Tomas if there was any word from him. They'd been friends, he said. He wanted to make sure Tomas had wound up okay wherever he went after the storm.

Since of course he'd written the letter in English, he hadn't known what would come of it, but two weeks after he'd sent the manuscript off, there'd been a phone call from a man, an editor, in Bilbao. His English wasn't very good but Henry listened to everything he said and then made him say it all again to make sure he understood.

Joaquim Xabier Otxoa had no brother by the name of Tomas. He had no brother at all, nor a sister. No one. The manuscript was a new work, not a work already known in *euskera*. A new work. A novel. Imagine. This man Henry had met was Joaquim Xabier. There could be no doubt. Still hiding, disguised now as a brother. A new work after so many years. A miracle, undoubted. Thank you. Thank you. Imagine.

Henry marveled at Tomas, at his performance. He asked if any of these novels had been translated into English, and the man told him no, though he hoped one day they would be. Our greatest writer, you know, he'd said, which was exactly what Tomas had told him, though Henry had not known then, of course, that Tomas was speaking about himself.

Two days later the man called back. "Yes, yes, Mr. Garrett, now it is very certain. I have read all to the end. You are there, in the story. You are there. Henry Garrett. Your name. You are there and the storm with you."

Henry tried to imagine it, tried to picture Tomas writing the final pages in the midst of the terrible storm. Where had he been? How frightened? How had he managed to continue writing, to find his way toward the end? Where, now, had he gone?

One day, Henry believed, his questions would be answered. Perhaps Tomas would do precisely what Henry had done, step by chance through the front door of the Ganesha Motel to find himself treated as Henry had been treated: with compassion and care, his squandered life restored to him, his every sin forgiven.

Meanwhile, Henry knew exactly what he would do. He would try to learn this strange and ancient language. He would try to memorize its syntax, its rules, its idioms. Gathered around him, scattered throughout Mohit's study, were dictionaries and histories, atlases and maps—everything he could find on the Basque Country, Euskal Herria, and its seven provinces straddling Spain and France. It might take years and years, he knew, but the clatter in his head had grown quiet, the faint murmurings of a distant city, and he was in no hurry now. There was nothing he felt himself rushing toward.

No matter how long it might take, he would make his way through the manuscript. He would work precisely as Latangi had worked on Mohit's great poem, translating word by word into English, carried forward by gratitude, attempting to decipher and then convey all the sorrow and longing the story possessed and its every moment, no matter how fragile or fleeting, of grace.

About the Author

Born and raised in New Orleans, John Gregory Brown is the author of the novels *Decorations in a Ruined Cemetery; The Wrecked, Blessed Body of Shelton Lafleur;* and *Audubon's Watch.* His honors include a Lyndhurst Prize, the Lillian Smith Award, the John Steinbeck Award, and the Louisiana Endowment for the Humanities Book of the Year Award. For two decades he has taught and directed the creative writing program at Sweet Briar College, in Virginia, where he serves as the Julia Jackson Nichols Professor of English. He and his wife, the novelist Carrie Brown, have three children.

LEE BOUDREAUX BOOKS

Unusual stories. Unexpected voices. An immersive sense of place. Lee Boudreaux Books publishes both award-winning authors and writers making their literary debut. A carefully curated mix, these books share an underlying DNA: a mastery of language, commanding narrative momentum, and a knack for leaving us astonished, delighted, disturbed, and powerfully affected, sometimes all at once.

LEE BOUDREAUX ON *A THOUSAND MILES FROM NOWHERE*

Set in Virginia, the state where I grew up, and New Orleans, a city I invent reasons to visit as often as anyone will let me, *A Thousand Miles from Nowhere* is tender and touching and sometimes uproariously funny. I think of it as an "Amazing Grace" story, the tale of a man who once was lost (or, more accurately, who deliberately lost everything he should have been holding dear) but then is found, in the most unexpected of places and alongside a cast of wonderfully bighearted small-town eccentrics. But for all of its deft humor, this is also a deceptively powerful story. The rich cadence of John Gregory Brown's language has the mesmerizing quality of a prayer, and his psychologically piercing portrait of a man trying to resist succumbing to the madness that took his father's life is as soul stirring and life affirming as anything I've read.

Over the course of her career, Lee Boudreaux has published a diverse list of titles, including Ben Fountain's *Billy Lynn's Long Halftime Walk*, Smith Henderson's *Fourth of July Creek*, Madeline Miller's *The Song of Achilles*, Ron Rash's *Serena*, Jennifer Senior's *All Joy and No Fun*, Curtis Sittenfeld's *Prep*, and David Wroblewski's *The Story of Edgar Sawtelle*, among many others.

For more information about forthcoming books, please go to
leeboudreauxbooks.com.